DOUBLE DOWN

5/05 B+T

Watch for a brand-new novel from
TESS HUDSON

Coming June 2006

DOUBLE DOWN

Tess Hudson

MIRA®

ISBN 0-7783-2178-9

DOUBLE DOWN

Copyright © 2005 by Erica Orloff.

www.MIRABooks.com

Printed in U.S.A.

First Printing: May 2005
10 9 8 7 6 5 4 3 2 1

Dedicated to the memory
of my much-beloved grandmother Irene Cunningham,
who taught me how to play cards. Wherever you are,
I am guessing you are playing 500 Rummy.

ACKNOWLEDGMENTS

A warm thank-you to my editor, Margaret Marbury, and to the wonderful team at MIRA Books, especially Dianne Moggy. An acknowledgment, also, to Donna Hayes for her encouragement, vision and kind words, and to Isabel Swift for her vision.

Thank you to my wonderful agent, Jay Poynor—you are a gem.

To my friend and twin separated at birth, Mark DiBona, thank you so much for all your advice and ideas, as well as sharing some colorful stories I put to good use.

Thank you to Writer's Cramp—Pam, Gina and Jon. It was great fun working on this book with your support and input. Now that the corny stuff is out of the way, you better show up next week with pages.

To my family, especially Maryanne, Walter, Alexa, Nicholas, Isabella and J.D.

To my circle of friends: Kathy L., Kathy J., Nancy, Cleo, Pammie and everyone who shares in the good times and bad.

And finally, to all the people in my extended family— Gloria, Joey; my immediate family—Walter, Maryanne, Stacey, Jessica; my late grandmother and "PopPop"; my cousins Lisa, Michael, Robert; my aunt Deanna and Uncle Joseph; and everyone who participated in our annual Thanksgiving poker games...what can I say? The heart of a gambler was born.

PR♥LOGUE

Thirty days.

Thirty days loom in the distance for me like a mirage in the desert. Before I ever get there, it all turns to just so much sand, and in its place are neon signs and immense pleasure palaces and gambling dens.

No, wait. That's Vegas.

Recovering alcoholics shouldn't buy a bar, and gambling addicts shouldn't live in Vegas. But I live here in this neon orgasm in the middle of the desert.

Sin City. Whoever coined that phrase knew what he was talking about. If you're a stranger to this town, with the right kind of cash, you can land here and, within thirty minutes, be ensconced in a hotel room the size of a house, with fourteen-karat-gold fixtures and three phones and two plasma-screen TVs in the bathroom alone, with fifteen call girls for company, a line of credit and "RFB"—casino code for Room, Food and Beverage, meaning it's all free because the casino knows you'll drop it all on the tables because you're a whale. A big fish.

But high rollers aren't the only ones who sin. Old ladies with buckets of coins sit at the slot machines until their asses are numb and they have carpal tunnel syndrome from pulling the one-armed bandit. Young girls with silicone-packed tits come here to make their fortunes, and soon find their fortunes are tied to whether or not they mind sucking on wrinkled, geriatric—but rich—cock.

For all that, you either hate this place, or you find it seductive, alluring and addicting. You can't leave. You're mesmerized.

So try as I might, I can't put thirty days together. Gamblers Anonymous. My home group gives out little bronze coins for thirty days. I want one. Badly. Like I want a cup of coffee in the morning or a shot of Jack Daniel's with a splash of Coke at night—though never at the table. But if I were laying odds on me, I'd say it's a twelve to one shot that I ever get that brass coin. I can't put thirty days together. I fall off my gambling wagon, my sponsor yells at me and I have to hang my head like some puppy dog that peed on the floor. And then I have to start over.

One day.

Twenty-four hours.

They tell me to take one day at a time. I can't take a minute at a time some days. My life is about math. The odds. Numbers. Twelve to one. Long shots. Over-under. And most of all, the odds of drawing an inside straight. Thirty days. One day. One hour. It doesn't matter, because I can't do it.

My name is Skye McNally, and I am a compulsive gambler.

♥ONE

"**I**'m dying, kid."

"Daddy...you said that last month. And over the summer. And last year. If I remember correctly, you said it the summer I turned seventeen, in some vague hope of forestalling the loss of my virginity."

"Yeah, but this time, I really mean it."

I rolled my eyes. My father was a perfectly healthy sixty-five years old. I balanced the receiver on my shoulder while looking in the cabinet for a clean glass to pour a shot of Jack Daniel's in.

"You're not saying anything, Skye."

"What do you want me to say? I know you're not dying. You're too goddamn mean and *way* too stubborn to die."

"Your devotion is touching.... Will you come back to New York? Will you come see me?"

Unable to find a clean glass, I took my morning coffee mug, dumped out the cold coffee, rinsed it once, poured myself a Jack, rooted in the fridge for a Coke, added a splash and sighed.

"Is that a no? I asked a simple question. Will you come see your old man? You're my only child. Is that too much to ask?"

"Honestly, Dad? Yes."

"I don't understand what I ever did that was so bad."

I looked at my watch—a Rolex I had once briefly hocked when I was on a losing streak—and took another sip of J.D. "Dad, I'd tell you, but I don't have all night."

"You deeply wound me, Skye."

"Hold on, I need to find a string quartet to play in the background. Let me shed a few tears for you, Dad."

"Will you at least think about coming?"

"Sure. I'll think about it…."

"If you come, we could go to a Mustangs game. I got season tickets—in a skybox. We could take a limo, drink our way out to the stadium. Live it up."

"A regular father-daughter outing."

"Come on…what are we supposed to do together?"

"I don't know. That's the problem, Dad. I have no idea what normal fathers and daughters do. I have vague recollections of girls at school going to Brownie meetings and, later, their fathers going to swim meets and crap like that. Not taking their daughters to illegal casino nights and teaching them how to deal blackjack. I learned to double down before I learned my multiplication tables."

Dad laughed. "Cards are a very good mathematical tool. You learned an awful lot hanging around me."

"Yeah, right. I learned that breaking a man's pinkie when he doesn't pay his bookie is a rapid way to get him to cough up some cash. A watch, maybe. His wedding band."

"Christ. Can we ever have a pleasant conversation? I'd like you to come home. Go to a game. You know the Mustangs have a shot at the Super Bowl this year?"

"I live in Vegas, Dad. I'd have to be in a coma to not know they're contenders. So, business must be good."

"Yeah. Nothing like betting for the hometown team."

"Listen, I'd love to discuss the spreads with you all evening, Dad, but I've got to go to a meeting."

"Still goin' to those, eh?"

"Sorry to disappoint you."

"I'm not disappointed. I just don't see how it's…an addiction. Gamblers Anonymous. Everything is an addiction these days, including those meetings. Why do you have to go talk about your problems with a roomful of losers? You win a *lot* more than you lose, Skye. You always have."

"Dad, can we drop this for the thousandth time?"

"All right, then, I'll let you go. And, Skye?"

"Yeah?"

"Your old man loves you."

"I know, Daddy. I know."

I replaced the cordless receiver and swallowed the rest of my drink.

Oh, to be the normal child of a normal father, not the only child of Sean McNally, one of New York's biggest bookies. Quality family time was something other people had on weekends. In the McNally household—just me and Dad after my mother died—my father had me sitting in the basement with a bank of phones, watching the football games on five different television sets and praying the teams made the over-unders and covered their point spreads. I served, for five dollars a day—a fortune when you're nine—as a waitress for the men who worked for my father, bringing down sandwiches and beer through a cloud of cigar smoke so thick it looked like the Hiroshima mushroom was suspended over their heads.

One fateful Saturday, my father's buddy, Eddie the Roach, motioned me over to him.

"Hey, princess?"

"Yeah?"

"Got a hot tip for you."

"I know this one. 'Never take a long walk on a short pier.'"

"Oh." He pursed his lips. "I guess I've used that one before."

I nodded. "'Bout a hundred times, Eddie."

"Yeah, Roach," Jackie Flanagan mocked. "Give the kid something useful. A real tip."

The Roach looked thoughtful. "All right, princess, come closer." I moved nearer to the Roach, who weighed a good 240 of mostly flab and reeked of some very cheap cigars. I tried to avoid crinkling up my nose. He had a double chin and a two-day stubble of beard. Sweat trickled down his cheeks and into the folds of his neck. "Look… see that game?" He pointed at one of the television screens.

"Yeah. Clemson."

"Right. Well, I have it on *very good authority* that the Clemson quarterback is in deep to his bookie. Big time. And so the quarterback has been *persuaded* to do his best to blow the game in the last quarter and screw the point spread. Bet on them to blow it and you'll quintuple your money. How's that for a tip?"

Right then, I took my five dollars in waitress wages and walked over to my dad. "Can I bet this on Clemson—to lose?"

"It's a proud day," he said. "The McNally heir, my own sweet daughter, places her first bet. Sure, sweetie." He took my five dollars and bent down so he was eye level with me. He was always freshly shaven, smelling of a musky after-shave. Around his neck was a gold chain—thin, not os-tentatious—and a St. Christopher's medallion. "Now, here's the first rule of gambling. Don't bet more than you can afford to lose. Can you afford to lose this five dollars?"

"Uh-huh."

"All right, then. You have a bet."

I watched the rest of the Clemson game. At first, it looked like Clemson would win. But in the last six min-utes of the game, the quarterback began blowing play after play. He would throw away a ball to the sidelines at the first hint of the defense coming after him. In the end, they lost. The feeling of excitement spread through me like a small jolt of electricity. I felt something magical hap-pen. I soon began plotting my bets every week, listening to the old-timers and my dad's cronies, reading all I could about teams, assessing rumors. A pint-size gambling ad-dict was born. It was only years later that gambling brought me to my knees.

I shook my head to chase away the memories. Seven o'clock. If I hurried, I could make a seven-thirty GA meeting. I didn't yet feel as if entering a church basement to listen to a bunch of people talk about how much they lost gambling was anything more than penance or pun-ishment. I kept waiting to "get it." Waiting for something to course through me—an ounce of gratefulness, a feel-ing of serenity, the feelings other people talked about in the rooms—something that could hold a candle to how I felt when I was gambling. But it hadn't happened yet, and most days I wondered if I should just give in. This push and pull of Gamblers Anonymous versus the allure of the casinos and betting made me constantly feel on edge.

I walked into my bedroom. All I had furnishing it was

a king-sized bed and a small dresser. My kitchen, living room, dining area, they all looked like furniture store displays. They were crisp whites and clean teak. My carpets were pale, white, spotless. I'd ordered everything in a weekend when I decided to stay here after a lost weekend. Surveying my bedroom, I had no pictures. No past, no future. That was my life here in Vegas. A perpetual purgatory. I felt that familiar longing. An ache, really. It starts in my stomach, and then I feel a restless nervousness. I paced back and forth, talking to myself in my head. *Don't go, Skye. You'll fucking hate yourself tomorrow. Don't. Don't...*

I said a prayer. *Mom, help me to not gamble. Please. Send me something, some sign, to stop me.*

But signs are in short supply in Vegas. Instead, people have lucky horseshoes and rabbits' feet, talismans to bring them luck at the tables. They worship Lady Luck as if she's real, a goddess of felt tables. I walked into my closet and picked out a simple black dress. A pair of high heels. I went into my bathroom and did my makeup. My reflection gave me a disapproving look, my big, brown eyes staring back at me. But I still went down to the parking garage.

The casino beckoned.

Within a few hours of my phone call with Dad, I was down eight thousand dollars. I didn't blame luck—Lady Luck is for suckers. I blamed the odds. It's all a numbers game. Life is a numbers game. Death is a numbers game. What do you think life insurance is? It's a gamble. You bet that you'll die quick and your family will get a big payoff, and the actuaries calculate that you'll live until you're wrinkled and gray-haired and pay into your policy so long that the insurance company will make money on the deal.

Still, as I sat there playing blackjack near midnight and watching the dealer take away my chips time and time—and time—again, I heard myself, this other half of me, speaking. *Time to cut your losses, Skye. The odds of making this back tonight are ten to one. You're on a losing streak. You've lost your concentration. You're taking risks and saying "hit" when you know you should stay. Get up and leave.*

I don't talk to anyone at the tables. Maybe because I talk endlessly to myself in my head. Some occasional small talk among gamblers is okay, but I'm not there to pick up men or socialize with tourists. I don't drink at the table, either. The tables are business. Well, both business and my drug of choice: the sound of chips clicking together, the feel of felt beneath my fingertips, the roulette wheel spinning rows away, the cheers and squeals around the craps table. I love the casino's smells, sounds, glitz. I love how it makes me feel. But in that moment, eight thousand dollars in the hole, I made a business decision to cut and run. I got up, tossed the dealer a hundred-dollar chip, and made my way to one of the bars off of the casino in the MGM Grand. I usually don't go to the Grand. I usually gamble at the Hard Rock, or even the Bellaggio. That, and I bet football. And basketball. Boxing. If sweating and athletes are involved, I'm usually betting.

The fact I had gone to the Grand was another sign I was off my game. Why had I gone to a casino where I almost always lost? I know what they would tell me in my Gamblers Anonymous meeting. I was *trying* to lose. I subconsciously wanted to hit bottom. The bottom was my purgatory.

From the bar, I made a call on my cell phone.

"T.D.?"

"Yeah, baby," T.D.'s deep, masculine voice made its way through the phone. He sounded like a deejay on the midnight-to-dawn shift.

"Feel like meeting for a drink? I'm buying."

"What's that sound?"

"What sound?"

"Don't play dumb-ass with me, Little Girl. I distinctly hear a *ka-ching ka-ching* in the background. You playin' the fuckin' *slots?*"

"No." Slots are a loser's game unless you have a whole

syndicate working for you keeping the seats warm until one of you hits the jackpot.

"You playing blackjack?"

"No."

"You're lying."

"No, I'm not. I *was* playing blackjack. But I just dropped a few grand, and now I'm calling my favorite sponsor to ask him if he wants to get a drink with me."

"Favorite sponsor," he snorted. "I'm the only one in Gamblers Anonymous who'd take a hard-nut case like you."

"Same difference."

He sighed. "Where are you?"

"The Grand."

"Damn you."

Thirty minutes later, T.D. walked into the bar, greeted a few old fans who stopped him for his autograph and made his way to my back table.

"I kept your seat warm for you." I smiled and slid over in the booth.

"Hmm," he grunted.

"Come on, T.D. Don't be mad."

T. D. Russell was once the toast of the NFL. He was an offensive lineman, meaning, simply, he was a monster. When he walked through a doorway, he was so massive people looked up to see if an eclipse had occurred. He was wide-shouldered and walked with a slight limp because he'd had his left knee scraped out four times. He needed to have a total knee replacement, which he kept putting off. At the height of his career, he used to pitch America's favorite luxury car, a brand of sneakers and a sports drink that frankly tasted like shit. Combined with his football earnings, this made T.D. pretty damn wealthy.

But then he lost it all. Or a lot of it, anyway. He still had a boatload of money, but he lost the endorsement deals, and any shot at the NFL Hall of Fame by getting caught betting on games. He swears to me, his best friend, that he never bet on the outcomes of games he played in. I believe him and I'd say that most football fans believe him, but Walter Hammond II, the N.F.L. Commissioner, doesn't. So T.D. is banned for life from the game he loves. Besides losing his status, the endorsement millions, he also lost one Mrs. George "Touchdown" Russell, aka his second wife. She liked being the wife of an NFL *star,* not the wife of an NFL pariah.

"Skye, when will you learn I'm not mad at you? I just know that when they're giving out the thirty-day coins, and *once again* you don't get one, you're going to whine— and I'm going to have to listen to it."

Our group gives out thirty-day coins. Then, if you get to ninety days, you get another coin. They're not worth anything but bragging rights. You did it. You made thirty days. Except me. Who's never made it to thirty days. Not even once.

I sighed and stared at my bourbon on the rocks. "I don't even think I can beat the system. I know the house always wins. This casino and all of the Strip is founded on the principle that the gambler will lose in the long run, and the house will win. As a bookie's daughter, my entire life was predicated on the house always winning. I just like how I *feel* when I play."

"See, there's your problem," T.D. said, wrapping his massive hand around the single-malt Scotch he had signaled to the bartender to hand him when he walked in. "You need to figure out how to *feel* that feeling doing something else that's not an addiction. Something that's safe, that's not gonna empty your bank account."

"But nothing else does it for me the way gambling does. When I was a little girl, T.D., my teacher once sat me in a corner and said I couldn't move until I solved this math problem. What's 1 plus 2 plus 3 plus 4—all the way up to 1,000. She figured I'd be there all day, which is what she wanted because I was this know-it-all little kid."

"Who grew up into a know-it-all adult. And a pain in my ass. How old were you?"

"Nine. Maybe ten. Bored out of my mind in math class. Always bugging her with questions. I wasn't a bad kid, just a smart one. And Sister Mary Elizabeth was tired of me interrupting her every time she tried to explain long division…or fractions, or pretty much anything. I tortured that poor woman."

"Why am I not surprised, Little Girl." He winked at me slyly.

"Yeah, well, I don't feel too badly for her. I'm convinced she had an altar to Satan in her supply closet. Anyway, I was staring at the paper when all of a sudden the numbers started doing a tango."

"A tango?" He gave me a look that said I must have just bet my last five dollars on a long-shot horse with a gimpy leg.

"A tango. A rumba. The hustle. They started pairing up and dancing across the paper. You see, number 1 went with 1,000. The number 2 went with 999. The number 3 went with 998, number 4 with 997. And so they spun off and danced together, and I realized if I multiplied 1001 times 50 dancing pairs of numbers, I would have the answer."

T.D. stared off into space, rolling his eyes upward at the

mental calculation. Suddenly his face brightened. "I get it. Very cool."

"Yeah. But that wasn't really the beginning. I've loved numbers before I could even talk, I think. I'm a freaky mathematical whiz. I used to tally my father's earnings faster than he could—in my head. He used to show me off like a trick pony, getting me to tally four or five three-digit—no counting on fingers, no paper—numbers in my head as a little girl. All his gambling regulars loved it. I liked numbers better than people—still do, except for you. And that translated to loving cards, and betting the over-under. The sad trouble is that the only time I am ever blissfully outside myself, just off in another world, is when I'm gambling."

"What about during sex?"

I scrunched up my face. "No. I'm always thinking of the odds that he's going to come before I do."

"You are very bad…or you've just had lousy lovers. Come on, now."

I shrugged. "My mind races a million miles an hour, T.D. And the only place it ever slows down is in the ca-sino. The minute I hear that *ka-ching,* smell the carpeting, see the movements of the croupiers as they hover over the craps tables, their tuxedos crisp, their movements theatri-cal, feel the energy…I'm home. Suddenly the world, which ordinarily zooms by me at this kinetic warp speed, slows down, and I finally relax. I finally breathe."

"You seeing a psychiatrist or something?" T.D. asked.

"No, why?"

"'Cause we got these little slogans in Gamblers Anon-ymous. 'Let go and let God.' 'One day at a time.' All that stuff. And there just isn't a slogan that is gonna fix you, Skye. You are hard core. 'Cause if someone thinks he can beat the system, then I can reason with him about the odds and all that, but if someone just is Jonesing for a numbers fix, that's a lot harder. You're not even saying to me, 'I can stop anytime,' like most of them. You're sayin', 'I just love how it makes me feel.'"

"Hard core or not, you're stuck with me."

"*I shouldn't* be stuck with you. You're supposed to have a female sponsor."

"I don't like any of the women in our home group."

"That's not it. You don't like people telling you they got rules. They told you to find a woman sponsor, and you came right on over to me."

"Hey, you took me on."

"I said it was *temporary*, until you found someone in a skirt to do it."

"But now you wouldn't know what to do if I found another sponsor."

"For one thing, I'd get to finish watching a television show. You're always callin' me from the casinos right when I'm settled down with the History Channel."

"But didn't I set you up with that cocktail waitress? Wasn't she gorgeous?"

"That's beside the point."

"No, it's not. I tried to repay the favor."

"You can't be bribing your sponsor by gettin' him dates, Skye. You've twisted this whole Gamblers Anonymous thing all up."

"But don't I have you over every Sunday to watch the games? And don't I make those little cocktail weenies you like?"

"Yeah."

"And that time you got all mad when the sportscaster referred to your gambling... Didn't I keep you from smashing your Porsche into the front doors of the local television station?"

"Yes, you did."

"So let's agree that we're both hard cases and leave it at that." I stuck out my hand.

T.D. shook it, and we nursed our drinks, watching ESPN on the TV in the bar. I had lived in Vegas for three years, and T.D. was the first real friend I'd made in this city. Vegas was a fantasy town, where problems paled in the flash and neon of hope. Silicone and celebrity, money and sex, gambling and cocaine swirled around and made it easy for people to dream, or to think that, say, stopping for a quickie wedding at the Chapel of Love was real. Look at Britney Spears. But it wasn't real. It was the seduction of Vegas.

I was a walking poster child for "What Happens in Vegas, Stays in Vegas." I'd had a quickie wedding myself. Flew here from New York. Got rice thrown at me by a justice of the peace. Filed for an annulment two weeks later—but never left Vegas. Still, the city wasn't real. T.D., he was real. The only other sort-of friend I had was Annie, though she was a worse hard-nut gambling case than even I was—she worked as a callgirl to support her habit, and she disappeared for weeks on end. She came to GA and sat in the back—like in high school when the cool kids always selected the back desk in the classroom. T.D. sat in the front row—and made me sit there, too.

I'll never forget the first time it occurred to me that gambling was a problem. I'd hocked my mother's watch during an all-night high-stakes Texas Hold 'em poker game in the home of a bookie I knew named Jimmy Jam. I was up for a while, but part of being a gambling addict is not knowing when to stop—kind of like an alcoholic who'll keep drinking until he pukes. I had gone through every cent I had, and I was sure I'd win the watch back. But when I woke up the next day—minus the watch, which I was very sentimentally attached to…past tense— I felt shame. According to T.D., shame can be a useful emotion. All I knew is that I felt like scum.

I looked up a meeting place for Gamblers Anonymous that night and went with a queasy feeling in my stomach. On a table in the back were pamphlets. And the walls had taped-up signs, with inspirational slogans. The Serenity Prayer was framed on the wall above the table where the guy who was running the meeting sat. Praying wasn't in my repertoire—unless it was an under-the-breath, "God, grant me an inside straight." I thought I had stumbled into a cult.

I picked up several pamphlets and shoved them in my purse. One was called "Choosing a Sponsor." That night T.D. spoke. I recognized him right away, so even though he said, "Hi, my name is George, and I'm a compulsive gambler," I knew he was the famously disgraced T.D. Russell. And I decided that someone who had been banned for life from the NFL was as good a sponsor as any. In fact, considering the shame I felt, someone who'd been dissected in every newspaper, sports column and talk radio call-in shows was *exactly* the sponsor I needed.

I badgered him until he agreed to be my temporary sponsor—which just ended up being a permanent thing.

"So what's the trick?" I asked him after that first meeting.

"What do you mean?"

"Well, how do you stop? I mean what's the answer? The magic ticket?"

"There's no magic. You have to take it one day at a time."

My heart felt like it was as mangled as twisted metal in a car wreck. I wanted a quick fix.

"*That's* your answer? Don't you have something better than that?"

"Nope." He stared down at me.

"Why can't I quit, like you?" I asked him as we looked at ESPN above the bar. "I feel like I should be cured by now."

"There is no cure. And you refuse to accept that you can't control your gambling without help from a higher power."

I hated his "Higher Power."

He looked at his watch. "It's almost midnight. Want to go get something to eat?"

"Sure."

I wasn't really hungry, but whenever T.D. rescued me from the tables, we had an unspoken agreement that I would accompany him to the Big Buffet House of Hunan, like all of Vegas, an open-all-night place. There I would eat an obligatory bowl of wonton soup and sit for hours while he made his way from one end of the buffet to the other. T.D. and I found the Big Buffet House by accident one night when we'd taken a wrong turn and T.D.'s stomach was growling, and we've been going there ever since.

We exited the MGM Grand, got his Porsche from the valet and drove to old Vegas—the seedier side of town, though it's on a bit of an upswing now, complete with a neon show that lights up the world like a Technicolor Jesus just made a sunrise.

"Mr. Touchdown." Mai, his favorite hostess, greeted us with a bow. She had long black hair down to the middle of her back and wore a deep blue kimono with a white orchid pattern.

She led us to our usual table next to a fish tank that had a single evil-looking moray eel we named Walter Hammond, after T.D.'s nemesis, and our regular waiter, Shen, brought us mai tais with little parasols. This is not the usual drink for either of us, but it is our usual at the Big Buffet House of Hunan because the bartender once bought us mai tais on the house because he was a fan of T.D.'s, and since then the entire place has been confused and thinks we like them. We'd hate to disappoint our friends at Big Buffet, so we drink them.

"Gotta pace myself," T.D. said, coming back with his first plate of food. The chef and assorted kitchen staff came out and began writing numbers down on a little pad. They all conferred in Chinese, with some Vietnamese thrown in, arguing among themselves. Busboys and waitresses joined in the act. The owner, Mr. Lee, even came over and began looking at the pad and motioning with his hands.

The Big Buffet has a house pool that bets on the number of trips to the buffet T.D. will make. If no one hits it, they keep the pool in the office safe until the next time. The highest it has ever gotten is eleven hundred dollars. That's a lot of friggin' wontons. And that's Vegas for you. Can't even go out to eat without betting on it.

"You realize the busboy is conspiring by refilling your water glass with every sip," I whispered. "He wants you to get bloated, so you'll quit early."

T.D. just smiled. "I am *very* hungry tonight. I ate dinner at six… So we're talking a good, solid seven hours ago. Water's not gonna stop me."

I watched him eat…egg rolls, sushi rolls, barbecued spare ribs. He went for fried rice, fried wontons and shrimp toast. Moo goo gai pan. Beef and broccoli. Shrimp in lobster sauce. He ate slowly, deliberately.

"See, T.D.—" I watched the kitchen staff in their white uniforms peering out every few minutes and giving hand signals for how many plates he was up to "—there's no escaping gambling in this town."

"I know. So you ever think of moving back East?"

"Wouldn't you miss me?"

He looked up from his sparerib and smiled. "I sure would, Little Girl. Don't look so hurt."

I actually had felt a stab of panic. "Good. Because I would miss you. I'd be lost without you."

"Well, I'm not leaving Las Vegas anytime soon."

T.D. would never leave, as far as I could see. He owned a sports bar called The Touchdown, and a well-reviewed restaurant called the Gridiron Steakhouse, which did a tremendous business and was our home away from home. It also supported T.D. in the style he'd grown accustomed to—twelve-person Jacuzzi, seven-bedroom house, one Porsche, two BMWs and a Bentley. Not to mention custom-made suits from Hong Kong and a personal masseuse who came to the house three times a week to try to help his arthritis.

"Then we're stuck with each other," I said, and smiled at him as I sipped my soup.

"You given any more thought to my offer?"

"Yeah. Still thinking about it." T.D. felt if I had a job—a real job—I might actually gamble less. I'd have something to do with my time other than read the sports page and call my bookie. He offered me a job as a hostess at the Gridiron. We'd be together, he'd be able to keep an eye on me, I'd get in less trouble. The only other real job I'd ever had my whole life was working in a casino—briefly. And running my father's bookie business. Neither of those did wonders for my gambling problem.

"It can be temporary until you figure out what you want to be when you grow up."

"Can't you just see me as a housewife with a bunch of rugrats?"

"Actually, I think you'd look cute with a little apron, baby slung over one hip."

I rolled my eyes. "You're delusional." I'd had two short-lived temp jobs since I moved to Vegas, but my word-processing skills left a lot to be desired. I lived off a monthly allowance from a trust. And gambling winnings—when I won, which all depended on drawing those aces.

He continued eating, and we continued talking. Two hours later, T.D. looked at me with total seriousness. "Nineteen plates. I think I'm nearing my limit."

"Can't even fit one more?"

He pondered this, took a sip of water. Then shook his head. "No. Nineteen."

Hand signals were exchanged back by the kitchen, and soon we heard a shriek and a cheer. A very short cook, a man we knew as Huang, came running out and hugged T.D. He was six hundred dollars richer. T.D. graciously congratulated him and signed his autograph on a menu.

We settled our bill, leaving a hundred-dollar tip on the table, bid Mai and the staff good-night, then went out to T.D.'s car. I had left mine at the Grand.

"Want a lift home? You can get your car tomorrow."

"Yeah. I'm tired."

"Wanna stay at Chez T.D.?"

"Sure."

I had my own room at T.D.'s, complete with changes of clothes and pajamas. We drove to his gated community and eventually pulled into his driveway. We entered the house through the four-car garage. The place is more like a palace. He has beautiful taste—though he kind of doesn't know when to stop. Why have an ordinary faucet when you can have one plated in ten-karat gold?

"Wayne Newton stop by lately for a cup of sugar?" I joked.

"Yeah, me and Wayne hung out watching *All My Children* today. He left just before you called."

In fact, we'd never met Wayne Newton, but T.D. was a serious *All My Children* fan. He'd been watching it for something like fifteen years and had a serious crush on Susan Lucci. His house was as Vegas as Wayne, though— and a little over the top. All right, a *lot* over the top. A waterfall cascaded in the foyer, and one living room wall was a massive saltwater fish tank. He also kept two "ferocious" felines, Fred and Ginger…adorable white Persian cats with pale blue eyes.

"I'm beat. And stuffed." He stretched his arms upward.

"You should be."

"You going to bed or taking a swim?"

"I think I'll go in the hot tub." I stood on my tiptoes and gave him a kiss on the cheek, went up to my room, changed into my bikini and went back down to the Jacuzzi. The desert night had a chill to it, and we were far enough from the city to see speckles of stars in the sky.

I turned on the timer and climbed into the tub. I felt the stress of the night wear away—the loss at the table, the fact that I had to start at day one again in my Gamblers Anonymous program, that my father was "dying" again. The tension loosened as I looked up at the Nevada sky.

Maybe I would go see my father. I knew that, sooner or later, he and I would have to make peace with each other. I didn't hate him. It was half my fault, too. If I hadn't been so intent on pissing him off by marrying his right-hand man, Jimmy Sullivan, in a lost weekend three years ago, I wouldn't even be here, floating in a desert hot tub, eight grand to my deficit. Then again, if Daddy hadn't been the world's greatest liar, hiding stacks of cash in the floorboards of our attic and making me such a little gambler that I asked the Macy's Santa if he had any odds on whether or not Rudolph would fly that year, then I wouldn't still be struggling to go a day without some kind of bet.

I went round and round it in my head, looking for reasons, excuses, detours. Exhaustion took over me, and I decided to go upstairs to sleep. I gave myself two to one odds that in the end, I'd go back to New York for a visit.

THREE

The next night, my home group gave out brass coins to Big Slim, Cowboy Hal and Louie Fish-eye for making thirty days, ten years and ninety days, respectively. The coins aren't worth anything. Just some pride. The ability to feel it in your pocket as you're tempted to instead dip your hand in to go play the slots. Bragging rights. If you go to another GA group, and it's an "anniversary night," you even get to raise your hand and tell them how long you have. Without gambling.

When Harry, who was running the meeting because he'd been elected to do that for the month, announced it was time to dole out the thirty-day coins, everyone in the room turned to look at me. And I stared right back.

Were they really that fucking surprised?

We admitted we were powerless over gambling and that our lives had become unmanageable.

Back to Step One—for me.

That was my problem. The whole step was riddled with land mines for me. Step One—measly Step One—

and I still didn't get it. I sat next to T.D. during the meeting and thought about it while Cowboy Hal, who had been in and out of GA for some fifteen years, talked about making ten long years without gambling. He hadn't been to so much as a fucking bingo hall. He didn't even play Lotto.

Step One. I admitted I was powerless over gambling. *Sort of.* I waffled. Like betting *both* the over and the under on a football game. So that was a problem, as far as T.D. could see. "Sort of" doesn't count. I had days—usually when I was winning—when I felt like maybe I wasn't powerless. All my life, when I'd been around my father, power had been as much a part of our lives as breathing—and it always seemed as if he had all the power. As a bookie, he had the power to break someone's legs, or maybe just a finger, if they didn't pay, the power to intimidate. And the gamblers lacked power. They were at the mercy of the odds, of what happened on the field or in the boxing ring. I grew up respecting the power of the odds, but I didn't know, not for sure, if I was powerless over gambling.

Add to that the fact that my life was only "sort of" unmanageable. As long as my father was far away from me in New York, life was at least somewhat manageable. T.D. and I were like an old married couple. We did our meetings, our dinners, our drinking. We spent holidays together, and never really asked each other why neither of us could make a relationship with someone else stick. I knew that for him, it was because he was particular about his house and his things and liked everything just so—he was kind of anal when it came right down to it. And as for me? I suppose I had grown to distrust authority so deeply that I didn't even like to sit down if someone offered me a seat. In short, I was disagreeable with almost everyone except T.D. We didn't sleep together, but we might as well have. We toddled along like some bastardized version of a granny and grandpa stepping off the bus from Century Village to try their hand at Sin City.

I knew I'd be a lot better off away from Vegas, with its temptations on every corner. But the only other place I'd ever lived was New York—and what waited for me there—in the parlance of GA—was even more unmanageable. I felt paralyzed to leave the desert.

My gambling usually let me pay my bills. I was thirty-one years old and got what was tantamount to an allowance from my mother's estate. She had married "beneath her," and though I saw her parents just a couple of times after she died, I was left with enough from a trust fund to live on. Some months I parlayed that allowance big time— I was, as gamblers say, "on a roll." But of course, you can't beat the odds forever, so some months life was *very* lean. I'd hocked jewelry and a television. And T.D. was always my backup. I could eat at his steakhouse seven nights a week if I had to, or wanted to. That's a lot of steak. Good thing I'm not a vegetarian.

They call what T.D. does "enabling," just as they call my train of thought "denial." As my sponsor, he really should let me hit bottom. We shouldn't even watch sports together. But we seem to understand each other innately. We need each other. Codependent and all. Another rule broken.

If I ever got in really big trouble, my father would bail me out. He's done it before, once covering me when I was twenty-six thousand in the hole. And my father was a big part of the problem. He helped me define *unmanageable*. My life was truly unmanageable when my father went to prison. My life was unmanageable when I had to collect money and oversee my father's business. So in the end, anything compared to that felt marginally more manageable. Comparatively speaking, there's family-member-in-prison unmanageable; there's come-up-with-bail-in-the-middle-of-the-night unmanageable; and then there's so-you-lost-eight-grand-playing-blackjack unmanageable. With this train of logic, I never made thirty days. This, after all these years, is my excuse. And denial is a river in Egypt. Oh, yeah—you hang around with these Twelve-Step types for long enough and you've got a fucking saying for everything.

Big Slim raised his hand when it was "sharing time." I wasn't much good at sharing in kindergarten, and I can't say I ever got the hang of it in Gamblers Anonymous. Sharing meant talking about your addiction, your week, what was going on in your life. Kind of like group therapy.

"I just want to say, I'm grateful to my Higher Power for helping me reach thirty days," Big Slim said. "I honestly never thought I'd see a month when I didn't go to OTB. It was like my home away from home. I knew all the regulars."

A few people nodded in agreement, in commiseration.

"For those newcomers who are wondering if it's ever possible to get past the shame, to get to a point where you're okay going a day without gambling—I'm here to tell you I'm a living miracle. I've been gambling since I was fifteen…and I've now gone thirty days without it, and it feels real good to have this coin."

I slid down in my seat. It wasn't just going without gambling. I mean, even I have had a week when I didn't gamble. It was the constant *thinking* about it. I wanted a week, two weeks, thirty days, when I wasn't constantly talking to myself, feeling this internal warfare of whether or not to call my bookie, whether or not to sit in on a poker game. I envied Big Slim. He looked like a Vegas old-timer, greasy-haired with a polyester shirt on. But he had something I didn't. He had a coin. He had peace of mind.

After the meeting, it was coffee time. Louie Fish-eye is the coffee person, and he makes probably the worst cup of coffee in the state of Nevada—so bitter your eyes well up. I went to the urn and turned the spigot, filling my foam cup. I added two heaping teaspoons of sugar, though even that wasn't going to help Fish-eye's coffee. I bet we could use his poison as battery acid.

I took a sip just as Cowboy Hal sauntered over to me in his big shiny belt buckle, beer gut, custom-made whip-stitched shirt—that snapped, how's that for fashion?—and ten-gallon Stetson.

"What's the story this time, Little Girl?"

I hate when he calls me "Little Girl," because only T.D. can call me that, but I humored him.

"String of bad luck at blackjack."

"Did you call your sponsor?"

"Yeah."

"Honey chil'…" He shook his head at me and dug around in his pants pocket for a quarter. "Here."

"What's this for?"

"Because for the hundredth time, y'all supposed to call your sponsor *before* you go to the tables, not after to come collect you like a dang booby prize."

"Well, thanks for the quarter, Hal. I didn't know you cared. Though a phone call costs more than a quarter these days."

He laughed, and then "wrassled" me into a bear hug.

Next, Connie came over. She had a year without gambling, but only sixty days without cocaine, and, by the looks of her, about forty-two minutes without alcohol. And T.D. wonders why I can't get a woman sponsor.

"Honey…" she slurred, wrapping an arm around me. "You'll get it. One of these days. Just like me."

Connie, about forty in the dim recesses of a smoky bar, fifty under neon and pushing sixty under the fluorescent lights of a church basement, was a hooker long past her prime. She wore Bonne Belle Lip Smackers, which I frankly didn't know they still made, and some kind of fragrance the average thirteen-year-old would reject as being nauseatingly sweet and babyish.

"Thanks, Connie." You know you're pathetic when even the trifectas feel bad for you. "Trifectas" are what T.D. and I call the triple addicts—gambling, drugs *and* alcohol. A lot of the people in Twelve-Step programs are battling more than one addiction.

And then there was Annie. She was an apple-cheeked Midwestern girl with dreams of being a showgirl, and she was naive enough to think she could beat the house when she arrived. By the time she realized she couldn't, she was broke. She worked as a stripper and sometime call girl, and Annie occasionally crashed on my couch when she hit bottom and bet all those dollars tucked in her G-string on a longshot that never came in.

"Hey, Annie." I gave her a hug.

"Hi, Skye. I'm working every night this week down at the Dollhouse. Come visit me?"

"Annie, you know I hate going there."

"I know, but I have a whole new routine worked out. I come on as a Native American with a headdress full of feathers and white leather boots…"

"Annie…you're a blonde. You couldn't look any *less* like a Native American if you tried."

"Hmm." She pondered this. "Maybe. But you know, it doesn't seem like any of the men notice."

"I guess not," I said, looking directly at her 40Ds.

The home group. A pack of real "winners" in a town full of losers. And the most depressing part of it all? *I* was the loser who couldn't get a fucking thirty-day coin.

After coffee time, T.D. asked me if I wanted to go to his steakhouse.

"Considering I'm down eight grand for the month, I'd say a free steak is in order."

"It's a good thing I know you love me like the real deal, Little Girl. A man could get a complex."

"Yeah, well, it's a good thing you don't ask me for a free blow job for every steak."

"What the hell?" He looked at me as we left the church basement where our meeting was held and climbed into his dark blue Bentley.

"Sorry. I was just talking to Connie and Annie."

"Oh," he said, as if that made perfect sense. Which it did. Because this is Vegas.

That's the thing about this town. The rules are different.

The Bentley was a smooth ride. He never let me drive it, though I could have my pick of anything else in his garage.

"Back to Step One," he said.

"Back to Step One."

"You decided whether you're goin' home to see your daddy yet?"

"Thinkin' about it."

"Good Lord. Haven't you gotten in enough trouble for this month?"

"No," I grinned. "Might as well go for broke. Bet it all, and let it ride."

"Given as we live in Vegas."

"Given as we live in Vegas."

"I don't know that going home is such a bright idea," he said.

"I *know* it's not a bright idea. On the other hand, he's the only family I have."

"And he wants you to gamble, Skye. He doesn't get the idea of addiction."

"Considering I can't earn a thirty-day coin, it appears I don't get it either."

"Little Girl...don't make me come find you in New York."

"Don't worry. I won't," I said. "I'm not going to go. I've made up my mind."

But of course, we all know addicts are born liars.

F♥UR

Late that night, again at Chez T.D., I couldn't sleep. Dinner had been perfectly grilled mid-rare Kobe beef. A bottle of red wine—an Australian shiraz handpicked by T.D.'s sommelier at his steakhouse. Actually, two bottles—one for me, one for T.D. I should have been sleepy, but I wasn't. And since as I was *staying* in my sponsor's spare bedroom, it wasn't like I could sneak off to the casino for a few hours.

I flipped through the myriad stations T.D.'s satellite dish offered. He has sports available 24/7. I could watch sumo wrestling from Japan if I wanted. But even naked jiggling sumo asses made me think of gambling. I'd lay odds on the bigger sumo to push the smaller guy out of the circle. I'd lay odds on whether or not the soccer fans in Italy would overrun the stadium. I'd lay odds I was in for a long night.

There were game shows.

Which also made me think of gambling. Would the blonde from the travel agency in Dubuque guess that C_L_FORN_ _, a place, according to Pat Sajak, was the state about to fall into the ocean to the west?

The Travel Channel was doing a special on the Bellagio. So, of course, that made me think of what else?

Gambling.

In frustration, I cruised until I found David Letterman. His gap-toothed grin usually soothed me to some sort of posthypnotic bedtime state. But it didn't work. I laughed at his monologue. I smiled at Paul Schaeffer's jinglelike keyboard songs. But instead of sleep, I inexplicably thought of my mother.

My mother didn't just marry down when she eloped with my father, she descended a fucking twenty-flight staircase on a bicycle.

Christina Wentworth was a blond-haired, blue-eyed cheerleader from South Carolina, where her grandfather was a senator from way back. She met my father while they were both at the Kentucky Derby. She wore a hat and was dressed to Southern-belle perfection. He wore a hat, too, though into its band he had tucked the racing forms. He was a few Scotches into a bender; she was two mint juleps into as tipsy as a Wentworth ever got. They literally ran into each other as my father turned away from placing his bets for the race. Five days later they were hitched.

How can I classify the reaction of the Wentworths? My mother's mother wore a black mourning dress for a year— granted it was from the House of Chanel. Her father forbade any of his other three daughters from mentioning my mother's name in mixed company. When I arrived nine months and eleven days after that first fateful meeting at the derby, the Wentworths softened only slightly at the news they were first-time grandparents. A trust fund was established. They flew to New York City to see me in my stroller. My father tried his best to show them a good time, but the Wentworths' definition of good time did not coincide with Sean McNally's. We never saw them again. Until my mother's funeral.

She was beautiful. It's funny how when someone has been dead a long time, they just sort of fade in your memory until you have only this misty image of them, like the ghost they've become. I remember that she wore a single strand of pearls all the time, even when she was cleaning the house. That she ran into my father's arms each time he walked through the door, and they never said goodbye without kissing on the mouth—something I and my childhood friends found gross. That she only wore dresses, never pants. That I never, ever saw her with curlers in her hair, and neither did my father, yet months after she died, I found a set of hot rollers in her bathroom and realized that was how she got her hair to flip up so perfectly on the ends. In my mind, she was suspended in time, the perfect icon.

Her death had been an accident. My grandfather Wentworth had prostate cancer, and with the tumor came a total reevaluation of his life. He said he wanted to mend fences. Wanted her and me to be a part of the Wentworths' lives again—even if that meant including my father. But rather than us all flying down there, my mother said she would go alone. Spend time with them. Then make plans for us all to be together. Maybe even a vacation in South Carolina. I think she knew that, prostate cancer aside, finding a way to reconcile what her world on Long Island had become with who they remembered her to be was not going to be easy.

My father wasn't thrilled about baby-sitting me for a weekend. Entertaining an eight-year-old kid during NFL play-offs time wasn't his idea of a good time. He wasn't pleased at all. But he never could say no to her. So we stood at a big plate-glass window and waved goodbye to her jumbo jet at Kennedy airport. Later, the small Cessna she ended up taking as a connecting flight to reach the Wentworth family plantation crashed. Both she and the private pilot were killed.

I think I've shoved the memories from those first days after her death way down inside. They live in the same place my gambling lives and mingle uneasily together.

My father, in between crushing grief and having to run his bookie business, didn't know what to do, let alone what to do with me. It was as if, in stunned silence, in grief, we had to figure out how to be father and daughter—and instead ended up being co-conspirators in gambling.

And the moment my mother died, I suppose…in a nutshell…that was when my father and I first started driving each other crazy.

Letterman was over. Flip, flip, flip. I usually switch over to Conan. T.D. knocked on my bedroom door.

"You up, Little Girl?"

"Come on in," I called out, punching my pillow and sighing over my sleeplessness.

He opened the door, and, as always when he invaded my room, I tried to keep from laughing. What would certain members of the NFL pay me, in cold, hard U.S. dollars, to obtain a Polaroid of George "Touchdown" Russell in the world's *largest* red silk kimono?

"Shut up," he said, without even looking at my face. Knowing it was contorted into a smirk. "I like the feel of silk on my skin."

"Yeah. Okay. You keep telling yourself that, big boy. Don't forget I've also seen you in a mud mask."

"I mean it—no lip. And what are you doin' in here,

Skye? Channel surfin' like a crazy person. I swear you have attention-deficit disorder."

"Among other problems. Why can't you sleep?"

He shrugged. But I knew why. There isn't an addict of any sort—gambler, alcoholic, coke fiend—who, when he stops, doesn't find himself wistful over what he's lost. The price he's paid for his addiction.

Me? I made a mess of my already messy personal life, creating the complication of an ex-husband, though the marriage lasted all of a nanosecond. And I've thrown away thousands upon tens of thousands of Wentworth dollars. I realize losing *their* dollars must give me some perverse pleasure. They set up the trust but haven't tried to contact me in years. I've also lost any shot at a normal life. I'm just not cut out for it, I don't think, regardless of how much therapy I try. I've lost, I sometimes fear, any chance of working things out with my father.

T.D. lost a lot of things, too. His addiction came with a price, like all addiction. You sign a Faustian deal. The thrill of getting high, gambling, sex, whatever, in return for your soul if you're not careful. T.D. was banned from the NFL, and has lost the ability to ever be in the Hall of Fame. And he's lost one Super Bowl ring out of two—ex-wife took it. And when I catch him some nights staring down at the ring he still has, I know he's thinking about the guys in the Hall of Fame. None of whom ever played better than he did.

"What a pair we are," I murmured, and moved over in bed. "Wanna sleep here?"

We occasionally slept in the same bed. Nothing ever happened other than us talking like a pair of seventh-graders at a slumber party, deep into the night. I think he sometimes liked knowing a warm body was next to him.

And frankly, I didn't mind a snuggle against a fifty-inch, hard-muscled chest myself.

"Yeah." He slid in next to me, and I curled up against the crook of his arm, his massive bicep serving as a pillow.

I sighed.

"What?"

"Nothing."

"Sounds like something."

"Nah."

"Skye…" he intoned.

"All right. All right. I'm thinking of going to New York."

"Which is always trouble."

"Yep. Last time I went home I drove there from a lost six months in Atlantic City." I was working as a cocktail waitress in a casino until my predilection for gambling got me in trouble. "I just needed a rest, and New York had always been home. Less than a week later, I ended up coming to Vegas on a dare and getting married."

Jimmy Sullivan, my father's second-in-command, was once nothing more than a punk kid from my old neighborhood. Lanky, with black hair that fell over his eyes all the time, he started out as a runner for my dad. He moved up the ladder, progressively trusted with more and more responsibility, following my father around, first like a puppy dog, then as an equal. In front of my eyes, he changed from this awkward juvenile delinquent into a man with an air about him that was part king, part junkyard dog, with a scent of sex about him, emanating from his now well-built frame. My father loved Jimmy as if he was the son he never had, maybe even secretly hoped I'd end up with his heir apparent. But Dad sure didn't expect us to elope for a quickie wedding, a mere three days after laying eyes on each other again.

"This time you can skip the elopement part."

"But I have to tell you, T.D., Jimmy makes my stomach tighten."

"I take it that's a good thing."

"It's a good-bad thing. He's so wrong for me, but I find him hard to resist."

"You're making me old before my time. If you go, you call me every day. Twice a day."

"I will."

"You're one big headache, Little Girl. You know that? Lots of issues."

"Yeah. But if you didn't have me, what would you do with all your time? Don't I make life more interesting?"

"*Interesting* is not the word I was looking for." He laughed, shaking the bed. I took the remote and flipped until I found an episode of *The Simpsons*. T.D. has a serious love of cartoons. We can spend Saturday mornings watching *Bugs Bunny* for hours.

After a while, I heard T.D.'s steady breathing. I leaned up on one elbow and looked down at his face. He had a wide slash of a mouth, strong cheekbones, a broad nose that looks like it's been broken a couple of times. A wrinkleless complexion, smooth and dark. I kissed his cheek. I knew in a few days I'd be running up his cell phone bill. Extensively. Not to mention mine.

Poor T.D. He really had no idea what he was in for when he agreed to sponsor me.

CHAPTER
FIVE

Five days later, I sat in first class on a direct flight from Vegas to JFK and found my thoughts drifting to flash paper as the flight attendant came down the aisle peddling drinks from a tray, and I waited for a bourbon. Actually, I ordered three of those mini-airline bottles.

Flash paper. I guessed I was maybe the only person on the plane who even knew what that was.

My father started in the bookie business long before technology. There were no cell phones or beepers. Forget the Internet. Just a bank of landlines in a dingy basement office, with TV sets scattered all around, men huddled near them, manning the phones, smoking. Some of them didn't actually smoke so much as chomp on the end of a cigar until it was a soggy mess. When they weren't smoking or chomping, they were eating, screaming, laughing (if all was going well) and cursing (if all was not going well—though often just for the hell of it, anyway). And buckets of water sat everywhere.

My father and all his guys wrote everything—bets and

bettors—on flash paper, sort of like bookie magic. They used code, but it still wasn't the type of thing they wanted the cops finding if we were raided. So flash paper was a sort of safety net. One kind of flash paper meant if they put it in an ashtray and took a match to it, *poof,* it all went up in flames should the cops be beating down our door. The other kind, the type my father used most often, disintegrated the instant it hit water. Thus the guys could dump it in a toilet, something my father had done more than once when he was in a bar, or they could dump the paper in the buckets of water we had everywhere, if we were in the middle of a raid. As a child, I maneuvered around the buckets expertly, occasionally peering in them, wondering why we didn't have goldfish like other families. Just buckets of tap water.

I don't even know if I ever asked Dad what flash paper was. It seemed like I was born knowing. I mean, he must have told me at some point, but so much of that life had seeped into my subconscious that I didn't recall a time when I didn't know the secrets of bookies, the secrets of my father.

Dad didn't rely totally on flash paper, though. Like me, he had an uncanny ability to store most stuff in his head, especially numbers. Which was good. Because if we were raided and everyone used flash paper to make all the evidence disappear, Dad—and later me—had to resurrect his books as near he could from memory.

As a kid, I didn't learn the first thing about how to fly a kite. I never even learned, oddly enough, how to ride a bicycle. I still don't know how. I didn't know the difference between Barbie or Midge or Skipper. Instead, I learned about flash paper. About "uncles" and "cousins." Back then, my father worried about the dreaded wiretap—

all bookies did. So nobody said anything on the phone that could tie either end of the conversation to gambling. When my father called one of his clients on the phone, he said everything in a rather transparent code—it wasn't like he was fooling anyone. "This is your uncle," he'd say. "I'm calling about you needing to bring two hundred pounds of shrimp to Thanksgiving." (Now, that's a lot of shrimp.)

I suppose I should have hated the life we led. When served with a search warrant, my pants were the number-one place to hide things. Children, not named in indictments or search warrants, could not be searched. But I just thought I was lucky. No homework. No Girl Scouts. Dad never looked at my report card. He didn't care what time I went to bed. He didn't care if I ate Twinkies for breakfast. Nothing boring or ordinary entered our lives. I lived in a world of men who were larger than life, who didn't follow the rules.

I missed my mother, though, ached for her. At night, sometimes, I would wake up in a half dream. I was sure she had been there in my room, stroking my forehead as I slept. She was so real, so tangible. But then I would wake more fully and realize it was a phantom dream. She was an echo, similar to the notes of a long-forgotten song, when you only can hum a bar or two. I longed to hug her. I desperately didn't want to be the girl at school whose mother died in a plane crash.

The human mind is extraordinarily resilient. Over time, I stopped having those dreams and I buried that ache, that physical pang, beneath the attention I got from a roomful of men, who patted me on the head and gave me an inside tip, and the excitement of Sunday's games, Friday night's fights and the worlds of horseracing and poker.

By the time I was ten, I could hold my own with a couple of my father's poker pals. We played, during football season, every Sunday, for quarter ante. I learned quickly that sometimes the cards turn against you. But I also learned to memorize every card on the table—a gift my father's crew didn't have, most especially after a six-pack, or two...or three. I learned to read a player's face. When to fold. When to bluff. I studied Larry the Lip and knew he got a tic in his left eye when he had a bad hand and should fold but was staying in for one last card. I often won. They didn't have Gamblers Anonymous for ten-year-olds. Come to think of it, they still don't. I never thought my life was diseased, addicted, distorted. And though as an adult, I didn't blame my father for my gambling compulsion, I knew he hadn't helped matters any. None of my childhood had.

The flight attendant gave me my little bottles of booze. I stared around me at the other passengers. They all looked like "citizens"—people whose lives were ordinary, or in the words of the first step of GA, "manageable." I drank my bourbon quickly, trying to drown out the memories that flooded my mind the closer I got to New York City....

"Prison? Please tell me you're kidding," I had screamed at him. All of eighteen, my black hair down to my waist, four earrings in one ear, three in the other. I was interested in clubbing and gambling, *not* running my father's operations while he served eighteen months.

"I gotta take the plea, Skye."

"The *plea?* You're taking a plea, and that's the best offer they got on the table?"

"Afraid so."

"And what genius turned on you?"

"Joey Smalls."

"Asshole."

"He'll get his." My father's eyes were murderous—and it wasn't the first time I ever saw that look. "Meantime, I gotta take the plea."

"Damn you, Dad."

"Come on, kid." He looked at me imploringly, pleadingly. As if I was the judge or the D.A. I knew better than to take his look seriously. He was a con man at best, something else at worst. And he wanted something from me. "I need you on this one."

"I don't know, Dad."

His face was handsome, angular. I guess he was around fifty then, still fit. He had a long but strong nose that seemed not to belong on his face; it was too regal for someone with an air about him that said tough guy, ex-con. His gray eyes unsettled people in their lightness against his swarthy complexion. His chin was reminiscent of Kirk Douglas's, with the little dimple in the center of it. He always had a five o'clock shadow and, unlike other men his age, hadn't seemed to lose so much as a strand of his thick black hair.

"Jimmy will help you," he said. "He can handle things. He can handle most everything. But I need you. I need family. I need people to know I may be gone, but my place in the business is not."

I crossed my arms and sat there sullenly. But life, like the odds, isn't fair. I knew that, so in the end, I nodded. He stood and kissed me on top of my head. He hadn't won me over with his sad-sack routine; I had been raised to value loyalty above all other qualities, and I was nothing if not loyal.

Soon, my life became a series of trips to a minimum-security prison. I got to pass through metal detectors and wait with the other felons' families and girlfriends in a crowded visiting room. I was struck by how stark it was. The walls were barren—just gunmetal-gray cinder blocks. A single large clock ticked away the minutes and seconds of visiting hours, its big black hands turning, indicating the one thing prisoners had—time. Time to think, time to regret, time to miss the outside. Dad and the other prisoners would enter the visiting room wearing orange jumpsuits that made them all anonymous numbers. Now I knew why men got jailhouse tattoos. Their arms were defiantly their own, and they made statements with the ink: love, hate, death, swastikas, children's names, girlfriends' names. Tattoos were a statement of their uniqueness. A statement that the prison could take away their names, their freedom, their possessions, but not their minds. Not their souls. My dad had two tattoos—my name in a heart on his right biceps, and a pair of dice on the inside of his left wrist.

Dad and I sat at a cafeteria-style table, and he gave me instructions, which I had to memorize, not write down. He seemed unbothered by his jailhouse experiences. He wore his uniform like a badge of courage. He never hung his head. He swaggered into that room. He told me he took book "in the big house." Convicts bet cigarettes. They traded with what they had.

I remember looking around at all the cons holding hands with their girlfriends, their wives. My father and I never held hands, and I only hugged him stiffly goodbye, my anger always in the air between us. I didn't want the mantle of responsibility. I didn't want the sleepless nights. I had to believe the swagger and his solid right hook would keep him from being shanked, would protect him. But at night, I would drink bourbon from the stress, wondering if he'd pissed off the wrong guard, the wrong con, worried what might happen if the bets he took went the wrong way.

After my weekend visits, Mondays were an orgy of numbers, figuring out the winners and losers on four thousand football cards—cardboard forms with all the NFL games listed on them. The cards bore the bullshit line "For Amusement Purposes Only" across the bottom to cover our asses with the cops in case they found them in a raid. Yeah…we fill out cards just to amuse ourselves. But that way, we could pretend the cards were nothing more than some harmless fun. *No one really bet any money, Officer.*

Bettors picked their teams. I knew each gambler was as unique as his technique. Some spent many hours calculating averages, yards rushed, reading scouting reports. Others bet their favorites, never betting against the hometown team even if the team was destined to lose. Some used superstition and Lady Luck. They looked for signs, betting on hunches and gut instincts. I even knew a few oddballs who bet on the colors of uniforms, whether the team mascot had a tail or not (betting on the tails every time)—and one guy even prayed to the Virgin Mary for "signs" on who to pick. Later on, when I went into Gamblers Anonymous, I realized that all gambling addicts were pretty much the same. They might choose their bets for unique reasons, but they all—we all—bet for the thrill. To quiet the buzz in their heads.

After we figured out the winners and losers from the cards, Jimmy and I spent the week gathering the cash from the various "cousins"—those guys who collected the book on the cards. We met on a rotational basis, never the same spot with the same guy. Never at the same time. I saw the inside of every Dunkin' Donuts in a thirty-mile radius.

I grew up even faster than before, the eighteen months of my father's sentence flying by in a whir of numbers and screaming at television sets until I was hoarse. The pressure on me was intense, and I hated every minute of it. I longed to be simply a gambler, back in my poker games, back at the track betting on a trifecta, not with Jimmy in a dirty bar waiting for a cousin with his losers' money. I ended up spending five days in the hospital with a bleeding ulcer. Bourbon didn't help it. Still doesn't.

And now, flying home to New York on the plane, I blinked hard. I thought it was the airplane making my eyes dry, but it could have been a tear. Either way, it felt like shit.

"Angel!" There my father stood, outside the gates, past Security, on the way to Baggage Claim, with an enormous bouquet of yellow roses. He was the king of grand gestures. I guessed there were three dozen in the bunch. I remember extravagant Christmases, birthdays of diamond tennis bracelets. My father was dressed in gray slacks, which I knew would be Italian and custom-tailored, black Ferragamo loafers, and a crisp white oxford-cloth shirt with his initials embroidered on the cuffs. He looked like he'd just had a fresh haircut. Over the years, he learned to spend in style.

Next to Dad stood my ex-husband, though, courtesy of our annulment, he was more like the man I married but didn't really. He still was as beautiful as I remembered. He stood with the same kind of commanding, tough-guy stance as my dad. They radiated a certain power. Not corporate boardroom power, but street power, the power that exalted them to walk into any room and defend themselves. They were afraid of no one. I took a deep breath and walked up to the two men.

"Hey, babe," Jimmy kissed my cheek, his lips staying there for a fraction of a second longer than a casual peck. "Long time, no see."

"Long time, no marry," I shot back, looking away, accepting my father's roses, and walking on toward Baggage Claim, leaving them both scrambling to keep up with me.

"How was your flight, Skye?" my father asked me.

"Long. I'm tired. Hungry. I have a headache." The combination of the dry airplane air and booze hadn't helped matters.

"Want to stop at Finnegan's for a steak and a beer?"

I nodded, not looking over my shoulder. I hadn't expected the sight of Jimmy to give me that old feeling. I hadn't expected to want to fuck him. I hadn't expected that seeing them both would make my old world of flash paper and bookmaking come hurtling back at me like a freight train.

The three of us fell into a stride together. *The three of us.* After my mother died, my father and I had eventually found a rhythm in our house, in our lives. When Jimmy came along, that rhythm didn't change much. He loved the world of flash paper, loved betting and poker. He loved the adrenaline rushes. And after a while, he loved me.

I thought, by staying in Las Vegas, I could forget the way I felt when I was around my dad and Jimmy. But I hadn't forgotten at all.

In a dark-wood back booth in Finnegan's, I cut into a rare filet mignon and shared a third pitcher of Michelob with my dad and Jimmy. My father kept smiling, grinning as if he'd just won a trifecta paying out odds at seventy-two to one.

"What?" I asked him.

"What what?"

"What are you grinning at?"

He threw his hands into the air, a gesture I often did myself—how had I turned into my father?—and rolled his eyes. "Can't a man admire his daughter? It's been three long fucking years, Skye."

I looked down at my steak, trying not to let him unsettle me. He did love me. Why couldn't he understand, though, what that love had cost me? Reams of flash paper down my pants. A childhood spent fearing police raids. It wasn't until my first Gamblers Anonymous meeting that I started, only vaguely, to understand my addiction. To understand that I had deserved a better childhood than that.

I remember telling my story at a meeting, and I drew pitying looks, even from the hard-core old-timers. As if my past destined me to a future fighting the compulsion to gamble.

"I'm sorry, Daddy," I whispered. "There's just a lot of water under the bridge, you know?" I looked up at him, composed again.

"Water. Like I don't fucking know that. Skye…angel… we've all been a team since I can't remember when."

"I didn't ask to be on the team. I didn't have a choice."

"Look, you think that anybody has a choice what family they grow up in? Okay, so we weren't Ozzie and Harriet. But you know, there were also some really good times in that 'water.'"

"Sure, I loved the Thanksgiving I had to bail you out of jail. I was laughing my way through your eighteen-month prison sentence. Oh, and it was a regular party hiding in the back seat of the car while you and Tommy Moe went to town with a crowbar on Johnny Four-eyes."

"Well, if we're dragging shit like that out of the closet, let's start with you marrying and then divorcing the best man in the world." He slapped Jimmy on the back.

"First of all, the marriage was annulled."

"Don't get technical on me, Skye. That's what my lawyers are for. Come on…you're home for the weekend. Let's just be together. A family."

I looked across the table at him. He was right. No matter how much I tried to reinvent him, to shoehorn him into the role of "Daddy,"—he was and always would be a bookie—and one you didn't want to cross. Something from GA must have sunk in. *God, grant me the serenity to accept the things I cannot change.* Anyone who thought she could change Sean McNally was crazy.

All the while Dad and I had been trading barbs about the past, Jimmy was giving me his best fuck-me gaze. His eyes were almost black. I never could see the irises for the pupils, unless his face was inches from mine. And his dark curly hair always drove me crazy, the way he looked boyish and roguish all at once.

Now that there appeared to be a truce between my father and me—if just a temporary one—Jimmy asked, "Marry anyone lately?" His grin was lopsided and smirky.

"Shut the fuck up, Jimmy. Don't remind me why we imploded," I said, but I was grinning, too. I could be such a tease with a pitcher of Michelob in me.

"I'd never do that. I miss you too much. I've sworn off all women since you left me."

"Yeah, right. You were leering at cocktail waitresses on our honeymoon, for God's sake."

"I was caught up in the thrill of Vegas," he replied. "But I really have sworn off women."

"He has," my father added. "Like a fucking monk, he is." Dad kept smiling. Like somehow he hoped Jimmy and I would reconcile. He signaled our waitress for another pitcher, and she brought it pronto. My father has a reputation, almost legendary, of being an obscenely big tipper.

"Who's driving us home?" I asked.

"I am," my father said, pouring himself another mug of beer.

"Dad—"

"All right. So you join this Gamblers Anonymous, and now you also have something against drinking and driving. A time-honored McNally tradition."

"Yes."

"I'll call—" He looked over at Jimmy. "What's the punk's name? The new kid?"

"Nick."

"I'll call Nick to drive us home."

"Okay." I helped myself to another beer.

Jimmy kept staring at me. "You look great, Skye."

"Thanks… I'm going to the ladies' room." I stood, and they both half rose from their seats across the table from me. Gentlemen. And gamblers and felons. What a combination.

I navigated through the now-crowded bar to the ladies' room. Then, after I finished, I left the bathroom and stepped outside the restaurant to call T.D.

"Hello, Little Girl." He answered his cell on the first ring.

"How'd you know it was me?"

"Caller I.D. Plus, you and my mama are about the only two people with this number. How's it goin'?"

"I'm drunk."

"I can tell."

"How can you tell? I've said about seven words."

"I can just tell."

"Fine."

"What else?"

"It's Jimmy."

"Don't sleep with him."

"I know. It would be a huge mistake. But those eyes. Those lips. That incredible male organ."

"More details than I need to know."

"Oh, please—you buy me tampons for Chez T.D. You live on details. It's how we are. We're detail people. You're my sponsor."

"I know. Which brings me to my next question."

"I haven't had *time* to gamble. I just got here."

"Well, you're drunk, horny…it's just a question of time before *all* of your vices kick in."

"Thanks for the vote of confidence."

"Don't mention it."

"I have to go. We're in the middle of dinner."

"Call me later, Little Girl."

"Fine."

"Don't pull your fuck-you attitude with me. Call me."

"I said fine."

"No. You said *fine*." He imitated my voice. I *did* sound snotty.

I laughed. "All right. I'll call you."

I went back to the table and finished my steak, ignoring my father's radiant grin and Jimmy's sex-starved gaze and wandering foot under the table.

After cheesecake for dessert with beer chasers, my father called Nick on his cell phone to drive us home. Nick got dropped off at the restaurant, and after my father paid the bill, tipping the waitress two crisp hundreds on a $190 tab, we piled into my father's Lincoln, he and Nick up front and Jimmy and me in the back. Jimmy grabbed my hand and squeezed it. Courtesy of all that beer, I squeezed back. Then I one-upped him and stroked the inside of his wrist with my index finger.

Nick navigated to my father's house—my childhood home. The poor kid looked very nervous with chauffeuring duties. He was probably all of eighteen or nineteen, maximum, with the lanky build the young Jimmy Sullivan once had. Punks. They all started out with my dad as punks. If they were good at what they did, they graduated from punk to tough-guy felon. The swagger began to have meaning behind it.

When the car pulled into the driveway, I was struck by how little the place had changed since I left. By how little it had changed since my mother died. The house was a shrine in many ways, and though I never kid myself about my father having had girlfriends since my mother's death, I know for a fact no other woman had ever slept in their bedroom, had ever even been inside the house. He always went to his girlfriends' homes. If you could even call them girlfriends. There was no commitment, no promise of a future to them.

"Home sweet home," Dad said, climbing out. "Jimmy, come on in for a drink."

Jimmy had Nick open the trunk, and then Jimmy carried in my overnight bag.

"You don't have much stuff," he said.

"Because I'm not staying long. I go home on Monday night."

"That's barely three days."

"Just enough time to avoid murdering my father and marrying you again."

"I see your sense of humor hasn't changed." He followed me up the front steps as I climbed to the entranceway. My father was already in the house, and Nick was standing at the end of the driveway talking on his cell phone, undoubtedly telling his buddy to come pick him up. Jimmy whispered, "That's what I always loved about you, you know."

"I know...." I cursed the Michelob coursing through my veins. I turned around and smiled at him, though. *Slut, slut, slut, slut, slut.*

My father appeared at the door to the house and held it open. He handed me a tumbler filled with bourbon and ice as I walked in. I took it and looked around. The couch was new, a Chippendale reproduction, but looked like the couch we had when I was still living at home. The pictures on the wall going into the dining room showcased a chronology of my life, from kindergarten to high school graduation. Me with two missing front teeth and a smattering of freckles across the bridge of my nose, my long black hair in two ponytails. Me, after my mother died, in third, fourth and fifth grade, sans ponytails, because my father couldn't figure out how to "do a ponytail." As I got older, with no woman around to teach me the basics of makeup application, I went bare-faced. Even in my prom picture—Jimmy at my side—I was devoid of makeup.

Jimmy came through the door, accepted my father's proffered bourbon and set my bag down in the hallway. The three of us walked into the den and sat down on butter-cream leather couches. My second-grade clay sculpture of a turtle in its shell sat on the coffee table, serving as a paperweight for the TV and cable guides.

"You following the Mustangs?" my father asked me.

"Who isn't?"

The Mustangs were a New York expansion team. With a new stadium, New York was one city that got a new team—along with two other cities. Owned by the two flamboyant brothers who started the River's End brewery, as well as an enormous chain of hamburger eateries, the Mustangs were decidedly less than a Dream Team for one long, agonizing season before they drafted Mark Shannon, he of the Golden Arm. Now, in a city with a love for all things sports, especially Cinderella stories, the Mustangs were poised to make it into the Super Bowl, this year scheduled to be played in sunny south Florida— Miami, home of South Beach, land of thongs and skimpy bikinis.

"I could kiss that Mark Shannon," my father said.

"Homo," Jimmy muttered, then winked at my dad. In truth, though, most of New York would kiss Mark Shannon if given the chance. The quarterback was six feet three inches tall, pure muscle, and had blond hair and green eyes. He was a commercial dream, and had endorsements rivaling any sports icon in the superstar universe.

"Call me a homo, but he always wins.... Pulls out these Hail Marys—yet doesn't cover the spread, so he's a bookie's dream, a veritable hard-on. He wins, which is good for business. But he does it very close—also good for business. And then once in a while, he obliterates the other team and decimates the point spread, so anyone who doesn't think he's covering the spread gets killed, too. Mark Shannon may just make it possible for me to retire to Las Vegas."

"What?" I tried to avoid the question coming out as a shriek, but, in fact, it had.

"Yeah. I've had it with New York winters. I want to retire someplace warm."

"What about Boca Raton?"

"Too Jewish."

"You're a poster boy of religious tolerance."

"Thank you." My father grinned. Then he looked at his watch. "You two stay up and watch Johnny Carson. I'm off to bed."

"Dad," I said. "Johnny Carson hasn't been on in years. It's Jay Leno now. And I hate him. I watch Letterman."

"Whatever makes you happy, honey." He stood and kissed me on top of my head. "Welcome home, Skye...the house doesn't feel like home unless you're here. 'Night, Jimmy."

"'Night, boss."

My father climbed the stairs of our big Dutch Colonial to the second-floor bedrooms. I tried to decide whether the Johnny Carson comment really meant he was confused and getting a little senile, or he was just manipulating me into *thinking* he was confused, and decided on the latter.

As soon as Dad was out of sight, Jimmy pulled me closer to him on the couch and kissed me, hard. I kissed him back.

"I've missed you, wife," he said, pulling back to look at me. "You really do look terrific. Like it was just yesterday, babe."

"You don't look so bad yourself." The Michelob was talking again. I leaned closer to him and started kissing him, then ran my tongue along his bottom lip, which always made him moan. Jimmy did not disappoint. And a Jimmy Sullivan moan, for the record, could make most women swoon.

We started making out, passionately. I bit at his neck and teased him, kissing him, then pulling away until he grabbed me.

"This is why I swore off women. No one else makes me practically come just by how she kisses me. God*damn* you, Skye."

Just as I was about to suggest we move up to my bedroom, my cell phone rang.

"Who's calling you—" Jimmy looked at his watch "—at this hour?"

"George Russell."

"As in the football player, T.D. Russell?"

"Yes."

"You fucking him?"

By now I was fumbling for my phone in my purse. I pressed Talk. "One minute, T.D.," I said. I covered the phone, and then looked at Jimmy. "Look, stick your dick

in your pants. You don't own me. It's Gamblers *Anonymous.*
So I can't say how I know him. But put two and two together, Sherlock. And no, I'm not fucking him."

I uncovered the phone and said, "Hello?"

"You fucking the man?" T.D.'s voice intoned.

I stood and walked into the kitchen, out of Jimmy's earshot. "Suddenly," I hissed, "everyone is interested in who
I'm fucking. T.D., I haven't been laid in almost a year."

"You drinking bourbon?"

"What, do you have surveillance cameras?"

"I can just tell."

"Fuck you."

"Don't get all nasty with me. Let us remind that thick
Irish head of yours of a few facts. Your father is a bookie…
big time. Correct?"

"Yes."

"This guy is his right-hand man. Correct?"

"Yes."

"You are a gambling addict. Correct?"

"Yes. Well, I don't know if addict is the right word."

"Denial."

"Okay, then. Yes."

"And you married this man on a drunken weekend
three years ago. Correct?"

"Mmm-hmm."

"Had it annulled. Correct?"

"Yes."

"Skye, don't make me come to New York. You gotta
stay healthy. Talk to your Higher Power."

"You know I hate that Higher Power crap."

"Skye, you are powerless. It's the Higher *Power.* God is
there to help you, if you'd just ask once in a while."

"I'm not particularly good at asking anyone for help."

"Please, Skye. Think about the consequences of your actions."

"Okay."

"You know this is because I care. Look…I gambled because I got caught up in trying to beat the house. I thought I was too smart for everyone else, Skye. For me, it was all about ego. But you…you are self-destructive. Don't do this. 'Cause you'll hate yourself tomorrow."

"I know."

"Love you, Little Girl."

"Love you, too. And thanks."

I went back out to the den.

"Come back and sit down." Jimmy begged me, patting the couch beside him. I could see a huge bulge in his crotch, and my mind immediately reeled backward in time to our hours-long lovemaking sessions.

"Jimmy…" I exhaled. "You have to go."

"What?"

"You have to."

He stood up and pulled me to him.

"Please," I begged him. "We'll both regret this in the morning. We can't be together."

He kissed me, biting my lower lip softly.

"Jimmy…"

"All right." He held his hands up and stepped back. "To show you what a gentleman I am, I'll leave. But tomorrow night, all bets are off."

All bets are off. Everything about our lives was a metaphor for gambling.

"What are we doing tomorrow?" I asked him.

"Your father and I have some things to do in the daytime, and we have tickets for Broadway tomorrow night, then dinner out."

"Broadway?"

"Your father is trying to show you a good time. Wait until tomorrow. I'll be back here at ten in the morning."

"Okay," I said, walking him to the door. I kissed him good night.

"And, Skye," he said, stepping down to the pathway that led to the driveway.

"Yeah?"

"Even if nothing happens between us this trip…your old man…he misses you and loves you."

I thought of the shrine to me in the hallway. The ceramic turtle that looked like it had barely survived a meat grinder—yet he had acted delighted when I gave it to him when I was a little girl. The doorway to the den still had the pen marks measuring off how I had grown each year.

"Yeah," I said. "I can hate him all I want for a lot of things…old stuff. But that…that, I never doubt."

I shut the door and went up to my old bedroom. It was stark, in some ways. No awards. No ribbons. No memorabilia of any kind. No nothing from my high school years. I had been too busy gambling as a teen to care what anyone my own age was doing.

CHAPTER

SEVEN

Jimmy and my father spent the day doing the things they do—collecting cards, visiting cousins, figuring out wins and losses from college games, and taking lots and lots of book for the New York Mustangs on Sunday. My father lived for seasons like this one. While New York had always been Giants and Jets territory, when the expansion team hit, it had occurred when the home teams were in a slump. And so sports-crazed New Yorkers embraced the new team more readily than any of the national or New York sportswriters thought they would—especially since the team had a state-of-the-art stadium. And when the Mustangs acquired Mark Shannon, and he started playing like possibly the best quarterback in the history of the game, well, New York went nuts. And so did my father and Jimmy—and no doubt other bookies. Business was good.

I slept in, got up around eleven and found my father had bought a dozen bagels from my favorite place—De Cicci's Deli—and cream cheese. He had made a pot of strong coffee, and he had even left out a bottle of Jack Daniel's in case I needed an eye-opening splash. I peeked in the bag of bagels and discovered he had bought six salted ones—my favorite. The others were his and Jimmy's favorites—onion. Six bagels was a stretch for me, but I took out one and sliced it open, spread on cream cheese and poured myself a cup of coffee. I skipped the splash.

I sat down in the den and turned on the television to ESPN. I ate my bagel and watched TV. Surprisingly, I was more famished than usual. Jimmy must have worked up my appetite the night before, so I made a second bagel. I looked at my watch. T.D wouldn't be up yet, and the whole day stretched out in front of me, alone in the house of my childhood.

I realized that there was no one else to call. No old high school friends to look up. No one to "catch up on old times" with. But I was facing, with my morning coffee, the truth that my whole life stretching backward through time was about ESPN, the odds, old gamblers who sat around and made fart jokes while we played poker, my father…and even Jimmy. But there were no normal people, no relationships with neighbors—my father always said they were too nosy. Nothing.

We didn't even have any relatives to speak of. On my father's side, he had one sister, who lived in Seattle with my two cousins. I think I met them once. My dad hated his sister. He'd given her money over the years—but she always stuck her hand out for more. My dad's parents had both died—my grandmother when I was thirteen, my grandfather the following year. The Wentworths hadn't contacted me in years. They had tried—a couple of times—to stay in touch, to influence me back when I was a teenager.

I recall one visit. My grandparents came to New York

my senior year of high school. They called and asked me to meet them for lunch at the Plaza. It was around Christmastime, and the entire trip was a shopping excursion for my grandmother.

I was seventeen. And I guess by being raised by my father, some of that swagger of his had passed along to me. I arrived in tight jeans, red snakeskin cowboy boots, a black turtleneck and a leather jacket. My ears were pierced multiple times. If I remember correctly, I may have smoked a cigarette in front of them. Suffice it to say, I didn't look or act like my two debutante cousins in South Carolina.

My grandmother asked polite questions. I gave somewhat sullen answers. They asked about school, and the honest truth was that I did okay, the work was easy, but I was truant so often that I barely scraped by. And I wasn't afraid to let them know it.

Part of me longed to ask them about my mother. I wanted to know what she was like when she was my age. I wanted to *know* her when all I had were very vague recollections, little frozen moments in time that I collected like precious gems in a velvet pouch, only bringing them out into the light once in a rare while. I think I was afraid I'd somehow lose those memories, they were so fragile. But part of me—the part that was one hundred percent McNally—wasn't going to give them the satisfaction of asking them anything. They had rejected my mother because of who she married. Along with that, they had rejected me when I was a little girl, and now, with my New York accent, my tough-girl stance, they were rejecting me again.

Lunch ended with my grandmother giving me a dry-lipped kiss on the cheek and promises to keep in touch. But we didn't. Before the disastrous Plaza lunch, they would call on my birthday, Christmas. After that, we sent Christmas cards. That was it. Not much of a relationship. When I was twenty-two my allowance from the trust kicked in. But I hadn't spoken to them in years.

Actually, my longest relationship—aside from my father—was with a deck of cards. I remember being weaned on games of high-low, then blackjack, then poker and all its variations—five-card stud, Texas Hold 'em, barn burn, seven-card stud. I even knew the stupid poker games like Follow the Whore and Night Baseball.

I knew more about cards than people. I looked around the house I grew up in, and I felt lonely. Though I wasn't hitting bottom, not by a long shot, I felt the urge to call T.D. To call my sponsor. Because whenever I feel things, I want to gamble. I want to take the focus off of me and instead put it out where I think it belongs. On a felt table. Even the smell of felt, or cigars, takes me far away from my loneliness and gives me a rush. It takes me to the thrill of that first Clemson game I bet on, or to a thousand thrills since then, moments when I forgot I was a motherless daughter, that I was a bookie's child, that I had spent way too much time collecting cards and figuring the odds.

I ate my bagel. I drank my coffee. I drank a second cup. And around twelve-thirty, I decided I could call T.D. and wake him. He answered on the first ring.

"You're up early," I said.

"I couldn't sleep."

"Why?"

"Lying here wondering if you're getting ready to elope again."

"Jealous?" I teased, though in reality, there never had

been more than sloppy New Year's kisses between T.D. and me—and a lot of bear hugs. I guess we had skipped over any attraction and went straight to friendship.

"Yeah." He snorted into the phone. "I just don't need to be calling up my divorce attorney again to straighten out an annulment for you."

"Will they grant you a second annulment if you marry the same guy as before?"

"Don't even fucking think about it."

"What about the lawyer? Does he give second-time discounts?"

"I am thinking of painful ways to kill you."

I sighed into the phone.

"What's up, Little Girl? What's *really* up?"

"Do you love me?"

"What? Love like how I love you or love like…you know…the whole big ball of wax?"

"Love like how you love me."

"Then you know I love you."

"I guess I do. It's just… T.D., I'm sitting here and realizing that there's no one else… Do you realize there's no one else I have to visit here? No old high school girlfriends. Because I didn't *have* high school girlfriends. I had Joey the Shark and Teddy Snake-eyes. And Jimmy. What kind of life is that for a kid?"

"Not much of one."

"I feel something."

"Skye McNally feels something. Will wonders never cease? And what is it you feel?"

"Sad. I feel sad."

"Well, that's progress, Little Girl."

"I know. I once had a therapist—a man with a Ph.D. and all—who spent six months just trying to get me to figure out if I was feeling anything or not. You know, like he'd start the session with this 'feeling wheel.'"

"A feeling wheel? What the hell is that?"

"A wheel with happy, sad, angry, lonely, angry—all these emotions on it. And I had to point to the ones I felt. Only I was never quite sure."

"I hope you got your money back from him."

"No. I didn't. He eventually shut his practice. Said it was because of the advent of managed care. I think it was having me for a patient. Oh, T.D., aren't we a pair?"

"Yeah." T.D. had told me one very *ugly* night, over the course of which we had polished off four bottles of champagne, that he was drawn to me out of the same lonely loner instinct I had. At one time, he had it all, had been a star. The adulation, the fans, the beautiful wife. And when he lost it, the shame had been so intense, the only place he had been comfortable, after a while, was Gamblers Anonymous meetings. The stories we heard there didn't have quite the Greek tragedy overtones that his did, but it was all about how much you lost—not money, but what you really lost by being an addict—and somehow he found peace there. Eventually, he stopped hiding from the rest of the world. When he stepped out again into the light of day, he found most of his fans didn't care. But the wall was up. And it took me knock-knock-knocking in my pain-in-the-ass way to tear it down.

"I'm going to try not to gamble *today*," I whispered. The emphasis was on "today." That one-day-at-a-time crap that drove me crazy.

"Good girl. Call me if you need to."

"I will."

I hung up the phone and went upstairs. I had *nothing* to do. Nothing. I found myself wondering what the odds were for the Mustangs game. I only had to call my father's cell phone and place a bet. Or call my regular bookie, Heavy Harry, in Vegas. I felt restless. The odds. My head was buzzing from coffee and wanting to gamble. I wanted to *do* something.

I roamed the hallway, staring at pictures of my mother that my father seemed to have in frames everywhere. I stared at them closely. Not a speck of dust was on the glass of the frames. That meant he still wiped them with Windex regularly, carefully aligning the frames so they hung straight. She certainly was beautiful. I wondered what my life would have been like with a little feminine influence. I remember when my father was off "working"—though technically, I wasn't sure you could call what he did work—I would sneak into his bedroom and take the smallest drop of my mother's Chanel No. 5 and put it on the inside of my wrist, just to have the scent of her near me. Sometimes I would go stand in her closet and rub my cheek against her blouses.

Still feeling antsy, I decided to take a bath. We were going to a Broadway revival of *Guys and Dolls*. Okay, the musical is about gamblers. But that's not why my father chose it.

As I filled the tub, I smiled at the thought of what all his tough guy friends would think if they knew my father was a sucker for musicals. I bet not even Jimmy knew. Sure, my father gave Jimmy a line about showing me a good time, but he was probably just as thrilled to be seeing the show.

I took my bath and tried to tamp down my yearning to gamble by thinking of all the lyrics to the musical *Oklahoma!* My father and I used to watch it on AMC every time it came on.

I soaked until the skin on my fingers wrinkled—I was on my fifteenth chorus of "Oklahoma." Then I did my makeup and pulled out the dress I was going to wear later that night. It was cut low in front, black velvet in the tight-fitting body, with filmy sleeves. I had brought a velvet swing coat as a protection against the fall chill in New York, though I knew my father would have a limo take us into the city and drop us right off in front of the theater. When it came to nights in Manhattan, my father's true gambler instincts showed. Most gamblers, most bookies, thrive on being big shots. And my father liked to show off with the best of them. They all tip big and live large. There's no such thing as a savings account. You buy the biggest and the best to show off your winnings—even if it means hocking your purchase a few weeks later.

I pulled on my bathrobe and went back downstairs to wait for my father and Jimmy. I needed someone, something, to distract me from the buzz in my head, that nervous energy that only gambling quieted.

"*Oklahoma!...*" I hummed to myself. Then I turned on ESPN again.

They were profiling Mark Shannon. He had played at UCLA, for all appearances the classic golden California boy. But in actuality he had been raised in a tough inner-city area around Pittsburgh, the only child of an unemployed iron worker and a homemaker mother. Shannon's stats were putting him to the top of lists of all-time greats. But as bright as his smile was, as perfect as his hair shone, as genuine as he was with kids—and not just for the cameras—he was known to sign autographs for hours in children's wards in hospitals and visit each kid—as long as there was no publicity associated with it—it was clear from the show that Shannon was an enigma. No one knew what made him tick, and he never talked about himself on the record. I knew that in media-hungry America, this just made the newshounds more rabid to get his story.

The buzzing in my head grew louder. I speed-dialed Heavy Harry and he answered, his voice a cross between a frog and a human—not surprising since he smoked three packs of unfiltered cigarettes a day.

"Yo."

"Hey, Heavy…it's Skye. I'd like to put down ten large on the Mustangs to cover the spread."

"You got it there, sister. That Shannon's been good for business. It's good to hear your voice. You swearing off those fucking meetings?"

"Nah. Just had the itch."

I hung up the phone. As if I'd taken a magic pill, the restlessness was gone. Suddenly, I felt downright serene. It was amazing how that worked. I told myself I would start fresh when I went home to Vegas on Monday. Day one. I would make it thirty days. Starting Monday. I was traveling. Travelers got breaks, like you don't have to go to Sunday mass if you're traveling.

It wasn't denial.

Even *I* knew I was full of shit.

CHAPTER

EIGHT

"Luck be a lady tonight."

In third-row-center seats, my father and Jimmy sat on either side of me and we watched the musical. Occasionally, I'd glance sideways at my father. He looked absolutely enthralled with the show, which had fantastic sets reminiscent of the movie *Moulin Rouge*. I even caught Jimmy, in a charcoal-gray Hugo Boss suit, no less, tapping his foot to the music.

After the show, the limo whisked us to Aureole for dinner. Jimmy and I held hands, much to my father's delight, and I found myself thinking less and less of Vegas, less of T.D., less of the Twelve Steps of Gamblers Anonymous, and more about how unbelievably sexy my ex-husband looked.

My father beamed all through the meal, which we washed down with pricey bottles of champagne.

"Skye...I have to tell you something, honey."

"What, Dad?"

"Well, you never listen to me, but every time I talk to you from Las Vegas, you don't sound happy. But tonight…tonight you look like a princess. And you look really, *really* happy."

I thought about it. Numbers were my territory. Feelings not so much. But my father was right. "I do feel happy, Dad. I shouldn't have stayed away so long." Being home was like slipping into a comfortable old sweater, something that made you feel warm and safe.

"You know, I'm getting old," he continued.

I rolled my eyes. "Dad, I hear that every time we talk on the phone."

"But it's true."

I looked across the table at my father. I was so used to him being in command. Even in an orange prison jumpsuit, his swagger told people not to mess with him. But now that he said it, he did look older.

Jimmy lifted my hand to his lips and kissed it. "This has been a night for the record books. I can't remember the last time I had such a good time. I didn't even mind the musical. Hey, are you named after Sky Masterson? From the play?"

"Yes, she was. It was her mother's favorite musical. I wanted to humor her mother. Part of the sacrifices of marriage," Dad said. I loved how he pretended *he* wasn't the one who was the musical fan. He would have leaped onstage and joined in the chorus of "Sit Down You're Rocking the Boat" if he could have.

"I promise I won't stay away so long next time." I smiled at the two of them. Okay, so they weren't Ozzie and Harriet. They weren't even the Osbournes. But they *were* the family I had.

"I'm glad to hear you say that," my father said. "Because I wasn't kidding when I said I was thinking about retiring."

"You should, Dad. You've worked hard your whole

life." I choked on the words a little bit. I wasn't sure if what he did constituted "hard work," but he certainly had been doing it a long, long time. He had started out running numbers as a fifteen-year-old on the Lower East Side of Manhattan. He worked for a guy who had a candy store that had once been a vegetable market with a chute in the back where they used to throw down old potatoes and spoiled vegetables. Only, after it became a candy store, the place really fronted for a bookie operation and people dropped money and bets down the chute to a cellar of men hunched over phones, radios and small black-and-white TVs. With buckets of water all around.

"Exactly. And Jimmy here will take over. And there is nothing that would make me happier than to know you were right there with him."

The comment just sort of hung in the air.

"D-D-Dad…" I stuttered. "I don't know what's up with Jimmy and me."

"No decisions." He waved his hands in the air. Then he reached over to the champagne bucket and poured me another glass. "I'm just saying that I would love to see you return to your roots, Skye. You were *born* for this life. It's in your blood."

"Because it was forced on me."

Jimmy gently stroked my leg underneath the table. I could barely think as his fingers moved up my leg. And the champagne wasn't helping any.

"You always say that, Skye, and sure, you never would have been down in that basement so much if we hadn't lost your mother, God rest her sweet soul. But I didn't hire a nanny. I didn't send you off to those fucking Wentworths. They wanted you, you know."

"Oh, really?" I gave him a doubtful look.

My father nodded. "They even offered me fifty thousand if I would let them raise you. Yeah…like I was going to sell off my own fucking flesh and blood."

"Fifty thousand?" Jimmy asked. "Jesus. That's cold."

"Ain't kiddin' it's cold. They tried to *buy* her."

"She's a hell of a lot of trouble for fifty grand, too," Jimmy smirked.

My father shook his head forcefully. "Sell her! But I didn't do that, see. I didn't. And so, no, it wasn't perfect. But it was a life, Skye. And you were good at it. Still are—those stupid meetings of yours aside."

"Remember all those Dunkin' Donuts meetings with O'Toole?" Jimmy asked me, laughing.

Chris O'Toole was a "cousin" who held the record of most doughnuts eaten in the presence of Jimmy and me. He ate twenty-three doughnuts—all chocolate glazed—washed down with a single large coffee. Doubly amazing, O'Toole was only five-foot-eight and weighed probably ninety-eight pounds, soaking wet. He had seen us staring at his doughnut consumption and told us he was desperately trying to gain weight. "It's a glandular problem," he had told us.

"That was the hardest year of my life." I smiled sadly. "Minimum security or not, it's not easy seeing your Dad behind razor wire." And right now, I was still trying to absorb that the Wentworths had tried to buy me into their lives.

"You were good at the life, Skye, because you have a head for numbers like nobody I ever met," my father said. "You can calculate those cards in your head in ways…I still don't understand it. And you ain't afraid of nobody. You don't take too much shit from anyone, either. All I'm saying is, I wish you'd come back east. Come take your rightful place. As my heir."

"I'll think about it."

"That's all I ask." Dad's eyes were moist. "Now, I know you must have saved room for dessert."

We ordered three of the most decadent desserts they had, washed down with still more champagne. When we left the restaurant and stepped outside into the night air, two limousines were parked at the curb. I headed toward ours.

"No, Skye," my father said. "*That* one is yours and Jimmy's." He pointed at an extra-long stretch.

We looked at him, puzzled.

"Come on. It's only twelve-thirty. The city ain't even awake just yet. You two go out dancing somewhere without me. Go on."

Jimmy looked at me, his eyes already dancing. I shrugged, and went over to my father to kiss him good-night. I held on to him just an extra bit longer. "I'm glad you never sent me to the Wentworths," I whispered in his ear.

"Me, too," he whispered back, clutching me tightly before releasing me.

He climbed into his limousine. "Have fun!" he shouted before shutting the door.

"Where to?" Jimmy asked me as we climbed into the back seat of our limo.

"You know," I said, "I think I'd rather go to a jazz club. Somewhere we can just talk."

"But you know what a good dancer I am…."

I smiled. "Oh, yes, I do. You're a regular John Travolta. That's also the way you first got me to sleep with you all those years ago when you robbed me of my virginity. Me, all of seventeen. You, a big, bad twenty-five. What would my father think of that, I wonder?"

"He'd kill me. You win. Jazz club."

He gave the driver directions to a place on the Upper

East Side, and we sped off into the night. Jimmy pressed the button for the dividing glass between us and the driver to go up. Ensconced in the dark in the back of the limo, he pulled me to him.

"Just so you know," he whispered as he kissed me softly near my ear. "I don't need dancing to make love to you."

And as he kissed his way down to the hollow of my neck and then still lower, I smiled and whispered, "No, I suppose you don't."

NINE

The next morning, I woke with a guilt hangover. And a touch of a regular hangover, too. But mostly a guilt hangover, because since I got the bright idea to visit New York, I had 1) bet on the Mustangs game; 2) spent all night making love to my ex-husband; and 3) had not checked in with my sponsor for twenty-four hours.

It used to be that I would lie to T.D., but somewhere along the line I had learned that the truth was simpler. I would have to tell him sooner or later that I woke up next to Jimmy Sullivan. I decided on later.

I watched Jimmy sleep. He looked so innocent, I could almost picture him twelve years ago on my prom night in a hideous tuxedo with a red-and-green-tartan cummerbund. I had told him, specifically, that my dress was all black, and that a simple, elegant black tuxedo would be best. But he'd ignored what I said, gone out in Jimmy Sullivan fashion and shown up in something that had the color scheme of vomit. His bow tie was polka-dot.

I remember I didn't speak to him all night—only

danced with him once. Come to think of it, I had only agreed to let him take me when my father insisted that I go to my prom....

"Why?" I had asked Dad.

"For the pictures."

That was Dad's logic for you. Every step, every lost tooth, every bad perm, was preserved in albums. And he needed the final pictures of high school to cap it all off. A prom picture. Jimmy had volunteered to take me, and I'd accepted. There had always been this undercurrent of attraction between us.

We'd gone down to the Jersey shore after the prom, telling my father we'd booked two rooms, which we had, but slept in one together. I had been a virgin, and Jimmy kissed me in a way that felt electric—I guess those years of attraction were bottled up and then set free. And after we'd had post-prom sex, Jimmy had fallen asleep. I remember watching him sleep then, just as I did now, and thinking he was beautiful, boyish looking, serene. It wasn't love I felt, but a deep caring and affection. An abiding feeling that when he was around, I was safe for a bit. I stared at him now. Time hadn't changed him much.

And so, here we were, in my old high school bedroom, and his eyelids fluttered, then opened.

"Hey, wife."

"Hey, Jimmy."

He rolled over and pulled me to him, our bodies touching. He had a morning hard-on, and that was Jimmy for you, always ready and willing.

"Last night was great."

"It was…great. Stupid of us, but great."

"Why do you say stupid?"

"Jimmy…you're a bookie. I'm a compulsive gambler.

This isn't the most intelligent relationship in the world. It never has been. We have a history."

"Have I told you since you went to Vegas you think too damn much?"

I slapped his ass. "Fuck you."

"All right." He grinned his lopsided grin and ground his body into me.

"Jimmy." I squirmed away from him. "We better get up. As it is, my father's going to be over the moon you stayed here. He'll be throwing rice before you know it."

"Is that so bad?"

"It's not going to keep me from getting on that plane tomorrow."

He leaned up on one elbow. "Promise me something? In all seriousness."

"What?"

"Think about what your dad said last night. We make a great team, Skye. We could have New York in the palms of our hands. I've got a few investments—a pizza parlor, a dry-cleaning business. Cash businesses. I'm set, Skye. We both could be."

"We're combustible, Jimmy. In bed and out. Do I have to remind you of the five stitches you have in your fore-head, courtesy of a thrown ashtray when I found that phone number in your pants pocket? On our honey-moon?"

"Shh," he whispered, then pulled me to him and kissed me. "What's a few stitches between old spouses? Just think about it."

I rolled my eyes, but inside something about him soft-ened me. "Okay. I'll think about it."

He slid out of bed and pulled on his dress pants and shirt from the night before.

"I'm going home to shower and change. I'll be back to watch the games."

"See you later."

"See you later," he said, making his way to the door. As he opened it, he muttered under his breath, almost out of earshot, "Love ya," then shut my bedroom door behind him.

I leaned over the side of the bed, feeling around for my robe. I sat up and pulled it on, then went downstairs in search of strong coffee. My father was reading the *Daily News* at the kitchen table, drinking coffee, eating a bagel.

"Hi, Dad."

"Coffee's over there." He looked up. "I see you and Jimmy had a good time."

"Yes, Dad, we did. The night was really wonderful. The play, dinner, the limo, the jazz club Jimmy and I went to—all of it. It was very, very sweet of you to plan a night like that."

He put down the paper. "See…coming home for visits isn't so bad. You might even find you like it here again."

"Maybe that's what I'm afraid of. Old habits die hard."

I poured myself a mug of coffee and added sugar and milk. I went and sat down opposite him at the kitchen table.

"Look, Daddy, maybe I was wrong for staying away so long. But I'm still getting on the plane tomorrow."

He frowned. "Why? You don't have a job. We McNallys aren't meant for real jobs—paying taxes. None of that. You could stay another week. We could go to a Mustangs home game. We could spend some more time together."

"Dad…I know this is hard for you to understand. But please try to really listen to me, to *hear* me. I'm trying to do the right thing. I'm trying not to gamble. I'm trying to make a life away from here. I don't like wondering when the police might come to haul you away again. I don't like the ulcer in my stomach. I don't like worrying about you—I never did. And neither did Mom."

"Leave your mother out of this."

I took a sip of coffee and nearly burned my tongue. "I'm sorry. Look, this is the only life you've ever known, and you've done an amazing job of it. I mean, in bookie terms, you're the Bill Gates or Jack Welch of bookmaking. You're up at the top there. But I want something more for my life."

"What?"

"That's the part I haven't figured out yet. Let's just enjoy today."

"Got anything riding on the game?"

"I told you, Dad, I'm trying to quit."

"So *do* you?" He cocked one eyebrow.

"Yeah."

"For or against the Mustangs?"

"I'm betting Mark Shannon obliterates the other team."

"That's my girl."

And there it was. My whole life I'd received attention for breaking the law and turning a blind eye to men who played a dangerous game of cat and mouse with the cops. I still received positive reinforcement for doing the very thing I no longer wanted to do.

I drank my coffee and asked him to pass the *Post*. We used to spend every Sunday just like this. From the time I was nine on. Coffee—I'd been drinking it since I was eight—the papers, scribbling down our bets, the odds, like two old bookies. I didn't fit in at school. Not only had I been bored out of my mind and years ahead of my class-mates in math, with a near-photographic memory of numbers, but I had a street sense that set me apart from them. I lugged coffee in my lunchbox thermos, not milk. I used to read the racing forms from Belmont while my pals were reading *Archie* comics. And by the time I was fifteen, I was sneaking Jack Daniel's in my backpack, which my father knew full well.

We ate out every meal, Dad and I, after my mother died. Greasy-spoon diners and fancy steakhouses. I didn't eat a green salad until I was in my late twenties. And here I was drinking coffee with Dad, looking at the sports pages, with ten large ones riding with Heavy Harry. The names of my bookies had changed over the years—Frankie Fingers, Mad Max, Heavy Harry—but not much else had.

"Catch it!" I screamed at the television, a sixty-one-inch plasma in the basement—where my father also had a full bar with a built-in keg and six desks with young punks, not so different from Jimmy when he was younger, manning the telephones.

Mark Shannon had just fired off a perfect spiral pass to his receiver, who was having an off day. The Mustangs were down with a little under a quarter to go. But then, just as I was ready to give up on them, the receiver caught it for a touchdown and the Mustangs were up and very much in the game.

I was sitting on Jimmy's lap. He kept surreptitiously kissing my ear when no one else was looking at us. His breath on my neck was driving me crazy. That, and the fever of watching a game. It was like looking at something down a long tunnel. My world shrank and grew smaller and smaller, closing in like a pin dot of light, until all I saw was the light of the football field, and the players on it. The game became my world. There was no other feeling like it.

"Yes!" I screamed at the television again when a defensive end intercepted the ball. Shannon ran on the field, called a quick huddle, and suddenly the Mustangs were up by twelve points. The spread was ten. If they held on, I would win.

I was aware of my body, and not just because Jimmy's hands kept traveling to my ass. Every nerve was alive, and before too long my addiction was telling me that the only time I was ever truly happy was at moments like this, with money on the line, and the thrill of a game undecided.

I heard T.D.'s voice in my head like a deep baritone Jiminy Cricket, a conscience, telling me I better leave New York soon before I was both married again and in the full throes of my addiction. I remember days when I was a bundle of raw nerves unless I had a bet riding—at OTB, on boxing, at poker. But T.D.'s voice faded away as I jumped off Jimmy's lap after the final play.

"They won!" I screamed, and hugged him, feeling his ever-present hard-on against me as our waists touched. He kissed me full on the mouth, and I could see the six young punks eyeing their boss, wondering what the hell was going on.

My hands shook. I was on a high. I ran over to my father, who was behind the bar, and I hugged his neck. "Dinner's on me tonight."

"Not a chance. But you can buy a round of drinks."

My father started lining up beers for everyone, including the young punks. I recognized Nick, our driver from the night I arrived. Everyone was happy for the Mustangs, and the odds of their ride to the Super Bowl looked better than ever. I went over and sat back down on Jimmy's lap, and we all watched the post-game interviews.

Mark Shannon was courteous to a fault. He had taken

off his helmet and was flashing his smile and answering questions on the way to the locker room.

"Does he look sad to you, Jimmy?" I asked.

"Sad? No way. The guy just fucking pulled one out from behind. He's on top of the world. He's the king."

"He looks sad to me."

Jimmy looked at the beer in my hand. "That your first drink of the day?"

"Second. No, third."

"Well, maybe it's gone to your head. 'Cause I think you're nuts."

But as I watched Mark Shannon make his way to the locker room, I couldn't help feeling that the Golden Boy of football looked like his dog just died.

Just before Dad, Jimmy and I left for dinner, my father got a call on his cell phone and I saw his eyes goes from laughing to murderous inside of three seconds. We were standing in the den, pulling on our coats. He signaled to Jimmy and then covered the phone.

"I have to take this downstairs," he said. He and Jimmy went down into the basement and left me alone. I moved over by the basement door, and I heard my father shouting into the phone, "You tell that little fuck-up that he better have his money here tomorrow or he's going to be limping for the rest of his fucking life. I'm through giving that cocksucker a free ride. You fuckin' hear me?"

I walked away from the basement door and back into the den. Sometimes I could almost forget that there was another side to my father's life, to his business. Strip away the laughter and the good times, the Super Bowls and big-money games when he came out on top, and there were the weekends he lost big and had to scramble to pay out his clients' winnings. And the threats—far from empty threats, too—that were necessary to keep his men and the gamblers in line.

I remember one time there had been no avoiding seeing my father for what he sometimes was. It was shortly after my mother died, and he needed to go to a meeting. He left me in the car while he met a man in a parking lot. He told me to lie down on the back seat and not to peek. But I did. I saw them arguing, and then the other man left that parking lot clutching his leg, crying in agony, after my father beat him with a tire iron. When my father came back to the car, he was sweating and out of breath, and ran his hands through his hair, taking deep breaths to calm himself.

He looked in the back seat and saw my face. "I told you not to peek," he said harshly.

"I couldn't help it. Why did you hurt that man?"

"Skye, remember this—" he had looked at me solemnly, his voice softer "—if I have to do something like that, it's because that man has no business betting the milk money. I try to be flexible, but in the end, you give losers too much rope and you hang yourself. You lose too much respect, and then you watch your business fall apart."

I hadn't understood. Not really. I'd been too young. But when I had taken over operations for my father when he was in prison, I had to tell Jimmy to order a guy to be threatened. Mike "Big T" Tomaselli was my father's number-one enforcer. He was almost as big as T.D., but not nearly as smart. He was like a lumbering mastiff dog. Usually, Big T just showed up and whoever was behind on their payments coughed up the cash. But I was filled with guilt. The man who owed us a few thousand dollars had already taken out a second mortgage on his house. He had four young children. But my father and Jimmy didn't see it that way. My father, when I visited him, sat in that orange jumpsuit, and again told me, "Big T doesn't bother anyone who holds up his end of the bargain. You can't afford to play with the big boys, you shouldn't be in the game."

Jimmy and I had talked that night in bed. My conscience wouldn't let me sleep, but Jimmy told me he'd take the order to Big T. "But don't feel guilty, Skye, you didn't force this guy to bet."

I remember that first rule of gambling—on the Clemson game. My father said never bet more than you could afford to lose. But people did. Desperate people bet even more. They got so far behind, they placed hopeless bets, trying to win back their losses and come out even.

I tried to reason that what my father did for a living was okay, and waited now for him and Jimmy to come back upstairs. The basement door opened.

"Hey, honey—" my father was all smiles "—ready for dinner?"

"Sure, Dad." I smiled sadly. It seemed all my memories of him were both bitter and sweet.

He drove us to an Italian place that was his Sunday-night haunt for as long as I could remember. The owner, Tony Tedesto, recognized me and gave me a kiss on each cheek.

"Skye, you look lovely," Tony said. "You been a stranger too long, no? Tonight, dinner on me. Welcome home."

He hugged my father, whispered something in his ear—I'm sure a bet—and then showed us to my father's regular table. Without even saying a word, my father had a Canadian Club in front of him, and Jimmy a beer. The waiter had to ask me.

"A Jack and Coke, please."

Crusty, warm Italian bread and butter shaped into pats that looked like seashells were brought to the table, and soon my drink was, too, and my father made a toast.

"To family."

"To family," Jimmy said.

"To family," I whispered. T.D. was my family, too, and he seemed so very far away.

We had a fantastic meal. I hadn't had good Italian since I left New York, I decided, and the veal I ordered was perfect. At some point after dinner, three Jacks and Coke to my credit, I reached over and held my father's hand. He cleared his throat and wiped at his eyes.

After delicious homemade tiramisu and a round of anisette, Jimmy drove us all back to my father's and then said he wanted to buy me a nightcap. I kissed Dad goodbye as he climbed out of the car, and he waved us off, looking pleased with how the day and evening had gone.

"Where are we going for that nightcap?" I asked Jimmy.

"My house."

The fact that I didn't protest was another sign that I had lost my mind in New York. In five minutes, we were at his place, a small ranch with a fenced-in backyard for his dog, Gunther, who was actually *our* dog. I had picked him out of a pet shop window when I was twenty. Gunther was looking old and tired as we opened the front door.

"Hey there, buddy!" I clapped my hands. "Come see me."

Gunther, a boxer, lumbered over to me, and I knelt down to pet him.

"He needs to be on a diet, Jimmy. Look at him."

"He's all right. Just a little thick around the middle."

"He's getting old."

"So are we. You're not that high school girl I fell in love with."

"And you're not the young boy with the dangerous eyes."

"You got better with age, you know."

"Thanks, Jimmy."

I scratched Gunther behind his ears, feeling like I might cry and unsure of why. Then I stood and walked into Jimmy's living room.

"Place hasn't changed any."

"Nah. I'm not home all that much…and what do I know about decorating?"

I laughed and then froze where I stood. There on the mantel of Jimmy's fireplace stood our wedding picture in an elegant heavy lead-crystal frame. We had paid $49.95 for the "portrait package" at the drive-thru chapel. We also got the "rice and (cheap) champagne package."

"You still have this up."

"Shit." He went over to the picture and shrugged. "I guess I never took it down."

"Oh, Jimmy…" I walked to him and kissed him. "I've known you since I was thirteen. And here we are all these years later still stumbling along, trying to figure out our lives."

"You're the only girl I've ever loved, Skye."

"You're the only boy I've ever loved. And I know you're terrible for me."

"Why? 'Cause I'm a bookie?"

"Yeah. And because you can be pretty damn addictive yourself."

He slid his hands up my sweater and then pulled it off of me. He unhooked my bra as we walked, him backward, me kissing him, toward his bedroom. My bra fell to the floor. His shirt was next. Within five minutes, we were making love.

I had to give Jimmy credit. He was a tough guy, originally from a rough section of Brooklyn, but when we were alone, he was a thoughtful lover. He kissed his way down my belly.

"When I'm with you," he whispered, "it's like coming home again."

I felt the same way.

Only in my case, home wasn't where I needed to be. And the person I was at home wasn't who I wanted to be.

ELEVEN

I told Jimmy I wanted to go to the airport with just my father, so he drove me home in the morning after we took a very sexy shower together. As he pulled into the driveway, he looked morose.

"Don't be so sad, Jimmy. I'll be back more often to visit."

"I didn't realize how much I missed you."

"I didn't realize how much I missed home, too."

We kissed in the driveway, and I promised to call him. I waved as he drove away, until his car was a little flash of black way down the street.

I climbed up the front steps and let myself into the house. My father was dozing on the couch. In his sleep, he seemed old, tired. I went upstairs to dress and pack, brought down my bag, then woke him gently.

"Christina?" he asked, as he awoke, my mother's name on his lips after all these years.

"No. It's me. Skye."

He sat up. "How long have I been sleeping?"

I shrugged. "It's almost time to go to the airport."

"Right. Let me find my keys."

He stood, stretched and went rummaging through several coats. I heard him opening drawers. "I can't find my keys!" he shouted.

I walked into the kitchen, where he was searching.

"Dad, I know you way too well, you sly old bastard. Not finding your keys to make me miss my plane? If you don't find them in five minutes, I'm calling a cab."

I squared off with him. He suddenly looked as if the proverbial light bulb went off. "Oh, *yeah*...they're upstairs on my dresser."

"Yeah. You just remembered. Go get them." I sighed. "And if you have a flat tire or sudden 'car trouble,' I'll kill you."

"Right." He looked sheepishly at me and trudged upstairs to retrieve his keys. When he came down, he had a small framed photo in his hand.

"Here's a picture of your mother shortly after we got married. I know she has blond hair and you have black, but you look like her. Same nose. Same eyes. I want you to have this picture."

"Thanks, Dad." I took it and stared down at the woman I barely remembered. I put it in my purse.

Dad pulled on his jacket and grabbed my small suitcase. "Will you come home for Christmas?"

"I don't know, Dad. I usually spend it with T.D. I'll think about it."

"Well, if the Mustangs make it to the Super Bowl in January, I have four tickets. You and me and Jimmy and old Lefty Canzonari could go. It's in Florida this year. Get away from the snow."

"I live in the desert."

"I forgot. Well, come with us, anyway."

"You're going with Lefty, too? Geez. I almost forgot about him."

"Yep. Still kicking. So what do you say?"

"Let me think about it, Dad. Either way, I promise to get home more frequently. And you know there are flights from New York to Vegas, too. You could come visit me. You've never even seen my place."

"I guess I always like picturing you across the table from me, reading the sports page. I can't picture you in that fancy place you have in Las Vegas."

"Trust me, it's a nice building, but it's not that fancy. You should see T.D.'s place. Now, *that's* fancy."

We walked down to the basement and entered the garage where my father kept his Cadillac. We climbed in, he pressed the garage door opener, and he eased his car out on the street, then clicked to shut the garage door again.

We both must have been feeling a little melancholy. I had wanted to talk some more on the drive, but I found myself at a loss for words. Dad looked worse than Jimmy had when he'd dropped me off that morning.

When we got to the airport, he pulled up curbside and hugged me across the front seat. "You need anything, you call your old man."

"I will, Daddy."

"All right…go on and get out of here," he said, managing a weak smile. I could see him pushing back his real emotions, but knew he would cry on the way home. Some tough guy.

I climbed out of the car, took my bag and went inside to wait at the security checkpoint line. Mixed with my sadness at leaving Dad and Jimmy, was the realization that I would soon be face-to-face with my sponsor, who was picking me up in Las Vegas. T.D. wasn't going to be pleased with me at all.

"You *what?*"

"T.D., pay attention to the road. You're swerving."

We were riding in his Bentley back to Chez T.D., and I'd blurted out my going to bed with Jimmy.

"It just kind of happened."

T.D. grabbed my left hand and held it up. "No ring. Thank God for that. You didn't marry him again."

"No, I didn't. But it was really nice. Even nicer was the fact I didn't have to make small talk during a date and try to get to know someone. You know, 'Where did you grow up? What was your family like?'—to which I'm supposed to say—'Oh, me? I grew up in New York. Dad's a convicted felon. Pretty ordinary upbringing, thanks.' I like that with Jimmy, he knows all the good, the bad and the ugly."

"Uh-huh. And the fact that he's a bookie didn't set off little alarms in your head?"

"Not really."

He sighed, then reached over and pretended to knock on my skull. "Hello? Anybody home in there?"

"Give me a break."

"Oh, Little Girl, I've given you more breaks than I've ever given anyone in my life. I didn't give my ex-*wives* the breaks I've given you."

"Oh, come on, didn't you miss me?"

"No."

"Liar. I know you did."

"You didn't check in every day," he scolded.

"I know. I was just so busy."

"And what else?"

"What do you mean, what else?"

"Heavy Harry came into my steakhouse to eat, Little Girl."

"Hmm." I had no good response to that little bit of news. "Did he order the filet mignon, like always?"

"As a matter of fact, he did. He also told me you must be a pretty happy girl, being as you just won a nice bet on the Mustangs."

"Did he say that? I mean, shouldn't bookies be a bit like priests and keep your confidences? Damn, he has a big mouth."

"Yes. I count on that. I even bought him an after-dinner brandy for speaking up."

We drove on toward T.D.'s house. "Are you mad?" I asked him.

"Not mad."

"Disappointed?"

"A little."

"I'm sorry. And I'm sorry I didn't check in with you. Was it so wrong to want to be with my father?"

"No. It's just that you have to learn to be with him without gambling."

"But that's our whole relationship. Once my mother died, it was all we had. That and an obsession with musical theater, though he'll deny that to his deathbed."

"People, places and things."

Another stupid Twelve Step saying. When you're struggling with addiction, you're supposed to avoid the people you're most likely to gamble with. Dad and Jimmy. The places where you'd most likely gamble—the casinos were pretty much off-limits to me. And the things. For instance, I don't buy the racing form, and I force myself to avoid the stats in the newspaper. I stopped buying *Ring* magazine, so that I wouldn't be tempted to bet on heavyweight boxing matches.

"Well, it's awfully hard when the people you love do the thing you should avoid, in a place you shouldn't go," I said.

"You have to decide how badly you want to stop gambling."

I looked out the passenger-side window.

Maybe that was the problem. When all was said and done, did I really want to stop? I mean, I wanted to avoid the shame. Like waking up minus my mother's watch because I'd hocked it. I had felt physically sick that morning, as if I'd had the world's worst hangover. But I also didn't want to stop the exciting part. I guess, if I got specific about it, I wanted to gamble—but just never lose. Though I suppose it was the risk of losing that made gambling exciting. T.D. was right.

How badly did I want to stop?

TWELVE

In an attempt to get back into T.D.'s good graces, I found myself five days away from getting my brass coin, despite really, *really* wanting to bet on the Mustangs. Twenty-five days without gambling. This was my personal best.

I told Jimmy about it on the telephone. We had taken to calling each other every other day or so since my visit.

"Five more days, and I get a brass coin."

"Is it worth anything?"

"What do you mean? In cash?"

"Yeah."

"No, idiot. It's not worth anything. I can't hock it, for God's sake. It's worth holding my head up and finally telling Cowboy Hal where he can shove his ten-gallon hat."

"So you're not going to place a bet on the play-offs this weekend?"

"What about *not gambling* do you not understand?"

"Everything about it. I gamble all the time—I'm worse than you ever were, and you don't see me with a brass coin or whatever the hell it is."

I was clicking through television channels when I abruptly stopped. "Right, Jimmy. That's because you don't think you have a problem."

"I don't have a problem. And neither do you."

"Let me ask you something, Jimmy. What do you do every time you see a cop?"

"What do you mean?"

"I mean, you're driving, and a black-and-white cop car is in back of you, lights flashing. Do you break out in a sweat?"

"Sure. Everybody does, whether they've done something wrong or not."

"No, everybody doesn't. T.D. doesn't. Lots of people don't. I want that feeling. You and Dad are always looking over your shoulder." I'd been thinking about the Serenity Prayer. I wanted serenity, something I'd never had.

"When are you coming home?"

"I still don't know."

"Don't you miss me? Don't you miss me fucking you?"

I sighed. "Yes. But I need to stay here for now."

"I think T. D. Russell is brainwashing you."

"No. He just wants what's best for me."

"So do I."

"I know," I said softly. "I better go. 'Night."

"Good night, Skye. I love ya."

I hung up the phone. Sunday were the play-offs. A few short weeks to the Super Bowl. The Mustangs were the favorites going in. It wasn't possible to watch ESPN and not have half the show be about the incredible American sports success story of Mark Shannon and the Mustangs. I felt that familiar buzzing. Heavy Harry was still in my speed dial.

T.D.'s advice for situations like this one was to tell yourself that you wouldn't quit gambling forever. Just for a day.

Twenty-four hours.

Feeling the urge to call Heavy, I decided to down two shots of Jack Daniel's and go to bed. If I was sleeping, I couldn't get into trouble. Maybe in the morning, I wouldn't feel so compelled to gamble.

Yeah. And I believe in the tooth fairy.

By Sunday I had $5,000 riding on the Mustangs, and I was lying to T.D.

"You coming over to the restaurant to watch the game?"

"No."

T.D., by virtue of owning a bar and restaurant, had the game playing on three plasma televisions in strategic spots throughout the restaurant. He was able, by working some mysterious and indefinable dance of faith, prayer and one day at a time—what he called "his program"—to watch sports like other people watch sports. He didn't even bet a dollar on the outcome.

"Why aren't you coming over?"

"Not hungry."

"You don't come here to eat. You come here to drink my Jack Daniel's for free."

"I sometimes eat."

"You have something riding on it?"

"No."

"Skye, if you have a bet riding on the Mustangs, don't call me when you lose. Or win. Don't call me when you feel guilty. You are now three days from that coin."

"I know."

"It's too late, isn't it?"

"I have to go."

And I hung up on him. And then, because I hurt for

both the coin I wasn't going to get *and* for hanging up on my best friend, I opened a fresh bottle of Jack and carried a six-pack of Coke over to my coffee table and settled in to watch the game.

Fuck T.D., I wanted to say. It was my business if I was soon to blow my monthly trust allowance on a football game. It was my business and always would be my business. But as I poured myself a J.D. over ice, I felt this pain searing through me like a heart attack. It had even started on the left side.

Five hours later, I owed Heavy Harry $5,000. The Mustangs had won, but they hadn't covered the spread. The bookies would be celebrating tonight. And me? I was just one Jack and Coke shy of what I call a bender.

Only one thing for a girl to do.

Pour another Jack and Coke. I was sinking toward bottom.

The next day, rather the next afternoon, my head pounded and that pain in my heart had grown to something like a boulder of remorse sitting on my lungs, making it hard for me to breathe.

I struggled out of bed and checked my answering machine. No one had called. Not Jimmy, who, I guessed, was on this side of a bender himself. Not my father. And not T.D. I had the distinct feeling no one loved me. This only made my head hurt worse, and it certainly didn't do anything for the boulder on my chest.

Had I imagined it? Had I really lost $5,000? I felt this urge to check the score again. The final numbers, the last-minute touchdown by the other team, the scramble for the loose ball. Maybe it had all been a bad dream.

I flicked on television and started clicking my way to

ESPN, stopping at CNN for what looked like a breaking news story that had to do with sports.

I assumed another sports star had screwed a waitress who was now claiming he was the father to her child, or had beaten his wife, or had gotten busted for drugs. They were human, after all, just making a lot more money than most. Just because they could run with grace, or throw like a rocket, their faults were held up to a magnifying glass. For the same reasons, people worshiped them and called them "heroes." They were neither perfect nor rotten. Just human, like me. Like my father. Like Jimmy. Like T.D. They weren't heroes. I had grown up without heroes, really. Whereas someone else might be impressed by a guy flashing a lot of money around, driving the most expensive car, I knew it was all a game.

I turned up the volume.

The Super Bowl was four weeks away. The Mustangs were guaranteed a berth.

And Mark Shannon, the pretty-boy quarterback, was missing.

As in gone.

As in the most famous face in all of sports, who hawked soda and sneakers, had disappeared off of Planet Earth.

THIRTEEN

By the end of that week, I was down $28,000, decimating my last remaining savings, blowing any chance of buying T.D. a good gift for Christmas, and the disappearance of Mark Shannon was the biggest sports story in the world.

At first, the team had tried to deny it. His disappearance was, originally, discovered by accident. A journalist who had cultivated the trust of the team's driver stumbled on the story early, that Shannon was AWOL with only four weeks until the Super Bowl. As one day slid into two and three, foul play was suspected. Literally, the world was looking for Shannon—well, maybe not in Bora Bora or some tiny South Pacific island where American football wasn't the most important thing to the entire male population, but pretty much everywhere else. Then came word Shannon had called his coach, wouldn't reveal where he was, but reported that he was, indeed, safe.

Now every amateur sleuth and investigative journalist in the country was trying to get to the bottom of the Shannon story. People were sifting through his life like archaeologists sifting through the sands of a desert ruin. No one was any closer to knowing where he was or why he disappeared. Drugs, scandal, violence and even gambling theories abounded with no evidence. Like any gambler who bet on sports, I was hooked on the story, but I also felt sorry for Mark Shannon. The media was hunting him like a bunch of lions surrounding a wounded zebra.

I felt like a bit of a wounded animal myself. My losses kept mounting. I was in a slump. Gamblers should never forget the odds are with the house. The odds are with the bookies. If they weren't, I wouldn't have attended the best private school on Long Island, and my father wouldn't have taken me on vacations to Las Vegas and the Caribbean with sumptuous hotel suites and new travel wardrobes.

It wasn't that I didn't know about the odds. I'd lived the odds for so long, I'd calculate the odds on T.D.'s Big Buffet House of Hunan plates in my head. I'd calculate the odds on anything. But I had stopped caring.

Going home had set off in me a feeling of inevitability. Why fight what was my birthright? T.D. was a different story. He had been raised by a Baptist minister father and a mother who played the organ for the church. They'd been poor, and when he first got into gambling, it was the lure of easy money…. Before he knew it he was hooked on the highs and lows. I was tired, I decided. It was easier to be a gambler instead of going to meetings and listening to people like Cowboy Hal talk about how they filled their days with meetings and coffee at diners to avoid going to the casinos. Seemed to me they just replaced their gambling addiction with one for caffeine and cigarettes and going to meetings.

T.D. kept calling me, but as my losses racked up, I was

too busy chasing them. That's what we call it. Chasing your losses. You think if you just get that one win—just one more—you'll be even again. It's all an illusion, of course. It's like chasing the mist. You think you can wrap your hand around it, but it's all smoke and mirrors like a David Copperfield show.

Heavy Harry kept calling my apartment, looking for his money, asking me, enticing me, to place another bet. Then there were calls from my father and Jimmy, asking when I was coming home.

I spent my nights drinking J.D. and Coke, alone. I spent my days reading the sports pages. I went out only to go to an OTB parlor. I ate takeout. I couldn't sleep. I felt a restlessness, and when I did sleep, it was the uneasy sleep of someone who's had too much to drink.

The fourth night of my self-imposed hiding, I felt a great melancholy. I climbed out of bed and went to my closet, where I stood on tiptoe and pulled down a box. It was a little bigger than a shoebox, and there, in my father's scrawl, the words Mom's Things were written on top.

Inside the box were the things no pawnshop would want. The things all people have that are priceless, yet worth nothing. They have heart value. I peeled back a piece of packing tape and opened the box. There was a macaroni necklace I made her for Mother's Day, and handmade cards. There were a dozen or so pictures of her and me. One was taken right after I was born, in the hospital. She was clasping me to her chest as she sat upright in bed. Something about her was so perfect. Maybe it was what they taught at finishing school in the South. I turned over the photos. She had put a note on the back of each one in her delicate handwriting: "Holding my precious lamb," "My angel loses her first tooth," "My sweet baby and me on Halloween." I found it comforting that she loved me so. That my memories were *real*. That I hadn't imagined the way she held me in her arms and rocked me, singing "Morning Has Broken," and lulling me to sleep—even when I was really a little too old for that. I thought about her and lay down on the carpeting, and sometime in the middle of the night, I fell asleep.

I startled awake with memories of my mother's funeral, with a small box of ashes where a coffin should have been. When the Wentworths came, rather than kissing or hugging me, they merely sized me up as one might look at a puppy in a pet shop. I was the mutt. The little dog that they wanted to take back to South Carolina and turn into a pedigree.

But that wasn't the worst part of the memory. It was Dad. After her death, he was completely shattered. He'd looked like a zombie, and I could hear him grieving for her in the night, not quite crying, more of a moan. It frightened me. He was the one who'd always made Mommy laugh, the one who was always so in control, so powerful. Maybe that's what scared me. I may, according to the Twelve Steps, be powerless of gambling, but in life we are powerless over…everything. Certainly death.

After the fifth night of uneasy sleep, the walls of my apartment started feeling very close. I had the urge to place a twenty-thousand-dollar bet, which I had no hope of paying, not having access to the bulk of my trust fund and only my monthly allowance. The trust was to forever preserve the principal.

I bought the paper to read about the search for Mark Shannon. And then I spotted it. It was buried on page 26B.

A small item about the body of a young woman discovered. Annie—from GA.

I sat down on my couch and clutched at my chest. She had been beaten. The cops were looking for her murderer, but I knew that her real murderer was gambling. Annie's bookie was a very, very tough guy named Mac G. The G stood for Grand. Which was the smallest bet he would take. I never liked Mac G. You hang around Vegas long enough, you hear stories, and he was not someone to fuck with.

I suddenly heard a sob escape from my mouth. I was crying. I was feeling…I was feeling so hopeless that I ended up falling to the floor and curling up into a ball, picturing apple-cheeked Annie with her face smashed in.

I don't know how long I lay there and cried. I cried until no more tears would come. I cried for Annie, and I cried because I didn't want to ever end up like her—someone who's lost everything—including her life. There's another Gamblers Anonymous saying: *There but for the grace of God go I.* I was raised to pray for football teams. But in my house, we viewed God almost like a talisman, a good-luck symbol, no more potent than a rabbit's foot. But I knew, there but for God, the fates, my trust fund, went I.

I called T.D.

"Hello, Little Girl. You done moping around and ready to come back to the rooms?" "The rooms" were GA-speak for the program.

"Did you hear about Annie?"

"No. What?"

I read him the item in the paper.

"Shit. Aw, damn, Skye. You know it was one of Mac G's boys. Had to be. That boy don't screw around."

"T.D….I admit it. I'm powerless."

"Good girl. Come on over to the steakhouse."

"Maybe. I gotta go."

"Call me later."

"Sure," I said. But I didn't mean it.

It was then I decided to get out of the city. To go somewhere. I showered and changed into jeans and a T-shirt, threw a couple of sodas in a backpack, along with some cash and went down to the garage. I wanted to take a drive in the desert.

CHAPTER
F♥URTEEN

T.D. had helped me buy my car two and a half years before. He'd given me a loan of one of his Porsches, and though I loved to drive it, I had decided I needed a car of my own. So we negotiated with a gambler named Snake Eyes Finnegan, who, coincidentally, was a rather squinty-eyed fellow with dark black eyes and no eyelashes—at least none to speak of. Snake, as his good friends called him, had a collection of more than thirty classic cars, and after taking some heavy losses at the tables, he decided to part with an old Cadillac convertible with a sleek baby-blue paint job and white leather seats. I fell in love with it, and it was tricked out with a killer stereo system. So, top down, denim jacket on to fight the coming desert nighttime chill, and stars above me, I drove out toward the sand, hitting the maximum the speedometer measured, not passing another car for miles.

I suppose there was something foolish about me driving off into the desert alone. A woman. What if my car broke down? What if I got lost? But a lifetime spent with hard-core gamblers, and the year and some-odd months of my father's prison sentence, staring down men who thought they could put one over on me, had taken away some of my fears. For instance, I wasn't afraid to ride the subway at night in New York or to wait in a dimly lit parking lot for a cousin to show up with a bankroll of money. On the other hand, I still had some classic fears—like of spiders and rodents, in particular rats, ever since one ran over my shoe in one of those dimly lit parking lots.

By the time I really hit the desert and started getting away from the neon of Vegas, the sky was pinkish with sunset. I felt a settling of my nerves I hadn't experienced since New York.

I thought about Annie. She kept saying she was going to stop hooking. She even talked of going home. But I knew she wouldn't. I knew once you slid down into places that were so dark they were hard to admit, that going home was impossible. The darkness would follow you. How could she sit at the family dinner table having sold her body to feed her gambling habit? She felt more "normal" with the rest of us sinners of Las Vegas. I ached that she must have fallen farther still.

I drove without even thinking of the road, that sort of subconscious driving when you're not even aware of your hands on the wheel or the miles you've driven. Eventually, though, my stomach reminded me that I hadn't eaten yet. Hungry, I regretted not having picked up a Big Mac or something for the road. Some thirty miles or so later, I saw a sign for a truck stop diner, its neon proudly proclaiming Joe's and below that Home of the World's Greatest Hamburger. Yeah, right. However, the growling in my stomach grew louder at the thought of greasy eggs and hash browns or a blue-plate special, so I pulled over.

The place was empty, except for a lone customer at a

back booth, his hat pulled down low, and a waitress, and I supposed someone in the kitchen—likely named Joe—to cook the food.

"Menu's on the blackboard there," the waitress said to me as I sat down at the counter. She had a bouffant and a tiny plastic tiara with glittering rhinestones stuck in it. I didn't ask.

"I'll take the number two. Scrambled. Hash browns. White toast. Cup of coffee."

"You got it, sugar."

She shouted back my order to the cook in the kitchen pass-through window. I looked at my reflection in the glass of the pie display directly across from me. Between a lemon meringue and an apple crumb, I glimpsed the absolute fright wig that was my hair. Only bald men should drive convertibles. Sure, it looks all sexy driving with your hair whipping around your face, but really…I looked like I'd stuck my finger in an electrical socket. My jet-black curls made Medusa's look well-coiffed. I smoothed my hair with my hand. When my coffee came, I was grateful for the warmth, and I curled my hands around the mug.

"Whatcha doin' all the way out here, honey lamb?" the waitress asked me when she brought my food.

"Driving. Just driving…"

"You from Vegas?"

I nodded, picking up a piece of toast.

"Well, you just be careful." She lowered her voice. "There can be some real creeps out there on the roads."

"I will." I smiled at her, then smothered my eggs with ketchup and devoured my meal. The hash browns were perfect, and I made a mental note to remember that this particular greasy spoon had food that was not so greasy and was actually pretty wonderful. Not only that, the music piping through the place was Elvis, and you can't live in Vegas without having a soft spot for the King.

"Anything else, sugarplum?"

"Just the check, thanks."

The waitress scribbled the total on a pad she pulled from her apron and handed it to me. I pulled out a twenty and said, "Keep the change. The food was great."

I headed out the door, a little bell on it jingling as I opened it, then pulled it shut behind me. The night air was still chilly, something most people don't realize, especially when the desert is so hot during the day. I headed over to my car and climbed in. I put the keys in the ignition. And nothing happened.

"Damn!" I tried it again. Nothing but a sickening sort of sound between a whir and a grind. That ruled out the alternator. My father may have been a bookie when I was growing up, but he had taught me how to check my own oil, how to jump a battery and the general basics of how an engine works. If the alternator goes, the car is usually silent. I voted for the battery and popped the hood.

"Need a jump?"

I let out a small shriek as the man in the baseball cap from the diner had sneaked up over my right shoulder.

I whirled around, my temper flaring, "Don't you know better than to creep up behind someone like that? Especially at night out in the middle of the fucking desert?"

"I'm really sorry. But you still look like you need a jump. My uncle is a mechanic, and I spent my life around cars. Why don't you let me have a look? I promise I'm not a serial killer."

"That's exactly what a serial killer would say."

"Trust me."

With that, he leaned under the hood. I squinted in the

darkness of the desert night, neon from the diner's sign illuminating the stranger slightly. I leaned under the hood next to him and tried to avoid staring. But up close, I was now almost positive. Except that it made no sense. But if it wasn't him, he had a twin. With his head under my hood, I could have sworn I was inches away from the ruggedly beautiful face of quarterback Mark Shannon.

FIFTEEN

I blinked several times. I pulled my head out from under the hood, and he did the same. "Are you…?"

He looked at me, as if sizing me up, figuring out if I could keep a secret. Then he slowly nodded.

"Do you know the entire world is looking for you?"

He froze for a minute, as if he had changed his mind about admitting who he was. "What are you talking about?"

"What am I talking about? The hat and that sort-of beard you've grown isn't fooling anyone," I said. "You're Mark Shannon."

"Mark who?"

"Do I look brain dead to you? Like I was born yesterday?"

He sighed. "All right…you got me."

"Can I ask what the hell you're doing out in the middle of the desert?"

He didn't answer.

"Okay, then," I said. "Ignore me and we can both stare at the gaskets on my engine."

"I'm sorry. Look, it's a long story.... I really don't want anyone to know where I am just yet. Here...um...seems now you know my name, but I don't know yours."

"Skye McNally."

"Skye. That's really pretty." He looked up at the stars that now scattered in the Milky Way across the sky. "Must be something to be named after something as magnificent as that." He swept his hand upward.

"Actually, I'm named after Sky Masterson in the movie *Guys and Dolls.*"

"Marlon Brando?"

"You've seen the old musical?"

"Scary as it sounds, I've seen them all. My mother loves them. I must have seen that damn movie a hundred times. But I never met anyone named after the singing Marlon Brando. Let alone a girl—um, woman."

"Yeah, well you haven't spent time with my father. Somehow, if you met him, it wouldn't seem all that surprising." I was trying not to stare at him.

"Let's see if we can't get your car started, Skye."

"Where's your car?"

"My car?" He took his hat off and ran his left hand through his hair.

"To jump the battery."

"Oh, yeah. My car is, at this moment, being towed to the nearest town. It was a rent-a-wreck, anyway. Literally. I figured no one would be looking for Mark Shannon in a 1994 Ford Escort from a no-name car rental place."

"If you were towed, how'd you get here?"

"Hitched a ride with a trucker, who, miraculously, was a bowling fan and had never watched an NFL game in his life."

"Bowling."

He nodded.

"Well, then what the hell are you doing offering to jump me when you don't have a car?"

"We'll ask the short-order cook. He must have a car parked around back."

"I'll go in and ask. If they look at you too closely, they'll be selling your whereabouts to the *Enquirer*."

"Right." He winked at me and put his baseball cap back on his head. It had the logo of Skoal chewing tobacco above the bill.

"You a tobacco chewer?" I asked.

"Nope. Disgusting habit. But this helped me blend in."

As he said this, he smiled. There was no mistaking the "Shannon smile," as they called it.

"Blend in. You. Uh-huh."

I pulled my jeans jacket more tightly around me and walked across the parking lot and back to the diner. Soon a cook by the name of Chicky was driving his beat-up old Duster around to my car, and between me, Chicky and the quarterback hands of Mark Shannon, my car was up and running.

"Thanks, Chicky." I stuck my hand out and offered him a twenty.

"Keep it. Okay, pretty lady?"

"Thanks."

Chicky drove his Duster out back again.

"Wonder why he parks it back there," I mused. "Not like they have to save the parking up front."

Mark Shannon laughed. Then there was an awkward silence.

"Well...I better hit the road. Um, do you want a ride?"

"I was hoping you'd ask me. Where you headed?"

"I was going to ask you the same thing."

He shrugged. "Nowhere. Anywhere. You ever get that feeling? Like you just want to be out there on the road not answering to anyone, least of all the things that keep you up at night?"

I stared at him. "More than you'll ever know."

CHAPTER
SIXTEEN

Next thing I knew, Mark Shannon, America's most famous quarterback—missing or otherwise—and I were driving without a destination. And playing Twenty Questions. We'd been playing it for more than half an hour. He'd picked, for his turns, Miss Piggy (which I said was kind of like cheating—she's not *exactly* a famous *person*, but rather a famous *porcine*), Yogi Berra and Joe Namath. When it was my turn, I picked George "T.D." Russell, Dan Marino and Willie Shoemaker.

"My turn to pick a person," he said. "Okay, I got one."

"Is it a woman?"

"No."

"Okay, so it's a man."

"Yes."

"Marlon Brando?"

"How'd you guess already?"

"I don't know. I figured you'd used up all your imagination on that terrible disguise you're wearing and there-

fore you would opt for something easy…and since we discussed Brando before in relation to Sky Masterson—"

"Come on…that's how you figured it out? What are
you? Psychic?"

"No. I'm a gambler. You sit around enough card tables
reading people for long enough, and you start to have
hunches. Don't you ever have hunches?"

"I thought I did," he said, and looked out the passenger-side window. "But now I'm not so sure. I'm not so sure
about anything."

"Well, it's my turn now."

"Got one?"

"Yup."

"Is it a man?" he asked.

"Yes."

"Still living?"

"No."

"A dead guy, huh?"

"Yes."

"Singer?"

"Yes."

"Frank Sinatra?"

"Yes. How'd you guess?"

"I thought maybe since he starred with Brando in *Guys
and Dolls,* that your mind might work that way."

"See, you do have hunches."

"I think you just gave me an easy one."

"I did. But it was fun, anyway."

The headlights of my car beamed far ahead on the
road, illuminating the flat expanse of highway.

"What's been your most embarrassing moment?" he
asked me.

"This car ride is taking on the mood of summer camp."

"Well, we'll start singing camp songs next…so come on, most embarrassing moment."

"I don't know."

"Come on." His voice was teasing.

"All right. I guess it was when I was on a date with this guy I really liked. I was a junior in high school and he had this bright idea to go to the beach and rent bikes and ride along the boardwalk. And I pretended that I knew how to ride a bike and made a total fool of myself."

"You don't know how to ride a bicycle?"

"Nope."

"That's downright un-American."

"No. It's very much Sean McNally."

"Who's that?"

"My father. For my father, career day meant showing a class of third-graders how to pick a trifecta ticket. Bicycles and baby dolls were way beyond his comprehension. I can't fly a kite. I've never been on roller skates—inline or otherwise. I never even owned a Barbie doll."

"Well, I'll have to at least teach you how to ride a bicycle."

"Not a chance. After said humiliating episode, I swore to myself I would never again get on a two-wheeler."

"We could get you training wheels."

"And that would be less humiliating how? A grown woman using training wheels. Don't think so, pal. Now your turn. Most embarrassing moment?"

"I was a rookie. And the guys on the team dragged all the rookies out to a karaoke place. Me and Frankie Wheeling, and Joe 'Big Bird' Reynolds, and Sammy Garcia all were dragged up on stage and we sang 'I'm Every Woman.'"

"What?" I howled.

"Yes. Exactly."

"I don't know if that beats me. You had company up there."

"Yes, but I did sing falsetto."

I smiled in the darkness, thinking about that sight—and sound.

Mark said, "Can I ask you something?"

"Sure."

"You said that you're a gambler.... What do you gamble on?"

"I don't know."

"You play the slot machines?"

"No. I play things where a little skill and intuition are involved. Not slots."

"Well, like what?"

"Anything. I'll take a bet on whether or not there's a gas station in the next twenty miles. Whether or not it rains tomorrow. Whether or not I can somehow pull an inside straight. I like blackjack. I like poker."

"Do you win?"

"Sure. But I also lose a lot."

"You bet sports?"

"Um…sometimes."

He looked out the window. "I was once offered a $100,000 to throw a game in college. Just to blow some passes in the final quarter."

"Did you take it?"

"No."

"Did you think about it?"

"Not really. Ego. I didn't want to have a tarnished game on my record. I know to most people, it's just a game. Just a bunch of guys putting on pads and playing on Astroturf. But to me, it's not."

"Well, you get paid millions to play. It's a job. It's more than a game."

"It's not that. I mean, believe me, coming from my hometown, I'm just thankful I'm not a laid-off steel mill worker. But then, when you grow up with few prospects for a life outside of a mill town that's seen its good days come and gone, a game can come to mean everything to you. It's all I've ever wanted to do. I play it for the love of the game. For me, it's something pure. And the money is a nice bonus, but man…it's not why I do it."

"Is that why you—I don't know, in interviews, you seem very…cautious. You don't seem all taken in by the whole superstar sports hero bullshit."

"You're the first person I've met in a while who calls it by what it really is—bullshit. I just want to play the game. I get such a rush when I'm out on the field. It's always been my escape. Man, I just don't get some of the guys who are just all about being spoiled. I mean, cutting rap records…partying. Girls in different cities. They all forget where they came from."

"You're not the typical NFL player. You sound like you're a pretty good man. I'm not too familiar with those types." I stifled a yawn. "I'm going to pull over to rest…or you can drive for a while."

"We can rest."

I pulled over to the side of the road, and then drove the car a little ways into the sand. I turned off the engine and looked up at the night sky. Off in the distance were craggy mountains.

"Help me with the seat?" I asked. My old Caddy's front seat could recline almost all the way back, though the exact technique for getting the seat to do that required some careful maneuvering and contortion of the body. After two tries, we got it to lie back.

The night sky was its own show. It reminded me of the time my father chaperoned my fourth-grade field trip to the planetarium and natural history museum. Of course, rather than properly watching his gaggle of nine-year-old girls, my dad slipped off to a phone booth to lay odds on the big Giants game. The other five girls and I, chaperoneless, somehow ended up in an exhibit of stuffed beavers. But in the end, after a reprimand to *both* my father and his charges by our pinch-nosed teacher, we did watch the stars come out on the dome of the planetarium, and I remember being awestruck and somehow believing, in my little girl way, that my mother was riding a star.

I was silent as I saw first one and then a second shooting star across the desert sky, which seemed endless.

"You gonna ask me?" Mark whispered.

"Ask you what?" I whispered back. I think both of us were awed by the sky and speaking in hushed tones, as if we were in a cathedral.

"Why I disappeared? Why I'm out in the middle of the desert—in a beautiful Cadillac, I may add, with a total stranger, looking at shootin' stars and playing Twenty Questions?"

"Figured if you wanted to tell me, you would."

"Anyone ever tell you you're different? Most people would ask a ton of questions."

"Most people aren't me. Put it this way, I grew up with a father who associated with people who didn't appreciate a whole lot of questions. At first I asked. When that got me nowhere, I learned to shut the hell up. If someone wants to tell you something, chances are he will. And if he doesn't, worming it out of him won't get you the real story, anyway."

"You're pretty smart for a woman driving around in the middle of the desert." He was silent for a few minutes, then he asked, "Do you think things happen for a reason?"

He talked in a thoughtful way, not like the sound bites I'd watched on ESPN repeated over and over since his disappearance.

"You mean, like fate? I don't know," I replied. "I lost my mother in a plane crash. Was she meant to get on that plane? Was I meant to grow up without her? I mean, why didn't she get the flu and cancel the trip, why didn't we get stuck in the world's biggest traffic jam on the way to the airport? Or 9/11. Why did some people run late that morning, or miss one of the flights? I don't know if I believe in that. It's why I like numbers. I like things that you can add up, that make sense in black and white. Even if I lose a bet, it's there in the final score—it's not up for discussion. It just is. I win or lose. How about you? Do you think things happen for a reason?"

"I don't know. The way you are with numbers...I was that way with football. It's all I ever wanted. You throw a pass, you take your team to first down, you find your receiver with a throw that hits him right in the numbers and he gets a touchdown. That world made sense to me. Take me off the field and I'm not so sure. Does anything happen for a reason? Does *everything* happen for a reason?"

"Look at that." I pointed at another shooting star streaking across the sky.

He slid over closer to me in the seat, our hands almost touching, and asked, "You believe in wishing on a star?"

I thought of my mother and the planetarium. "Not really. But I sometimes catch myself wishing, anyway. It's a habit."

"What do you wish for?"

"I wish for people to be different sometimes, I wish for miracles. I wish for signs that…I don't know, that my mother is still with me. I wish for things that really can't be. Isn't that what all people wish for?"

"I suppose so."

I turned my head to the side. He looked at me and brushed a stray curl away from my cheek. Then, without saying anything more, he leaned in and kissed me. I couldn't explain it, but I felt connected to him, out in that desert. I kissed him back. He kissed his way to my ear and whispered, "Maybe tonight happened for a reason. Maybe I want to believe that."

We slowly slid down until we were lying, cramped like two sardines, face-to-face on the seat. We continued kissing until my eyes could barely stay open. I rolled over on my side and he spooned around me. I felt safe, and realized safe wasn't something I was used to. I was used to looking in the rearview mirror and wondering if a cop was tailing me.

Turning my face to the sky, I said, "I feel like this is our own private theater."

"Me, too. This is the first time I've felt at peace in a week. You know, you never did tell me why you are out here in the middle of the desert just driving."

"I needed to be alone. A girl I know died."

"I'm sorry. How?"

"She was beaten up. Murdered. She was a gambler and she turned tricks to support her habit. It's not a very healthy profession."

"God…I'm so sorry."

"She was someone I sometimes wished for. That she would stop what she was doing. Selling herself. She thought Vegas would be like Oz. But it's not the Emerald City. The Yellow Brick Road has a lot more twists and turns to it."

"You said your mother died. How old were you?"

"Eight."

"I wish I'd known you when you were eight. I would have been your friend."

"Thank you."

And then, wrapped in the tight embrace of Mark Shannon, America's enigma, I fell asleep.

CHAPTER

SEVENTEEN

The next morning the sun rose hot in the desert.

Mark stirred first. "I have sand in my mouth."

"Me, too," I said, my throat feeling as if I'd swallowed gravel. I also had sand in my hair, my ears, my nose. Some grains even clung to my eyelashes. I remembered waking in the night to a strong wind.

"I thought spending the night in the desert was going to be romantic."

I shook my head. "Not unless you like waking up to a woman who looks like she's survived a plague of locusts." I felt my hair as I struggled to sit up. "Windblown convertible hair, day two. Not a pleasant sight."

"You look beautiful."

"No wonder you can do commercials for Hi-Power sports drinks."

"What's that supposed to mean?"

I imitated him on the commercial: "Mmm! Tastes great and gives you the energy you need."

"It does."

"It tastes like piss, Mark. And I—" I tilted the rearview mirror "—do not look beautiful."

"To me you do."

I rolled my eyes again. "I don't know about you, but I am in desperate need of a shower."

"Since I've been hitching around out here, I've discovered truck-stop showers."

"I'll pass on the free invitation for athlete's foot and other fungal nightmares. I don't know how you feel about heading back to civilization, but we can go to Vegas, and you're welcome to stay in my condo for a couple of days until you figure out what, exactly, you're doing."

"Yeah...there's that."

"Look, I haven't asked you any questions. And I have to guess that for a guy who loves the game as much as you do to disappear, it has to be more than an existential crisis or something. The big question is, do you plan to go back to your team before the Super Bowl?"

"Yeah, I'm pretty sure about that. Just haven't figured out all the particulars."

"My condo has a parking garage. I can easily sneak you in without anyone seeing you. We can put the top up."

"Sounds tempting."

"What? A shower without black moss growing up the walls? A bed instead of a Cadillac seat with a broken spring?"

"Don't forget real food, not truck-stop food."

"I said nothing about real food. All I have in my fridge is Coke. And maybe a jar of half-sour dills. Maybe. Don't pin your hopes on that or anything."

"And then there's you. Sand-encrusted eyelids and all."

I smiled and looked at him. Somehow the sand and

sweat induced by the early morning sun made him look *better*. It was almost enough to make me hate him.

"Yes. Don't forget Medusa hair and seat impressions worn into my cheeks."

He leaned over and kissed me. His tongue brushing along my lips, which felt cracked and dry. Would it have killed me to pack some ChapStick?

"Mark…I am not kidding. I need a shower, and if I never see another grain of sand it will be too soon. Of course, I live in the Nevada desert, but you get the idea."

"Vegas it is, then. I'm trusting you."

"*Trust* is a pretty big word."

"I know. But last night was, well, like I said, maybe you were meant to find me at Joe's diner."

"Didn't they have good food?"

"Yeah. Best meal in a couple of days."

I put my keys in the ignition. "I've got to pee in the worst way."

"Me, too."

"Next gas station."

Thirty miles later, which felt like an excruciating eternity, we stopped to use the rest rooms at a small gas station with pumps that looked like they were from 1950, and then we headed on to Vegas. Mark rested his hand on my thigh as I drove, and both of us were lost in our own thoughts. I kept thinking about Annie and the Twelve Step expression: *There but for the grace of God go I*. More than ever, I realized, in a way that settled into my heart, that I had to stop gambling. It had stopped being fun. Maybe it had never been fun, but more like my own little drug. A way not to feel. A way to make the past go away. I wished, more than anything, that Annie had been able to learn that, and I winced silently when I thought of how terrified she must have been at the end.

I still had no idea why Mark Shannon had disappeared, but I did know he wasn't ready to talk to anyone about it. When we reached my condo, I parked in the garage to my building, and we luckily encountered no one on the way up to the fifth floor.

I unlocked the door to my apartment and swept my hand aside. "No black mildew in the showers, but home sweet home."

Mark Shannon stepped in the door while I held it open. Out of nowhere, he was promptly and violently, with great noise and a sickening thud, tackled into a wall and then crashed onto the floor. Busted plaster filtered through the air.

I screamed. And then I heard it. The deep voice of many a late-night phone call: "What have you done with my Little Girl?"

And when I turned on the lights and waved my hand through the air to try to see past the plaster dust, there, sitting *on top* of Mark Shannon, the most famous quarterback in the world, was my sponsor. All 275 pounds of George "T.D." Russell.

EIGHTEEN

Mark promptly belted T.D. with a left hook that landed on T.D.'s cheek. While I screamed "Get off him, T.D.!" the two of them engaged in something that looked like a cross between World Wrestling Entertainment, the TV show *Cops* and a boxing match. The two of them were grunting, and they crashed into my teak coffee table, splintering it instantly. "Stop!" I shrieked. I started hitting T.D. on the head, and then smacked Mark, but I was leery of getting too close and getting a black eye myself—something I was certain Mark would be sporting in a few hours. They fell against the couch, tipped it over, and then Mark slammed T.D. into my breakfast bar, where his shoulder left an impression in the plaster.

I raced into my kitchen and filled a pot with cold water, running back and dumping it on the two of them. That stopped them. Both sputtered and said "Hey!" in tandem. T.D. looked up at me from the man whose chest he was now straddling, looked back at the man beneath him, returned his gaze to me and back again.

"Has she kidnapped you?" He furrowed his brow as he asked Mark, whose shocked faced was turning red from the weight of T.D. on top of him.

"Um…T. D. Russell, right? If you could—" Mark's voice was strained "—get off of me, I'm sure we could explain."

"Ahh. Where are my manners?" He slid off of Mark, and they both stood. T.D.'s left cheek was already swelling, and he had a cut on his upper lip. Mark's eye was puffy, and his hair was pasty with plaster and water.

Mark stuck out his hand. "Maybe we should start over. I'm Mark Shannon. And no, she didn't kidnap me."

"Surprising. I would put nothing past her. T.D. Russell…and I'm sorry. Hope I didn't break a rib or anything."

Mark patted his sides. "Doesn't feel like it. Ever been sat on by Two-Ton Taylor? Now there's a man who could crack a rib or two."

They both laughed. Then T.D. seemed to realize I was 1) in the room; and 2) no longer AWOL. His face changed, sort of the way a father whose teenager has stayed out until dawn first is angry as curfew is blown off, then gets worried, then panicked, then ready to call the cops as the hours tick away and thoughts of twisted steel wreckage dominate his thoughts. Then, when the kid finally shows up, there's a rush of hugging and relief—followed by the biggest ass-chewing-out the kid's ever gotten. I was pretty sure I was about to be on the receiving end of a major verbal reaming. So I did what anyone would do in my shoes.

"Drink, anyone?"

"I'll take something." Mark smiled brightly, picking up on the fact that T.D.'s mood had darkened.

"Make yourselves at home, gentlemen. I'll get us drinks."

"It's eleven o'clock in the morning, Skye," T.D. said sourly.

"Practically happy hour."

In the kitchen, I checked out my reflection in the blackness of the microwave. God, I needed a shower. I poured three Jack and Cokes and brought them into the living room. The two of them had righted the couch again and were sitting there. I handed them each a drink. "No need for coasters. I no longer have a coffee table."

"Sorry about that," Mark said, taking a sip of his drink.

I chugged my drink in about three gulps. I was parched. T.D. stirred his with his index finger.

"Now, let me get this straight. You did not kidnap Mark Shannon."

"Correct."

"This is not gambling-related."

"Correct. You should be very happy about that."

"All righty then. You are not maimed or harmed in any way."

"A little sand in my ears, but no."

"Fingers not broken?"

"Umm, no."

"So nothing—no catastrophe, disaster, fire, accident—prevented you from dialing my number. You want to tell me what possessed you to pull a disappearing act, right on top of Annie's death, and make me worry like this?"

Mark shifted uncomfortably in his seat. "Is this like a lovers' quarrel or something? Have I gotten myself in the middle of something?"

"Oh, you've gotten yourself in the middle of something all right. Her crazy life. You got a sandy ass, too?" I guessed T.D. saw my hair was full of desert grains of sand.

Mark looked sheepish. "Kind of."

"I don't suppose she told you that I'm her best friend, and she is supposed to check in with me every day."

"Best friend or parole officer?"

"Oh, my man. My foolish, foolish man. This woman is trouble. She's a rebel. She hates authority. She doesn't know how to follow rules. That car? Not even registered. She don't even have a license. *Not licensed to drive a car.* She tell you she can't ride a bike? If you know what's good for you, you'll take your sandy ass and march it back to your team."

"T.D.!" I protested. "I am not *that* bad."

"You worried me near to death. I haven't slept. I haven't eaten. I had tickets to Cirque du Soleil, and I gave them to the hostess at the steakhouse because I was driving around looking for you. I even went to Big Buffet House of Hunan, thinking I might find you there. Only ate two plates. Threw the entire betting pool off." T.D. had stopped looking furious and started looking hurt.

"I'm sorry," I whispered. "I just needed to think about things…and Heavy Harry was looking for me. And Annie. Poor Annie." I didn't know her all that well, didn't know all her demons, but nobody deserved what happened to her. It made me wonder, briefly, if my father had ever had a woman beaten, and I decided to not even go there. Not today. "T.D., I just wanted to get out into the desert and look at the Milky Way. I wanted to be away from this fucked-up city. And then I ran into Mark."

T.D. turned to take a good look at America's Most Wanted Quarterback. "You do realize like every person on earth is looking for you, right?"

Mark nodded. "I'm just not ready to go back yet."

"You're as nuts as she is."

"Possibly. If you don't mind me asking, what's going on

between the two of you? Does he live here?" Mark turned to look at me.

"No. I have a key," T.D. replied. "And after a while I came here, thinking maybe she fell asleep and there was a gas leak. I didn't know *what* to think."

"T.D., I've never even used the stove. And it's electric."

"I know. Then I was envisioning a serial killer."

"You read entirely too many true-crime books."

"Anyway, Mark…" T.D. said, "Skye and I are just friends. She's like my little sister. My incorrigible little sister I'm tempted to put into juvenile hall."

Finally, T.D. smiled. He winked at me and then grinned, and Mark, who'd been leaning forward on the couch, looking tense, finally relaxed and settled back into its soft leather, draping his arm across my shoulders.

"I don't suppose, Mark," T.D. said, "you're going to tell me why it is you vanished."

"No. I can't say anything just yet. I've actually got to make a phone call to a friend of mine. You just have to believe me that I felt like I didn't have a choice. I left temporarily, and then it was a mess, and now I don't quite know how to go back to the team without having to do a sit-down with Barbara Walters."

I glanced over at T.D., who nodded silently. He'd told me that at the height of the allegations against him, much of which weren't true, he'd just wanted to hop a flight for Fiji and disappear. An idea that was attractive to me right now, if it didn't probably entail more sand in my ears. I desperately wanted a shower.

"I hear you." T.D. clasped his hands together. "Now that I know my Little Girl is safe, if just as exasperating as always, I'm starving. You two want to go grab something to eat? We could do lunch at the steakhouse."

"T.D.," I said, "we can't. He's still…I don't know what you'd call him. A fugitive from the NFL. So we can't go parading him out in public."

"True," Mark nodded, "though digging into a T-bone sounds pretty good. Anyway, we both need a serious shower."

"Tell you what?" T.D. grinned. "You go shower and I'll order us some takeout. I don't own a steakhouse for nothing. How do you like your meat cooked?"

"Medium-rare."

"Twenty-ouncer?"

"Oh, yeah."

I shook my head. Being friends with T.D. had inured me to how much a guy that size could eat. I'm no calorie-counter, but when breakfast is a twelve-egg omelet, we're talking a serious appetite.

I stood and said to Mark, "Come on. Let's get this sand off of us." I led him down the hall to my bedroom and into the master bath, which, like much of Las Vegas, featured over-the-top excesses, such as a marble shower stall big enough for four. And a chandelier.

Alone in the bathroom, I handed him a terry-cloth robe I kept on hand for T.D. Mark and I had kissed for hours the previous night—but we'd kept our clothes on.

"I'll let you shower first." I smiled. "Shampoo's there in that basket. Soap." I opened a drawer in my vanity. "Shaving cream in here. Razors."

"Who'll scrub my back?" He winked at me and pulled me to him. Close up I noticed how much his eye was swelling.

"Poor baby," I whispered, touching his burgeoning bruise.

"Nothing I don't get on a typical Sunday." He wrapped

his arms tighter around me and kissed me. Hard. His tongue found mine, then he kissed my lips gently and made his way with small flicks of his tongue down my throat.

"Aren't you getting sand in your mouth?"

"Mmm-hmm. What do you say we shower all this off together?"

I assumed Mark Shannon could have his pick of any cheerleader—heck, any female—anywhere. For a moment I was wary.

"I don't know," I whispered.

"I know I disappeared, and you may think I've lost it, but I'm trying to make sense of a few things, and the one thing—the one thing that has made sense in the past week of my life—is how I feel when I'm with you. I feel connected to you, and it has nothing to do with the moonlight in the desert or the stars. It's me and you."

I stepped back silently, stripped out of my clothes and started the shower, finding the line of demarcation on the round hot-cold knob between piping, burn-your-skin-off hot and chilly. Mark soon joined me. It felt good to be next to him in water, not sand, and I took in the sight of his perfect body. He had six-pack abs and just the right amount of hair on his chest. For the record, I'd seen his chest in an antiperspirant commercial. Oddly, I didn't feel awkward being naked in front of him. Something about him induced a feeling of comfortability. We kissed a long time under the shower spray. He didn't ask me any questions about being tackled by T.D., or why T.D. and I were such good friends, or even why T.D. thought I was crazy.

And I didn't ask him how long he planned on staying, because part of me would have been happy if he never left.

NINETEEN

"Hello? I'm still sitting here," I pouted.

T.D.'s right hand was bandaged where he'd cut it on the vase they'd smashed, and Mark, now sand-free and close-shaven, sported a shiner. Yet, in the way of men, I suppose, it was all forgotten now. They were eating enough food for a party of twelve and laughing as if they'd known each other their whole lives. As for me, I seemed to be forgotten as every anecdote revolved around the almighty game of football. Now, if this involved action that could help me win a bet, it might have been okay. But it was all about hulking idiots.

"Sorry, Little Girl, it's not every day I get to talk about the good old days." T.D. quickly lapsed back into his story. "…his center, Johnny 'Tailhook' Rothko, came out of the navy to play for the NFL. Me and ol' Tail-hook…now, we got into some trouble when we played together a few years back."

I rolled my eyes.

"Hey," T.D. asked Mark, "is Tailhook still dating that stripper with the tattoo of an angel on her shoulder?"

"Nah, he's not datin' her, he *married* her, found Jesus and they've got four kids—including a set of two-year-old twins."

"You're shittin' me."

"Am not. He won't even let us call him Tailhook anymore. So now we call him Johnny Jesus. He's a deacon in his church now."

"Well, I'll be….Johnny Jesus." T.D. shook his head.

"Hello? *Hello!* Guys, I love football as much as the next gambler, but if I hear about another jock-strap prank I'm going to throw up."

"Sorry, beautiful," Mark said, and grinned at me. He then dug into seconds on the *pommes frites* the restaurant had delivered us. I was used to T.D.'s displays of gastronomic fortitude, but side by side, bite for bite, their intake was nauseating. I felt like I was watching one of those food contests they have out on Coney Island.

I had stopped eating forty minutes before. Mark showed no sign of stopping. Guess the desert made him hungry. I watched him as he laughed with T.D. and was surprised that I felt something stirring in my belly, stronger than the flutter of a butterfly, almost a pounding.

"So tell me, T.D., how is it you two became friends?" Mark asked before inhaling another bite of steak. I was fairly certain between the two of them they had eaten an entire steer.

T.D. raised an eyebrow and looked at me. I nodded. We thought alike, always in sync. It's Gamblers *Anonymous,* and you're not supposed to break confidentiality. You would never break the confidentiality of another GA member—especially without their permission. But we understood each other. It was okay. Besides, I was never one to follow the rules.

"She came to my Gamblers Anonymous home group. She had eloped, gambled her way through Vegas and annulled her marriage in the space of five days…actually, the annulment took a little longer to unravel. I had to have my lawyer help her. And she felt like it was time to stop gambling."

Mark put down his fork and listened. He wasn't a typical guy where that was concerned. T.D. wasn't, either. They listened in a way I wasn't used to. With my father and Jimmy, one eye was always focused on the television sets that ran 24/7 on ESPN. You learned to talk *over* them. To stand in *front* of them if it was really that important.

T.D. continued. "You just get weary, Mark. I know I did. Tired of the lies. Of Monday coming and needing a calculator to figure out just how broke you are. And so, anyway, in GA they tell you *specifically* if you're a woman, you go and get yourself a woman sponsor. But one thing you'll find out pretty damn quick about Skye is she don't listen to nobody. So she asked me to be her sponsor. And I vaguely recall we went on a two-day drinking binge as we shared our life stories. And the rest is history."

Mark looked directly at me, as if he could see *into* me. I wasn't sure what he was looking for. A sign I was cured? A sign that I could be trusted? But he just nodded and reached across the table to hold my hand, then kissed my palm.

"You two make a cute couple." T.D. smiled. "If I was going to let my Little Girl hang out with someone, I suppose you'd be all right. You have a mean left hook, too. That sometimes comes in handy when you're around Skye."

"Shut up, T.D." I felt a pang. T.D. and I were very unlucky in love. My last date had been with a guy who'd

rummaged through my purse looking for cab fare, and
T.D.'s last date had been a reconciliation attempt with the
ex Mrs. Russell that had ended, as near as I could remember, with her driving her custom-painted Porsche in 360-
degree circles around his front lawn. He had to have it
completely resodded. I wished I could find T.D. a suitable
girlfriend—preferably one who didn't try to relandscape
his lawn and who also liked me. My attempts at setting him
up with every barmaid, Hunan hostess and cosmetic sales
associate had all failed miserably. It would be so wonderful if we could each find a relationship. I knew he'd never
approve of Jimmy—and deep down I understood why.

The restaurant had sent over two entire pies—one a
chocolate mousse and one a key lime, which was their signature dish. They knew T.D.'s sweet tooth well.

"I'm stuffed," I said, and then watched with amazement
as the two of them each took a fork and dug in. Mark took
aim at the key lime, and T.D. the chocolate mousse. "What
must the food bills at training camp be like?" I mused aloud.

"I always started with two dozen eggs and a strip steak,"
T.D. offered.

"Your veins must be like pure Valvoline," I said.

"Me," Mark began, "I always start with one of those
huge mixing bowls—you know the giant stainless ones?—
filled to the top with a jumbo box of corn flakes. Whole
milk. I hate skim. A quart of orange juice—no pulp. And
then sometimes I like a nice six-egg omelet with mushrooms and cheddar, some green peppers. And I usually
have half a cantaloupe."

"That is just wrong."

"We should take you to Big Buffet House of Hunan,"
T.D. offered.

"We can't take him anywhere, T.D. You forget every

tabloid in the country is looking for him. Hell, even the legit papers want a piece of this story."

"How soon we forget." T.D. took another bite of pie. "God, I love a good graham-cracker crust."

Mark looked first at me, then T.D. "I guess now that we've eaten, and gotten to know each other better, I should tell you guys what my story is."

"Only if you want to," I said. I'll admit, I was very curious, but I also had lived a life whispered about—albeit not on a global scale. I had kids try to be friends with me because they heard rumors about my father—and on the flip side, there were kids who avoided me precisely because of who my father was. Either way, I didn't like strangers analyzing me, and I assume Mark Shannon felt the same way. Though I suppose at this point, sandy encounter and all, we weren't exactly strangers.

"I do." He leaned forward and put his elbows on the table and sighed. "I haven't laid this all out for anyone."

"You know, part of GA is we have to tell our story at meetings sometimes," T.D. said. "There's definitely something to be said for letting it all out. You're as sick as your secrets, and I don't mean that in a bad way. Usually when you let your story out, you feel better."

I rolled my eyes. "They have a whole boatload of slogans in Twelve-Step programs."

"And she doesn't like any of them," T.D. said, staring me down.

"Honestly?" Mark said quietly. "I've had this bottled up for too long." He exhaled. "All right, then, here goes… A while ago, I started having some physical symptoms. The team doc kept it real quiet. I begged him not to tell anyone. I mean, here we were in a bid for the Bowl, and man, I was sick."

"What kind of sick?" I asked.

"Well, at first, I thought I was crazy. I started seeing halos around things. Like lights. And all of a sudden, I had a tough time distinguishing colors. I saw spots."

"Did you go get your eyes checked?"

"Yeah, yeah. Did that. But I seriously thought I was maybe crazy. I have two cousins who'd been diagnosed with schizophrenia."

"Oh," I winced. "I'm so sorry."

"Yeah. And it starts with a psychotic break. Usually when you're younger. A lot of times when you're under severe stress."

I suddenly feared that this man I was attracted to was sick, but then realized that so was I, in a different way. I reached out and patted his arm. "You can't get much more stressful than going for the Super Bowl, being in the media glare all the time."

"Well, part of the stress was trying to keep it from the media, even from the other players. Big time. I mean, you've seen the stories since I've left. Everything from alien abduction to—no offense, you two—gambling."

I tried to broach it tenderly. "Did you go to a psychiatrist?"

"No. T.D. will understand. You kind of spend your life being trained to suck it up."

"Shit, yeah," T.D. said. "I've played with concussions so bad I didn't even know my own goddamn name."

"And that was part of it, too. I was confused. Felt all fuzzy. I wasn't hungry. I was nauseous. I threw up some days. Had diarrhea—not fun when you're suited up. Christ, I was a mess."

"So, did you have a workup?" T.D. asked.

"Well, remember, I was trying not to let on. All I wanted

to do was play this game. And I'm not saying I'm the most important person on the team, but the guys needed my leadership. We're a young team—an expansion team—and some of the guys are really kids. I needed to set an example. So I kept it quiet, just talking to the team doc. His name's Jack Henson."

"What'd the doc say?"

"He said he ran blood tests and everything, and it was stress. In my head."

"Well, could you take something for the stress?"

"No, because it wasn't the stress. I mean, I just knew it wasn't. I lived for the game. I breathed it. I'd been under stress before."

T.D. and I looked at each other. If it wasn't stress, why'd Mark go AWOL? I looked at Mark, urging him on.

"One night, I threw up three times. I just knew something was up."

"Ulcer?" I asked.

He shook his head. "I'd had a GI workup…. Look, guys, what I'm about to tell you, you've got to swear to me you won't tell a soul. For your own safety."

I nodded. T.D. said, "You got our word, man."

"All right. That night, I suddenly had this feeling. It came over me from out of nowhere. I thought…what if the doc, what if he's bullshitting me?"

"Why would he do that?"

"I don't know, but he kept sloughing it off. Granted, I was the one to ask *him* to keep it quiet. But…I'm worth millions to the team. You'd think he'd want to be super thorough, not just tell me it's stress."

"Okay," I said, "so why would he be bullshitting you?"

"Look, I'm not paranoid. I don't know, I had a hunch. So I called this childhood friend of mine. Mike, he's good people. He grew up in the same tough neighborhood I did. Kept up straight As, got a scholarship, went to medical school. We keep in touch. He came out to the desert to a Native American reservation and started a clinic. No one knows, but I've bought him an X-ray machine, an ultrasound machine…I write him a check each Christmas so indigent people can get care."

I looked at Mark admiringly. That impressed me more than his touchdowns.

"So I asked him if he could do a workup on me if I flew out here. On the lowdown—without word to anyone. He agreed."

"And?"

"He looked at all my symptoms as a whole. Then he did a tox screen."

"For drugs?" T.D. asked.

"Yeah. All the usual suspects came up negative. I mean, I could have told him that. But then he did some obscure ones. I mean, I told him to look at everything. And I meant it. I wanted him to think like someone, I don't know— like a real detective. Even if he thought it was schizophrenia, I wanted him to tell me. I also wanted him to think what he might look for if someone was trying to do me harm."

"Harm? You really don't trust this Doc Henson."

"It was how he talked to me. Like this radar came up when I asked him for details." Mark leaned back in his chair.

"And? Did your friend Mike find anything?"

"Damn straight, he did."

"What?" I leaned forward.

"Digitalis toxicity."

"What?" T.D. asked. "My grandmama took digitalis. What the hell would you need digitalis for?"

Mark held up his hands in front of him. "Nothing. That's the conspiracy, man. I don't need it."

"I don't understand," I whispered, feeling a little chill come over me. This was starting to sound scary.

"Digitalis dropped into a sports drink is colorless. You can't smell it. You can't taste it. You add too much and the person can get heart arrhythmia, but you do it little by little and the person can seem crazy, experience all that confusion I had. Stomach problems."

"Holy crap, Mark. Is your friend sure?"

"Hell, yeah. He ran the tox screen from it a second time. And, I got to tell you, the drug could have killed me. I could have gotten a heart arrhythmia during a game or a practice and had heart failure, and no one, not the M.E., no one, would have thought to do a tox screen for digitalis toxicity. Henson could have killed me."

"How do you know it was Henson?" T.D. asked.

"He could write prescriptions for it. He had access to me, to what I was drinking. And he was gaslighting me, man. He was making it out like it was all in my head. I mentioned the confusion to him. I mentioned my cousins. He played into that. Looking back, I can see he was manipulating me."

"I need a drink," I whispered, and went and got the bottle of Jack, which I poured straight into a glass. "Why? I don't get it."

T.D. shook his head. "I know why…and you know why, Skye."

"How the hell would I know why some crackpot doctor wants to screw with the star quarterback of a Super Bowl team—" And then it dawned on me. "Oh, Christ. Gambling."

"Yep. Rig it. I'm not open to a bribe, but you can get

me sick enough so that I either play sloppy, or they have to go to the second-string or third-string guy."

"Mark, it can't be." But even as I said it, I knew it could be. I knew the amount of bookmaking taken *legally* in Vegas was in the millions upon millions for football. And the amount taken in *illegally* had to surpass that, with the mob involved, no less. The figure, the money floating on one game, was likely a hundred million or more—way more. So why wouldn't someone try to fix it?

"So why don't you go to your coach—go to McBride? You have the tox reports from your friend. That's proof."

Mark shook his head. "I already thought of that. The problem is I have no idea how deep this goes. It could be the doc has gambling debts, or it could be it's not just him. I know for one he plays golf with the commissioner. He knows a lot of people. And if they—whoever's involved—were willing to mess with something as potentially deadly as digitalis, then what's next? What if they try to take me out with a bullet? I went into hiding so I could get a handle on this. I didn't leave so I can't play the game I love. I left so I could get well and be sure I *stayed* well so I *can* play the game I love."

"So now what?"

"I hired a private eye. A guy named Joey Rialto that I'm positive I can trust. He's looking into the doc's private life. And I've contacted a top security guy—bodyguards. And when I go back, I tell my coach I want my own personal physician—no team doc. As for the rest of it—what I found out, I keep to myself. For now."

I sat at the table as waves of shock ran over me. "This is huge, Mark."

He nodded. "I know. Eventually, I assume I'll actually have to go to the FBI."

T.D. shook his head. "You're lucky that quack didn't kill you."

"I am. There're a lot of people who are going to be pissed at me for not handling this some other way. I needed to figure out a plan. I needed to clear my head, which I can tell you was pretty damn fuzzy for a while. I've been playing ball since I was four years old in a peewee league. It's all I ever wanted. It was my ticket out of the steel mills. And in the end, football has brought me everything I've wanted, but it hasn't meant that I get to escape all the bad stuff."

"No one gets a free ride, Mark," I said.

"I guess I just had to figure that out for myself."

"Mark, you have to be really careful," I said. "Right now, I'm going to make some coffee. I think we could use some."

I went into the kitchen and started a pot, and the three of us sat at my table for hours. We were letting Mark Shannon piece together a plan to keep himself safe, away from the prying eyes of the rest of the world.

CHAPTER

TWENTY

"Honey, I want to come to Vegas."

I was staring at the perfectly sculpted naked ass of Mark Shannon as he slept on his stomach, and I was listening to my father tell me he was about to do something very, very stupid. Well, maybe not stupid, but definitely inconvenient.

"Dad—"

"Now, don't try to talk me out of it. Me and Jimmy want to come and visit. We want to see where you live. Meet George Russell. Take you to see Wayne Newton. You know, 'Tiny Bubbles...'" he sang.

"Don Ho."

"What whore? What are you saying?"

"Don Ho, Dad. Don Ho sang 'Tiny Bubbles.'"

"Oh. Well, I want to visit, anyway."

"*Now?* Now you decide to visit after three years?"

"I admit at first I thought the whole Vegas thing was temporary. And I was respecting your wishes when you said you needed some time to figure out your life. I fig-ured it was some kind of therapy bullshit. Anyway, it was

so good to see you, honey, and we miss you. *I* miss you.
And what man can't use a getaway to Vegas?"

"Well, you can't come. Not right now, Dad."

"Why not?"

"It's the play-offs. You can't leave your business. What
sort of bookie would you be if you left your business in
the busy season? Do *I* always have to be the responsible
one?"

He was silent, as if he were mulling this over.

Mark rolled over and said, "Good morning, angel."

"What was that?" my father asked.

"What?"

"That sound? That voice? Do you have someone
with you?"

"Dad..."

"Well, who was that?"

"I can't say."

"Here we go again. I'm trying to build a relationship with
you, and you're shutting me out. You're putting up walls."

"Dad, this sounds suspiciously like the time we briefly
entered family counseling."

"What about Jimmy?"

"I have to talk to him."

"He'll be over in two hours. What do I say to him?"

"Nothing, Dad."

I rolled my eyes at Mark, marveling yet again that even
with bed head, he looked irresistible.

"Are you coming to the Super Bowl with us?"

I stared at Mark. Frankly, it looked like the Mustangs
were a lock for the Bowl. At least if he could play one
more game to clinch it. But attending the Bowl with my
ex-husband sounded like a rather stupid idea. However,
the word "yes" left my mouth.

"Wonderful! Then I don't feel so badly that I'm not coming to Las Vegas. Now, do you want to tell me who this guy is you're with?"

"Mark Shannon, Dad," I said in the most sarcastic voice I could muster.

"Fine. Obviously, you want to be difficult, Skye. I'll call you tomorrow."

I hung up the telephone and slid down under the covers, sliding my arms down Mark's body. If we stayed together past this little lost weekend or whatever you wanted to call it, I would either have to give up my desserts at T.D.'s restaurant or start doing sit-ups.

"How come you don't have a girlfriend?"

Mark rolled on his back, and I settled into the crook of his arm. He stared at the ceiling. "You don't often meet people who like you for you. I mean, you meet these girls…these beautiful girls, yeah, but they hand you hotel keys in bars and they show up on the doorstep of your hotel room wrapped in a towel…and man, it's just not my style."

"Come on," I teased. "Naked women on your doorstep? How could that not be your style?"

"I won't lie and say I never just went for it, but you get over that pretty quickly. At least some of us guys do. You start to want to find someone with some substance. Someone who's not there, next to you, just because of your money or your fame. Someone to play Twenty Questions with. Someone you can tell your secrets to. Fame is actually kind of lonely."

"I know about lonely. I told you, I'm a compulsive gambler. I've used gambling to keep the world at bay, so I didn't have to feel too much. Only, my days are kind of empty. And my nights are filled with trying not to gamble, or sometimes *not* trying not to gamble—and that's when I get into trouble. I ran away from New York because I thought I needed to get away from my father. But I didn't have anything here. I'm on a first-name basis with the people in my GA home group, but I wouldn't consider them my friends. Not really."

Mark wrapped his arms around me, my face nuzzled into the base of his neck. "I'm your friend. I can't thank you enough. I feel a lot better after talking to you and T.D. last night. A lot better. He's a really good guy."

"Yeah. He's my one best friend. Best ever."

"And I don't have to worry about you two? You know, hooking up or anything?"

"Nope. I think if we tried, we'd laugh so hard we'd fall out of bed."

"Good. I don't mean the falling out of bed thing. I mean I don't want you and me to be just this…fling. This means something to me, however strange it is how we got together. We have time to figure it out. That's if you're willing to figure it out with me."

"T.D. wasn't lying. I have a lot of things to figure out, Mark. But there's definitely something between us," I said, kissing him.

"I've thought about it. I'm going to go back to my team. I'll hop a flight tomorrow. They need me, and I'm going to have to deal with some pissed-off teammates."

"I figured you would go back sooner or later. Sooner being better. I mean, either way it's going to be a shit storm when you do."

"But I'll try to keep you out of it as much as possible. I mean, when they ask me where I've been. I think I'm just going to say I lost it. Pressure. Something. My coach, McBride, my gut's telling me he's a good guy. I'm not going to mention the digitalis and the doc, but I'll let him know I needed some time. He'll help me in all the insanity."

A cell phone began ringing—Mark's. He leaned over to the bedside table and picked it up. He read the caller ID. "It's Rialto."

He had been waiting for this guy's call. I listened to one half of the conversation—Mark was saying a lot of "uh-huhs" and "I hear yous." After about ten minutes, he hung up.

"It's bad, Skye."

"How bad?"

"The doc is in for 400,000 big ones to his bookie."

"Who's his bookie?"

"Guy by the name of Big Easy Marino. Ever hear of him?"

I felt queasy. "He's my dad's rival. They pretty much stay clear of each other. My father's got a lot of loyal union book. Anyway, Marino, he dabbles in some other stuff. Brutal guy. And I got some bad news for you."

"What?"

"Bookies don't let someone have a line of credit that big without taking your car, your boat, your house in the country. If they let the good doctor run up a tab like that, there's no *way* he can even pay the vig—the interest. So he's screwed. He'd have to have a million to ultimately pay it off. He's in deep. So that means Big Easy probably had this plan all along."

"I've really got to watch my back," Mark said. "I better get on the phone to McBride."

I began kissing his neck. "Before you leave…one more time for the road, cowboy?"

He laughed. And then obliged. Then the two of us took a long, leisurely shower. Afterward, Mark called his coach, who was treating him for now with kid gloves. No doubt McBride was happy to have contact with Mark, but scared shitless he'd lose him again. McBride said they were sending a "fixer."

"You realize that sounds like a mafia term," I said to Mark after he hung up from McBride. "Or like you're fixing the score."

"This is the guy the team calls when someone gets a stripper pregnant, gets caught with underage girls, sleeps with the wife of a movie star... runs away with a beautiful gambler." He smiled at me. "You know, he'll arrive with a PR agent, a couple of bodyguards. A driver. We'll keep this low-key, and your name won't be mentioned. We'll play it off like I needed a rest from the media scrutiny. I don't know. That's what fixers are for. They figure out an angle to make the whole thing smell like roses."

"Great. This fixer is worth his weight in gold if he can get you out of this jam."

"When can I see you next?"

"I don't know."

"How about coming to New York this weekend?"

"Okay...let's go down and get the paper. They always have flight specials in today's travel section."

And it was that simple. We had a plan. We had a fixer.

And we still managed to fuck it up.

By Monday morning, my face was plastered in newspapers and on TV from one end of America to the other. Actually, according to an Internet search, my face was plastered as far away as Bora Bora.

From the Las Vegas newspaper: Shannon's Gambling Woes: The Bookie's Daughter

The paparazzi who was hiding in my parking garage was a very rich man.

And I was a hiding at T.D.'s house while satellite dishes were erected on his freshly resodded lawn, which led to the following *People* magazine cover: Love Triangle with T. D. Russell: How Will It Affect the Super Bowl?

And Jimmy Sullivan was on a plane heading to Vegas.

CHAPTER

TWENTY-ONE

My father's exasperated voice echoed in my ear over the telephone. "Skye, you do realize my business is based on anonymity. I don't advertise my services. People find me. Discreetly. Front-page headlines about you—and me—is not the kind of discreet referral I'm looking for."

I rolled my eyes and silently cursed at the heavens—or at least at the ceiling of T.D.'s spare bedroom. My father was not amused by the sight of me and Mark Shannon running into T.D.'s house with jackets over our heads on CNN.

"Dad, I'm sorry. I'm really, *really* sorry. But c'mon, Dad, you've had your run-ins with the law. It's not like I did this on purpose. It'll blow over."

"Blow over? One of the biggest sports stories in a decade—after Kobe and O.J. It's not going to blow over. People will be telling their *grandkids* about this one."

"The team's called in a fixer. Some guy who can make this all go away—or at least settle it down. Give it a week."

"Darlin', this is going to last to the Super Bowl and beyond."

I had no comeback, because I knew he was right.

"And—" he continued his little tirade "—what about poor Jimmy? Did you stop to think about that? About him? Imagine how he felt? He's thinking you two are getting back together, and you're off banging a quarterback."

"Nice, Dad. Very nice. I'm not 'banging' him. Next time, could you put it a little nicer? I'm your daughter, remember?"

I heard the sound of shattered glass, and I guessed he'd hurled a dish at the wall. "Damn. Skye, look, I didn't mean that. This is just a mess. Jimmy's a mess. When he's a mess, my business is a mess. Just tell me one thing, Skye."

"What?"

"Do you love this guy? This Shannon guy?"

"I don't know, Dad. I just met him, really. I've never been too good at relationships, anyway."

"I know you like I know the back of my hand, Skye. I can hear it in your voice. You really like this guy. Or at least you're starting to think so."

"I guess so."

"I knew it. It was like when your mother fell for me. Messy. Well, then…hang in there, kid. It'll all work out."

"A minute ago you were telling me people were going to tell their grandkids about this."

"They are. But that still doesn't mean it won't work out for you and this quarterback. Just do me a favor?"

"Hmm?"

"Go easy on Jimmy. He's nursing a pretty major broken heart."

"Sure, Dad." I swallowed hard. Another minute and I'd be blubbering. "I've got to go."

I hung up the phone, and Mark walked into the bedroom. He knelt on the floor in front of me. "What's up, Skye? You're crying."

"I'm not crying."

"Okay, you're not crying. Your face is just wet."

I managed a smile. "I just talked to my dad."

"What'd he say?"

"Put it this way, he can't back out of his driveway for all the television vans. That makes doing business a little difficult."

"You know, I think we were both just in this place where we needed to talk to someone, to connect with someone," Mark said. "I don't think we thought past the week. I don't think I thought through what a mess it might be…dating a bookie's daughter. And I guess I underestimated how quickly people would find out."

I winced. "He's got a record. He's not a minor league bookie. I guess I didn't think it through, either. I've hurt him."

He leaned in close to me and kissed me, salty tears mixing in our mouths. "It's okay. We're just making the fixer earn his money."

"Does this fixer have a name?"

Before he could answer, the doorbell rang. T.D. called out from downstairs, "Mark! The team guy is here."

"That would be the fixer," Mark said, standing and taking my hand. "And his name's Leon Krakowski."

"You're kidding."

"You know him?"

"No. That's just a helluva name."

"From what I've seen of him in action, he's a helluva guy. Come on."

We walked down T.D.'s teak staircase, holding hands as if going to our execution. And there, waiting for us in the foyer, stood a five-feet-two-inch man, about sixty years old, in a fedora and an expensive gray suit, smoking a cigar that looked almost as big as he was.

"Leon!" Mark smiled.

"Good to see ya, Shannon. Is this the dame?"

"Yes. This would be Skye." We reached the bottom of the staircase. I smiled and tried to look innocent.

"She's a looker, all right. Well, kids...we got a mess that needs fixin'."

T.D. motioned toward the kitchen. "Why don't you all go in there and sit down. My housekeeper made a fresh pot of coffee."

"Can you trust her?" Leon asked.

"Who?"

"Your housekeeper. She won't sell you up the river to the *Enquirer*, will she?"

"Nah. She's been with me for ten years. Comes each day for a few hours. Her grandson takes care of my pool."

"A little money can turn people's heads."

"Not her," T.D. said. "You all go on in there. I'll be in the den."

"Not so fast, big man," Leon said, chomping on his cigar and reaching *way* up to pat T.D.'s shoulder. "You're in this mess, too."

"Me?" T.D. stared straight at me as I scrunched up my eyes and avoided looking at him.

"Yes, you. Everyone thinks this is a love triangle. Don't you read the papers? Half of Vegas is quoted as saying you and Miss Gorgeous over here are a couple. You've been seen everywhere."

"Yeah, but—"

"I know what you're gonna say," Leon said, his large bushy gray eyebrows knitting up and down. "'But,

Leon—'" he took on a mocking voice "'—there's nothing going on between me and her.' Listen pal," he said, back in his own voice, "the truth has no place in this mess. Tabloids aren't interested in the truth. The media isn't interested in the truth. Katie Couric ain't interested in the truth. You are all in this mess together. And you got me—" he smiled a big grin, cigar still between his teeth "—to get you out of it."

We moved into the kitchen and sat down. T.D. immediately brought over a tray of lunch meats and rolls. He always eats when he's nervous. He and Mark immediately began making immense sandwiches piled three inches thick with cold cuts.

"I ain't hungry," Leon said. "But I'll take a bourbon if you have it."

T.D. got Leon a bourbon, and brought over three chilled Heinekens for me, him and Mark. I swallowed half of mine in one gulp.

"All right," Leon said. "First of all, Mark, you've got a sit-down chat with Katie Couric on *Dateline.*"

Mark groaned.

"Look here, pretty boy, what Leon says, goes." Leon spoke of himself in the third person. "That's the word from the coach—you know it and I know it—so let's forget the moaning and groaning."

"I just hate that whole heart-on-the-sleeve routine."

"Cry me a river, Shannon. I didn't go AWOL. You did. The way it plays is this—you go through the whole bit about how you spoke to McBride about taking a little R and R. We have the offensive coach saying you were having stomach problems. They thought it was stress, an ulcer. You weren't technically AWOL. You just took off to get out of the media glare. And then you talk about pretty woman over here. One thing led to another and you were swept up in a romance. It would help if you two were going to get married. Any chance of that? Engagements seem to get people all happy."

Mark looked over at me. "Well, um, you realize we just met a few days ago. It's a little early for that—not that this is a fling. It's serious. It's kismet. It's—I don't know what it is."

"Okay. Can you at least say she's your girlfriend?"

Mark looked at me, and I nodded.

"Okay. Good enough. You're in love. Blah, blah, blah. Roses. Balloons. Flowers. Puppy dogs. Rainbows. Love. Now, big man." He turned his gaze to T.D., who was mid-sandwich bite. "What's your part in all this? You and pretty woman used to be an item?"

T.D. laughed, a deep baritone laugh that started in his belly. "Nah. Me and Little Girl, we don't have a thing goin' on, Leon. Never did. She's *way* too much trouble. Evidenced by the two hundred vans outside my house with satellite dishes."

"So what gives?"

I nodded at T.D., who said, "I'm her sponsor. We're in Gamblers Anonymous together. You *did* hear about my gambling, right?"

"Yeah, yeah, yeah. That was a mess. You shoulda had ol' Leon back then. You'd still be in the NFL. Christ. She's a gambler *and* a bookie's daughter. That's rich. All right… the Twelve-Step thing can make for good TV."

"No. It's anonymous," T.D. said. "One of their principles is you can't say you're in Gamblers Anonymous to the media."

"Principles," Leon snorted. "All right, then. Let's say you 'took her under your wing' as she tried to get over her traumatic childhood. Her gambling woes. Oh, I like that."

He looked at me. "Heard about your mother. The press is camped out on your grandmother's lawn in South Carolina, too. Sorry, kiddo. Tough breaks. Dad's an ex-con, Mom gets it in a plane crash. Doesn't sound like it was a picnic." Leon said all this with lightning-fast speed.

I spoke up. "I'm not too keen on having my life splashed on the cover of every magazine in the supermarket."

T.D. snorted. "It's a little late for that. You stand in line recently? Every tabloid has you featured on the cover."

"Well, we don't have to feed into it."

"Yes, you do," Leon said sternly. "You feed the monster. Only you feed the monster what *you* want the monster to eat. That's the way it works."

I rolled my eyes, feeling as if I were an engineer on a train hurtling down the tracks who'd suddenly discovered the brakes were broken.

"Okay, pretty woman. Now it's your turn. Do I have all the facts? You're a bookie's daughter. You're a recovering gambler. And now you're Mark Shannon's girlfriend. When was your last bet?"

I stared at T.D. "Last Saturday."

"You ever bet on Shannon?"

I turned crimson. "Yes. But to win, not to lose."

"Like that'll make all the difference. You place these bets with your old man?"

"No. My bookie. Heavy Harry."

"Does Heavy Harry have a last name, perchance, Princess Catastrophe?"

"Weinstein. He operates sports book out of an office on the Strip."

"Will he talk to the press?"

"Doubt it."

"We just have to fucking pray not. All right, then. Next you have to meet with the commissioner of the NFL, Walter Hammond II, or Walt Squared as I call him. You have to swear to him on a stack of Bibles as tall as me that your father and Shannon have never met—they haven't, right?"

Mark and I shook our heads no.

"And that Shannon has nothing to do with gambling. Then Hammond will let Shannon play in the play-off game and the Super Bowl, which looks like a lock. Right now, Hammond's official stance is it's a maybe...but you don't sink the greatest sports event in humankind for a girl. No offense, honeybun. You're hot but not hot enough to derail the countdown to the Bowl. So you all have to grovel in front of Walt Squared, and he'll stretch out the drama a bit. Say it's an investigation. Then Shannon will be cleared *just* in time to play. You follow?"

"I follow," I said quietly. My world, while never in control, had never been so out of control as in this moment. *We admitted we were powerless over gambling—that our lives had become unmanageable.* I felt sick to my stomach. Mark had finished his sandwich and now he held my hand in a death grip. My life was completely and utterly unmanageable and I swore to myself I wasn't ever going to gamble again. Not just for the next twenty-four hours. Forever. If I had felt shame before, humiliation at showing up at GA and revealing to my home group that I had gambled again, I couldn't imagine how I would feel showing up after my dumb luck—and yeah, I'd blame it on luck, fate, whatever—had propelled the details of my life into a news story.

"All right, then." Leon clasped his hands together. "We've covered everything."

With that, the doorbell rang. T.D. stood and went to the door. "I already told the press it was gonna be 'no comment,'" he muttered. I downed the rest of my beer.

"Jesus H. Christ," T.D. shouted, and we heard the door open, loud commotion from the press outside, then footsteps in the foyer.

Next he stood in the kitchen doorway, with Jimmy Sullivan by his side.

"Oh, my God," I whispered.

"Who's this guy?" Leon asked.

"Her husband," Jimmy said angrily.

"I think I'm gonna need another bourbon," Leon said hoarsely. For the first time, all color drained from his face.

CHAPTER

TWENTY-TW♥

"Her husband?" Mark turned to look at me, his eyes registering shock.

"My *ex*-husband," I said firmly.

"Well, I'm not giving her up," Jimmy said, striding over to me. "Pack your fucking suitcase, Skye, you're coming home with me. Back where you belong. Back with the people who really love you, the people who'll die to protect you. In New York!"

"Now, wait a minute," Mark said.

"You shut the fuck up, pretty boy," Jimmy snapped, and swung at Mark, landing a clear shot on his left cheek. Mark pounced from his chair and went for Jimmy, knocking him against T.D.'s breakfast bar and sending the platter of deli meats sailing through the air. T.D. stood, knocking over his chair, and rushed between them, holding them each at arm's length.

"Hold on, boys, hold on."

Jimmy was still swinging wildly. "Just let me kill him!"

Mark shouted, "Just try!"

"Christ, this gets better and better," Leon chimed in.

Mark's face was turning red, and Jimmy, though outsized by a good sixty pounds, was ready to fight to the death. "Jimmy!" I shouted. "Settle down." I picked up Leon's bourbon, which was all ice now, since he had quickly polished it off, and I hurled the ice at Jimmy's face. That got his attention.

T.D. looked Jimmy in the eye to settle him down. "Need a drink there, to go with your ice, buddy?"

Jimmy finally stopped moving and took a deep breath. "Hell, yeah. Something strong."

"Bourbon?"

"Fine."

"I'm gonna let go of you, and you're not going to hit him. And Mark, you just sit down next to Skye. When I say three, you both back off. Agreed?"

"Agreed," Mark said.

Jimmy said nothing.

"Jimmy!" I urged.

"Fine. Agreed," he said like a whiny five-year-old.

"All right, then," T.D. intoned. "One…two…three."

Like two prizefighters retreating to their corners, Jimmy backed up and Mark sat back down next to me.

T.D. went to the counter and started making Jimmy and Leon bourbons. I called out to him, "As long as you're bartending for them, I'll take one."

"Me, too," Mark piped up.

T.D. took the bottle of bourbon and four clean glasses and brought it to the table. He refilled Leon's drink and made fresh ones for himself, me, Mark and Jimmy.

"To my Little Girl." T.D. lifted his glass. "The only person on Planet Earth who could create an international incident of this proportion."

"I'd hardly call it an international incident, and it's not like I planned this," I said in my own defense.

Leon shook his head. "They're leading with this story in Prague, for God's sake."

"What?"

"That's what I hear. Walt Squared is monitoring the press coverage."

I downed my bourbon and poured myself a fresh one.

"Skye, wife, darling," Jimmy said through gritted teeth, "can I please speak to you in private?"

I touched Mark's thigh, rubbing his leg. "I need to take care of this," I whispered. I was willing him to be okay with me going upstairs with Jimmy.

"I know what we have," he whispered back. "Go ahead."

I nodded and stood, downing my second bourbon. Leon threw his hands up in the air. "I'll wait for you two to settle whatever it is you're settling, so I know whatever the hell *else* I need to clean up."

T.D. looked at Leon. "Do they pay you by the mess?"

"I wish."

I stood and walked over to Jimmy. "Come on. Let's go upstairs to talk."

We climbed T.D.'s staircase. I gazed out the massive window as we got to the top. You could barely see lawn for all the reporters and paparazzi.

I took Jimmy by the hand and led him to the guest room where I always stayed, and shut the door. He enveloped me in a tight hug in an instant.

"I love you, Skye. Don't do this." His lips were on my neck, his tongue tracing its way to the hollow of my throat. I felt a burning in my gut from both his kiss and the bourbon.

I pulled myself away, trembling. "Jimmy, I said I didn't

plan to do this. If I could, I would undo it all in a minute, beginning with my trip to New York. I shouldn't have gotten involved with you again."

"Don't say that."

"Jimmy, when I'm with you, I get a love hangover."

"What are you talking about?"

"When we're together, I'm always aware you're not good for me, Jimmy. It's like drinking a bottle of bourbon. The first couple of drinks are smooth, and you may want the next one and the next one, but you'll pay for it in the morning."

"You're talking crazy. Come home with me, Skye. You know we're meant to be together. We've known it since the first time we met."

"I was a kid when we met, Jimmy."

"You can't deny you love me. You can't deny what happens when we're in bed together. You can't deny how we *feel* together." His eyes were pleading. I took a good look at him, dark circles under his eyes, face drawn and tired looking. In my insides, my heart, my belly, it was killing me to know I was hurting him.

"No, Jimmy. I can't deny any of that. I do love you. I love you as much as it's possible to love someone else. I will always love you with a part of my heart. I can't deny that when you're inside of me, I go somewhere far away, someplace exquisite. I know how we feel together, like we belong." I reached out and stroked his face, then ran my fingers through his hair.

"Exactly, baby."

"But…I also know something else, Jimmy. I don't want to gamble anymore. I wasn't even sure of that until this past weekend. When I was with Mark, I never thought about gambling. I can't explain it. I just never thought about it. Not once. And when I had to tell Mark and Leon downstairs that I bet last weekend, I was *ashamed*."

"Why? I don't fucking get it, Skye. What is so fuckin' wrong with gambling?"

"For some people, nothing, Jimmy. But for me, everything. It consumes me. Everything I do some days is just about gambling. It takes over my life, Jimmy. My mind. It's like my own portable prison. Compare it to people and alcohol. One person can have a glass of wine or two with dinner every night; another person will try that and start a spiral downward until they wake up with their head in a toilet bowl and no memory of the previous night."

"Okay. So you want to stop. Then I'll stop gambling, too. Big fuckin' deal. I'll get a job."

"You have a job, Jimmy."

"No, I'll get a real job."

I shook my head. "What? You going to go manage a McDonald's? Work for the post office? Tie yourself to an office?"

"It doesn't matter. I'll take any job to be with you, Skye."

"Jimmy." I moved closer to him, my voice quiet but strong. "You do what it is you do. It's part of you. My father couldn't stop being a bookie. It's what he is, who he is. But I have a chance here to be more than a gambler. I'm not sure what that is. But I'm going to try, Jimmy."

"But you love me," his voice cracked.

"Yes, I do. I love you. The part of me who is a gambler loves you, Jimmy. The part of me who gets into these manic moods and spends all day at OTB, or at the track. But I'm just not willing to let that part of myself be *all* of me. I never knew, until this weekend, that I could want, *really want* something more than what my life is. But I do.

It's like I've been suffocating, and for the first time, I can really breathe."

"Skye…" His shoulders were slumped, and he pulled me to him. "I need you, baby doll."

"I know. But I need *him,* Jimmy." I started crying, the sobs rising up from my chest in racking gasps. It wasn't just Mark causing the tears. It was the memories that got stirred up like a hornet's nest when I went to New York. Memories I didn't like to think about—that I gambled to avoid thinking about.

"Shh, baby. Don't cry. You know I hate when you cry."

I held him closer. That was my Jimmy, being protective and kind to me even as I was twisting the knife in his back.

"I'm sorry, Jimmy. I never should have come home. I never should have made love with you."

"Come on, now, I wouldn't have traded that for anything, Skye. We never got to say goodbye properly when I left Vegas after the wedding. The doctors stitched up my head in the ER, and you walked out and went back to the hotel. I was so hotheaded I took the next plane home. Remember?"

"Yes, I remember." I laughed a hollow little laugh. "You know, Jimmy, that doesn't say much for us being good for each other when one of the most significant weekends of our lives features emergency-room stitches."

He took his hand and lifted up the lock of hair that always fell on his forehead. "Still got the souvenir." He leaned his forehead down to show me his scar, pale white and a little jagged. I kissed it.

"Promise me something?"

"Hmm?" I looked up at him, my nose running.

"If it doesn't work out with him, give us another shot?"

"I'll say yes, Jimmy, but if you love me, you shouldn't want what's bad for me."

"Bourbon's no good for you, but I don't see you giving up that, either."

I laughed.

"I'll always love you, Skye. I'm never gonna marry anyone else. Someday, I think, you'll be back. You think you're not a gambler, but you are. Deep down. It's in your blood."

And suddenly I felt peace. I was glad he'd said that. I realized Jimmy would never understand the part of me that wanted to be free of this giant albatross around my neck. I rubbed my face. "I need a tissue," I said, and moved away from Jimmy and into the bathroom. I blew my nose and came back out to Jimmy, whose hands were in his pockets as he stared down at the ground.

"I better go home, Skye."

"You can't leave now," I said. "Look!" I pointed out the window through the blinds. Two helicopters flew low to the ground outside. "They'll eat you alive out there. I'm not even sure how you got in safely. Better to wait out this thing."

"With him?" Jimmy looked at me forlornly.

"He's not a bad guy, Jimmy."

"Fuck!" He kicked the dresser. *"Fuck!"* I saw his anger and knew that anger was better than feeling sorry for himself. He took a vase and threw it across the room. Then he grabbed a second vase and threw it. I winced.

"Sorry, Skye. I feel better now."

"That first vase was worth a thousand dollars."

"Jesus. Fuck!"

"I'll explain it to T.D. somehow. Let's go downstairs."

"I'm going to get good and drunk," Jimmy said.

We left the room and walked down to the kitchen. I noticed a second bottle of bourbon was now on the table. If Jimmy was planning on getting good and drunk, he had plenty of company.

CHAPTER
TWENTY-THREE

I was still a prisoner in T.D.'s home. And the time was approaching when Mark would have to leave and face the phalanx of reporters and media. I felt like a swimmer in shark-infested waters watching fins encircle me. The plan, designed by Leon, was fairly simple. Mark would do a press conference, and I would have a private meeting with Walt Squared, arranged by one Leon Krakowski, fixer extraordinaire. After that, if need be, I would give a statement to the media. Inwardly I cringed. In the meantime, unbeknown to Leon, Jimmy and Walt Squared, was the fact that the team doctor was in deep to Big Easy, and Mark, T.D. and I couldn't be sure of Mark's safety. Because we had been entrusted with the big secret, I suppose that placed T.D. and me in danger, too.

All night, Jimmy, T.D. and Leon sat around the kitchen table and drank bourbon. Jimmy told stories about my teen years, about my father. About prom night. I just kept my mouth shut and held on to Mark's hand in the den. We were within earshot, watching the round-the-clock coverage on ESPN, CNN and MSNBC. Finally, I turned off the news.

"I can't take it anymore. Everything's for sale. My past, yours, my father's. I mean, how many times are they going to run my father's old mug shot?"

Near dawn, Mark and I went upstairs and shut ourselves in T.D.'s guest room to say goodbye. He was going back to his team to prepare for the play-off game, and I would be where I was a week before…taking it one day at a time and trying not to gamble, with the added pressure of trying to avoid the press and the feeling of incompleteness when I thought of being without Mark. It was funny, in a way. My life with Jimmy was about what we shared in the realm of gambling, about falling into step with a life I knew so well. But with Mark, I couldn't explain how utterly lost I felt at the thought of him leaving. It was silly. As a rational person, I knew it was the extraordinary situation that we found ourselves in that made us closer that much faster, but it felt real. It felt as real as chips and cards on a felt table.

Mark took my hand, pressing my palm against his. "Your hand is so tiny in mine."

I looked at our hands. His were the large, strong ones of a man who wrapped his palm and fingers around a pigskin football and spiraled it in front of millions every Sunday during the season. I took his hand and turned it around. His knuckles were crisscrossed with the scars of endless tackles against hard turf and frozen fields, little white scars I wanted to memorize. I kissed his hand, holding it up against my cheek.

"I wish it was just us again out under the desert sky," he said, pulling me to him.

"Me, too," I said softly, loving how I fit against him.

"Remember how I said I wondered if life made any sense?"

"Yeah."

"I know this sounds stupid, but it feels like fate that I ran into you in that diner," he said.

"It doesn't sound stupid."

"All I wanted was to figure out what was wrong with me. To make sure I wasn't paranoid. That what I thought was happening to me physically was real. I didn't want to drag you into this. And I sure as hell didn't want to drag T.D. into it. Or, for that matter, your ex-husband."

"Jimmy's not so bad. He's just hurt right now."

"You guys have a long history."

I nodded. "Long and colorful."

"Are you sure things are okay between you and him? Is it really over?"

"I'm sure."

"Are you sorry you ever met me?"

"How can you say that?"

"Well, you've been dragged through the mud. And I still need Rialto to do some digging before I can discover the truth—the real truth."

"My father didn't raise me to back down from anything."

"So, are you ready for this circus?"

"No." I gave him a tiny smile. "Then again, are you ready to face all the dirt they'll dredge up about my father and me?"

"Sure."

He kissed me, and I felt my insides swoop down like the big initial plunge on the roller coaster out on Coney Island, the Cyclone. Mark pulled away, and together we went downstairs. He and Leon, as well as four body-guards, who'd apparently arrived in a dark Hummer with tinted windows, then went downstairs to T.D.'s garage and climbed into the Hummer. When they drove off, the paparazzi swarmed around them like a hive full of bees around a flower. I was surprised they didn't run anyone over.

I watched Mark and his entourage drive away, feeling ever more certain that where Mark Shannon was concerned nothing was going to be easy. T.D. and Jimmy and I were left in the house. Jimmy was in full hangover mode, five o'clock shadow covering his chin, hair a mess. T.D. didn't look so great, either.

"Look, you two," I snapped. "We're all going to get cleaned up and get out of here. I'm tired of feeling like a monkey in the zoo."

We each cleaned up, trying to wash away the insanity of the last couple of days. Jimmy had arrived without so much as a toothbrush, never mind a change of clothes. Classic Jimmy. A hundred pounds lighter than T.D., Jimmy was unlikely to be able to borrow something. So he wore one of T.D.'s robes while I washed his clothes. At 5:00 p.m., I got a call from Leon, who was in a limo on his way to training camp. Mark, he said, was in a separate car with his coach on his way to the press conference.

"I thought you said you told me everything."

"I did."

"Turn on your television."

"What channel?"

"God, you're a headache. Take your fucking pick."

I covered the phone and yelled to T.D. to turn on his plasma TV.

"Oh, shit!" I felt my body go numb as I fumbled to reach the couch and sit down, not trusting my knees.

There, in living color, was my mug shot.

TWENTY-F♥UR

"You still there?" Leon asked me.

"Uh-huh," I whispered, my voice hoarse.

Jimmy materialized with a big glass of bourbon, still wearing T.D.'s robe as we waited for his clothes to dry. He looked at the television and dropped the bourbon on the floor.

"You want to tell me about this?" Leon shouted through the phone. "The Smoking Gun Web site found it. They find all the dirt."

I looked up at Jimmy and then over at T.D. and shook my head. The words of the first step of Gamblers Anonymous again rang in my ears. *We admitted we were powerless over gambling—that our lives had become unmanageable.*

My life was officially unmanageable. I hadn't ever gotten to Step Two, and I wasn't sure they had a step for how insane this was all getting. "My father was in prison—" I spoke softly into the phone "—and I was running his bookmaking operations. We had scheduled an illegal casino night, and we were raided. I got busted for dealing blackjack. Eventually, I pleaded guilty to a misdemeanor."

"Not a great picture of you," Leon said.

"I suppose it isn't." I looked at my mug shot on the TV, I was wild-haired and angry, my eyes glaring. I had all my earrings in—there must have been four or five in each ear—and I looked like a punk. Or a streetwalker.

"You know, I'm a sucker for a love story, but this may possibly be beyond even my help," Leon said. "You may want to consider distancing yourself from Mark. Permanently."

"What?"

"If you care about him, you will. You think the NFL is going to let its star quarterback get involved with someone with ties to organized crime?"

"Organized crime?"

"Your father and Jimmy and, yes you, are all criminals—"

"Hey—"

"Skye, it ain't gonna help the current situation to tap-dance around the obvious. You've all committed crimes. And the crimes were organized."

"As opposed to disorganized?"

"It's obvious you've got ties to the mob. All bookmaking is connected in one way or another. If you care about Mark Shannon, and his career, I'll advise you to tell him you went back to your husband."

"Ex-husband."

"Same difference. Not too many ex-husbands come flying out to Vegas just because their ex-wife has a boyfriend."

"Have you spoken to Mark?"

"No. But his press conference comes on in thirty minutes. In the meantime, your meeting with Walter Hammond is scheduled for tomorrow at four o'clock in his offices. A private jet will be waiting at the airport to fly you to New York. Try to avoid being arrested between now and then."

"That may be difficult," I said sarcastically.

I hung up the phone on Leon. T.D. didn't say a word. Neither did Jimmy.

Later, we all stared at the television screen as Mark Shannon sat down in front of an army of reporters and started fielding questions, sixteen or so microphones near his face. He handled the reporters gracefully, blaming his disappearance on personal problems. When pressed, he said those problems did not involve me or gambling. Then one of the reporters asked him about my arrest record.

"I didn't know about that at the time I got involved with Ms. McNally."

Ms. McNally? He sounded like Bill Clinton denying "relations" with Monica Lewinsky.

"And does that arrest record change your plans?"

He froze for a moment, then his brow furrowed. "I— I don't know. That's all the questions for right now. Thank you."

Then he stood as a cacophony of voices screamed out, "Mark! Mark! Just one more question."

I looked over at Jimmy. He put a hand on my shoulder. "If he has to think about anything, Skye, fuck him. You deserve better. I accept you for who you are."

"Of course you do." I felt small and ashamed. What had seemed like hope and renewal yesterday, now felt like cold, hard denial. "Because what you are, I am. What I am, you are."

Jimmy knelt down in front of me. "What is going on with you, Skye? The girl I knew would spit nails over this. Fuck them all. That's what my girl would say. Fuck them all."

"I'm ashamed, Jimmy. It's a part of my life that has

been out of control, and I don't want to be out of control anymore. I want my life to make sense. I want it to be simple…."

He stood and flopped into T.D.'s leather recliner. "What do you think, T.D.?"

"I think she won't know anything until she meets with Walter Hammond, and until she talks with Mark Shannon again, away from the glare of flashing bulbs. And I think that Little Girl here is finally getting it. That we're powerless and it's our Higher Power who can help us. The home group may have to throw a party."

"My name is Skye, and I'm a compulsive gambler."

"Hi, Skye," the home group members sang out in a chorus. I sat next to T.D., my nerves wrecked.

"Um…I think I finally get Step One."

Spontaneous applause broke out.

"All right, all right," I snapped, then I took a deep breath. "Look, I have gambled my whole life, and I assumed my habit was something I could simply put aside, tuck away in a box. I could stick the box on the top shelf of my closet, and take it out when *I* wanted to play with it. When *I* wanted to gamble, I could *decide* to gamble, and when I didn't, all by myself I could decide not to. But it didn't work that way. Not by a long shot."

Cowboy Hal looked at me sympathetically. He held the gavel tonight. He was running things. He put it down and cupped his chin in his hands and listened.

"Gambling," I said, my voice quavering a little, "took on a life of its own. It became bigger than the box. It *ate* the box. It was this monster that needed to be fed nearly every day or it would make me restless and anxious, lonely and depressed. But I kept thinking I had the power. I kept thinking my life was manageable."

T.D. patted my leg. I looked over at him and sighed. "I guess some of you have seen my face on the news. So much for any anonymity. But I've learned something from that, too. Before…anonymity meant I could sneak off to the casinos and no one would have to know. It was a cloak for my lying. It was a way to hide my shame. Now I realize in this basement hall, anonymity made it a safe place. Safe enough that I should have taken my box off the closet shelf and brought it here, and opened it so I could see the monster—my gambling habit—wasn't all that powerful after all…as long as I talked about it. As long as I brought it out into the light."

Cowboy Hal dabbed at his eyes. "Skye, I want to thank you for sharing. That was really beautiful. I think you've actually gotten Step Two: *Came to believe that a Power greater than ourselves could restore us to a normal way of thinking and living.* I've seen you in this room for a long time, girl, and I'm proud of you."

"Thanks, Cowboy Hal. I'm not sure that I would ever use the word *normal* when referring to myself, but… thanks."

He nodded at me and winked. "And now, I would like us all to observe a moment of silence for Annie. For those of you who come to this meeting regularly, Annie was in and out of here, struggling in her battle with addiction. She was a beautiful girl, the type who always had a kind word for everyone. She was murdered. The police haven't caught her physical murderer yet, but they will.

"But I think we all know that it was gambling that did her in. It appears she had huge gambling debts she could not pay. She serves as a reminder that this addiction, this disease, doesn't know when to stop. It can bring you to your knees the first time you lose the money in your savings account, or the first time you run your credit limit up to the max. That's called a high bottom gambler. Some, like Annie, like me, like Fish-eye over there, they're low bottoms. That means we had to sink real low before we admitted we were powerless. We'll lose our house, our car, our families, our jobs, our self-respect, even our freedom—we end up in jail—before we finally accept. So…for Annie and all others like her, let's have a moment of silence."

We all bowed our heads. I talked to Annie in my head: *You're finally in a better place where you don't have to worry about gambling. You're free of it, once and for all.*

After we shared our moment of silence, we had our coffee—still the worst coffee in Vegas. T.D., Cowboy Hal, Louie Fish-eye, a guy who sometimes came to our home group when he worked late and couldn't get to his regular meeting, another guy named Deacon Jack, our treasurer, Bill, who worked at a church and sometimes tried to talk some "Higher Power" into me, they all clustered around me, patting my back, telling me to stick with it, that I was finally getting it. For the first time in a long time, something had pushed aside the shame and was making room in my heart. Something that felt like serenity. Even though my world was coming apart, inside I was okay, for now. And that was a very good feeling. And I had a hunch it was going to come in handy over the next couple of weeks.

"Drink?"

This morning I had flown in a private jet, on which a flight attendant had offered me caviar and chilled vodka, to New York. I had been hustled into a waiting limousine, and then driven to Walter Hammond II's luxurious office in New York City's Trump Towers. I now sat across from Walter Hammond as he waved a hand toward the well-stocked bar in his office.

"Bourbon, please."

"A woman after my own heart." He stood and mixed my drink, made himself a Scotch, and then sat down opposite me again, the two of us facing off across a desk polished to a sheen. The entire office was set up to convey power. The space was cavernous, the furniture stately. An unsmoked cigar sat in a Waterford crystal ashtray. Walter Hammond was bald, with a port-wine stain on his scalp that sort of looked like the state of Florida. He had a wide girth, and at least two chins protruded over the top of his crisp white shirt collar. The window behind him offered a view of dusk setting on Manhattan.

"Well, now," he drawled, "we seem to have an itty-bitty problem."

"Which is?" I asked, trying to avoid navigating the map of Florida on his head.

"Sunday is the play-offs, and I need to decide whether to allow your lover to play." He pronounced *lover* like *lovaaaah*.

"That's your choice."

"Now, Mark, he told me he's not givin' you up."

"He did?" My heartbeat quickened.

"Why, yes, he did. So now, I have to decide whether that boy's involvement with y'all has anything to do with gamblin', 'cause if it does, that's it for him." His Texas accent annoyed me.

"It doesn't," I stated. "Gambling is my own problem. He didn't even know about it when we met."

"Yes, but then y'all made the unfortunate decision to

camp out in Mr. George Russell's home—and that boy surely did have a gamblin' problem."

"He's not a *boy,*" I said, the racist connotations clearly escaping Walt Squared. Or maybe not.

"I don't like your tone, young lady. Fine...*man.*"

"And T.D. had even less to do with all this."

"So you say. Now I'm going to need something from you. I'm going to need you to swear, in an affidavit, that your relationship with Mark had nothin' to do with gamblin'."

"And then what?"

"Then I let your boyfriend play in the Super Bowl—if the Mustangs make it there—which I expect they will. The last thing I want is the league's number-one quarterback not playin'. You know why? 'Cause then if the other team wins, all we'll hear is that it's because Shannon didn't play. Makes it all ugly." He pretended to cringe. "Makes the win less glorious, less powerful. It *undermines* the league."

"And that's it? That's all you need?"

"One more thing. You keep away from Mark till season's over."

"So I become enemy number one and am hounded by the media, and I have to stay away from Mark...while you get to play your precious game."

He grinned as if he'd just won the lottery (though Walt Squared was so wealthy even that probably wouldn't have mattered). "That's about right. You may not understand this, but I can *crush* you. And your father. I got friends in all sorts of places. And you are a whole lot of trouble. A lot more trouble than I expect a piece of ass is worth."

At the mention of my father, my insides fell to the floor. Sean McNally wasn't about to win any awards for Father of the Year, but I didn't want to see him sent off to prison again.

"And then there's that ex-husband of yours. I see by his record he's done six months' time. He could do a lot longer if I bring him down."

I looked Walt Squared in the eye. We were playing a game of chicken, and so far, I was losing. Then the brakes slammed in my head. I may have sworn off gambling, but I wasn't stupid. For the first time, the odds didn't matter.

I wanted to take control.

"No. I won't sign your little affidavit. I won't swear on some stack of holy Bibles this isn't about gambling." I said it calmly and firmly, and watched all the color drain from Walt's face, the map of Florida now redder than ever.

"What do you mean, 'no'? I thought you said your relationship with Mark Shannon had nothing to do with gambling?"

"I did. But I won't sign whatever it is you want me to."

"Why not?" I watched his eyes, formerly jovial and sparkling, turn icy.

"If I don't sign it, I shut down the league. I shout from the rooftops that Mark Shannon was in bed with the mob, literally and figuratively. And I don't have to stay away from Mark. So you can fuck yourself, Mr. Hammond. You can fuck yourself. I'm not some naive young girl who doesn't know what's at stake." I stood to leave.

"Now, hold on. What the hell is it you're up to? You're willing to watch your father maybe go to prison, for what? What is this? Some weekend fling of yours?"

"No. I want something in return."

"I might have guessed a little NFL slut would want something. What is it?"

I held on to my integrity and ignored the "slut" comment. "I want you to lift the ban on George Russell getting into the Hall of Fame. I realize you can't do it while all of this is going on. But you can do it a year from now. In writing. In a contract we both sign. If you don't reinstate him, I go to the media with that contract, with your signature on the paper, and your stay as the commissioner of the NFL is finished."

Walter Hammond II had a vein near Orlando on the state of Florida on his head, and it began to pulse. He stood up and put both hands on his desk. "I will not be blackmailed by some whore who's fuckin' a quarterback."

"Suit yourself."

"Son of a bitch!" Walt Squared picked up his glass of bourbon and hurled it across the room at the wall. The crash was loud, and I wondered what the secretary outside his door was thinking.

"I'll just blab to *Dateline* that the NFL is rife with gambling," I said as I walked toward the door. Considering Mark thought the team doctor was in deep with the mob, I wasn't far off. In the end, when the season was over, Walt Squared wouldn't know what hit him—not when Mark finally came forward.

"No you won't," he replied. "You're in love with Mark Shannon. That's the word I've got. And you won't tear him down. Not for this."

I stared at Walter Hammond. "Yes, I will. Don't tempt me. I've been staring down worse men than you my whole life." My voice was firm.

"You strike a nasty little bargain."

"So do you."

In the end, he shook on it. And in the space of twenty minutes, I was for the first time eternally grateful that I had spent a lifetime staring down tough old men with their gambling debts. Because I had faced down Walter Hammond II, and one year from today, T.D. would be eligible for the Hall of Fame.

TWENTY-FIVE

Walter Hammond II's secretary drew up papers, which I signed. I took my copy, and Walt Squared, practically spitting nails—forget nails, spitting *spikes*—took his copy.

Afterward, I took a cab to my father's house on Long Island, where TV trucks lined the street. I raced, bulbs flashing, to the front door and Dad let me in. I hugged him.

"I'm so sorry, Dad."

He led me into the den. "No…I guess I'm sorry. Kid, you haven't had a chance."

"What do you mean?" I sat down on the couch.

He sank heavily into his leather recliner. "I mean, all this time, all these years…I told myself that what I did for a living didn't matter as long as I raised you to be, I don't know, a strong person. A person who did right by people. I told myself—" his voice caught "—I told myself that the Wentworths couldn't have done better."

"And they couldn't have."

He shook his head. "If the Wentworths had raised you, you wouldn't be in this mess. You'd be a woman with a fancy education, a fancy job and a fancy husband. Hell, you could have had Mark Shannon and been one of those NFL trophy wives."

"Dad…" I sat down opposite him. "I have resented my upbringing as long as I can remember. But in actuality, the world of the Wentworths is a world where loyalty is in short supply. It's a world inhabited by people like Walter Hammond II, who make slimy back-door deals and yet appear, to all the world, like they are gentility. It's like the men of Enron, and the white-collar criminals. They hide behind the trappings of legitimacy. I may not want to be a gambler anymore, but I'm not ashamed of who you are.

"The NFL makes their money on the backs of young men who are swayed by fortunes and a love of the game, and don't know right from wrong because they've been led through a system. Passing grades in high school, scholarships to college. Hookers. Bribes. Cars. They're given it all. It's rife with sexual assault, drugs, bullshit. The NFL. It's a system, Dad. And now the system is trying to pretend that gambling isn't a part of it. It's hypocrisy, Dad. They act like the legal bookmaking in Vegas isn't corruptible, when you and I both know it is. I've known it since my first bet on a game, Dad."

My father looked at me. "You're not angry with me, then?"

"No."

"What about Mark Shannon? How does he feel about all this?"

"I don't know. We haven't spoken. He was sucked into the whirlpool. I need to talk to him."

"Skye?"

"Hmm?"

"Jimmy got back around two o'clock this afternoon looking like he'd been on a bender."

"I know. I'm sorry about that, too."

"But you love this Shannon guy?"

"I don't know. It was like we had this one perfect night out in the desert. We talked about everything and nothing. We talked about things that didn't matter—aimless conversation…and yet it was all very real. We connected. We didn't talk about football or gambling, but about ourselves as people having nothing to do with any of that. And for that one night, everything was right with my world, Dad. But I don't know if back here, back in real life, if we can ever have that again."

My father stood up and walked over to a bookshelf that was lined with photo albums. He plucked one from the shelf and came and sat down next to me. He opened up the album, and there on the front page was a picture of my mother on the day they met at the Kentucky Derby.

"She sure was beautiful," I whispered. My mother had an elegance I don't possess. She was the perfect blonde in a Grace Kelly kind of way. Even when I'm dressed up, there's always something askew about me—whether it's my curls sort of wild around my face, or my freckles that seem less than classic, or the simple fact that I have lipstick on my teeth. I'm never the whole package. Not the way my mother was.

"We fell in love at first sight," my dad recalled. "I saw her and that was it. I'd never once thought about marriage before her. Not once. But the minute I laid eyes on your mother, that was it. We had a perfect day at the Derby together, and then I asked her to dinner, and we had a perfect meal. I can't tell you what we ate, or where we ate. But it was perfect."

"And then you eloped."

"Right. And suddenly we had to deal with reality. We had to figure out how to make the magic we had at the Derby translate to real life."

"But you did it."

He looked at me. "It wasn't easy. First of all, your mother didn't know how to cook, clean or even do laundry. The Wentworths had servants for all of that. I was doing all right with my business, but I couldn't afford that kind of lifestyle."

"Come to think of it, I don't really remember her ever cooking."

"We lived on takeout. She eventually figured out how to make a burnt roast. Always burnt." He smiled and laughed to himself a little. "And I had shirts with iron marks. And she shrunk my favorite golf shirt, among other things. Turned another one pink by washing it in hot water with bleach and one of your baby blankets."

"What did she think of your chosen profession?"

"She said she married the man, not the job. She hated the late nights. She hated that she couldn't tell anyone what I really did for a living. She hated my poker games and the guys hanging around. I didn't understand why she liked shopping so much, or why she was homesick for the South. She liked to go to bed by eleven o'clock and get up early, and I liked to stay up till all hours and sleep in."

"Were you happy together?"

"Over the moon, Skye. Over the moon. Because when we were alone, or we were with you, and it was just us in this house, there were no two people more connected."

He wiped at his eyes and then shut the photo album. "You and Mark just need to figure out how to be together away from all the craziness."

★ ★ ★

Mark sat in a leather armchair, in a denlike setting artfully arranged with football trophies. Katie Couric had been nixed in favor of a guy with NFL hosting duties. It was time for Mark to bare his soul on national television. My father and I sat together and watched. I was a nervous wreck—for Mark.

"Was that fair?" the interviewer asked him. "You're on a team—you play as a team. Was it fair to abandon them? What does that show about your ability to lead your team if you bail on them like that?"

"Well, Bob, no, it's not fair. But I had a private meeting with the team, and I explained what happened, and the guys have been very supportive."

"What did you say at that meeting?"

Mark shrugged. "I'd rather keep it between me and the team."

"And this all had to do with what? Pressure? Media scrutiny?"

"I hadn't been feeling well. The doctors thought it was stress-related. I had discussed with my coach taking a couple of days to see my own private doctor. This is the playoff season…we didn't want word getting out that I was hurt. So I backed off from the team, the media, and it just sort of got out of hand."

"And is this physical problem better?"

Mark nodded. He kept clenching his jaw, and through the television screen, I had this urge to race down to the studio where it was being filmed and go and touch his cheek, tell him to relax, offer comfort.

"And what about your connection to this Skye McNally, a woman who has an arrest record for gambling and a father who's a convicted bookie, and how all this is timed with your disappearance? You realize how this looks, don't you?"

"Look, when I meet someone, I don't ask for her résumé. I don't ask if the person has a record. Perhaps it shows some poor judgment on my part, but that's all it was. Poor judgment."

I looked at my father, then took the remote control and switched the television off. *Poor judgment. Was that all I was?*

TWENTY-SIX

The sportscasters and talking heads were brutal. True to his word, after Mark bared his soul on television, and after the team issued a press release and had another press conference, and after I issued a denial, Walt Squared let Mark Shannon play in the play-off game on Sunday, the game that would clinch a Super Bowl berth for the Mustangs if they won.

Mark played terribly. And the media was merciless.

My father, Jimmy and I watched the game, along with my father's runners and the usual punks that surrounded him. True to my oath, I had no bets riding on the game—didn't even feel the itch. I watched just to see him play. Each time they showed a close-up of his face, I ached.

"Jack," the sportscaster in the booth said to his co-anchor, "I'd say Mark Shannon has a lot on his mind."

"You said it, Bill. I'd say the events of the last ten days, among the strangest in the annals of football history, have taken a toll on Shannon. His head does not seem to be in the game."

And there was my mug shot again. "This woman is at

the center of the swirling controversy. Was Mark Shannon involved with bookmaking operations? The office of the commissioner has officially cleared him, but the controversy has yet to fully subside…and this with the Super Bowl right around the corner."

The score was twelve to seven, and the Mustangs were losing with two minutes to go and possession of the ball.

"I think I'm gonna be sick," Jimmy said.

"Why?"

"'Cause if he blows this, I'll remember it was my ex-wife who single-handedly caused the self-destruction of the Mustangs."

"I had help."

"Nonetheless, you will go down in history as the one who destroyed the hometown team."

The Mustangs' head coach called a time-out.

"Bill," the announcer said, "the Mustangs are in a do-or-die situation here. And Coach McBride is in a bind. The Mustangs' second-string quarterback has a rotator-cuff injury. And their third-string, Kyle Beckwith, was arrested a month ago for rape, and they have him benched pending trial. Could it be the Mustangs are the new bad boys of the NFL? Their tight end, Ricky Jervis, was busted for cocaine possession. I mean, what is going on here? Prior to this scandal, Shannon was considered the all-American dream."

"If McBride had another option, I am quite certain he would be pulling Shannon. The guy's head is just in the clouds."

"All right, their time-out is over. It's now up to Shannon."

I stared at the television screen and willed Mark to throw a winning pass—or at least make first down. "You realize, Jimmy, if they lose, I won't be able to visit New York ever again. I will be the most hated woman in New York history."

"Yes."

"You don't have to agree with me."

"I know. But you will be."

I covered my eyes. "I can't watch."

But I could still hear the announcer. "Bad snap, Jack. Bad pass, but my God, there's Vinnie Tate heading toward the end zone…and…and he catches it! Un-be-lieve-a-ble! Mark Shannon throws a lousy pass, and Tate saves the game! The Mustangs are going to the Super Bowl!"

"Well, Bill, let's hope before they get there that Mark Shannon gets his personal life and his love life together."

"I'm sure all of New York wishes that, Jack."

I uncovered my eyes. Mark was going to the Super Bowl. I was happy for him, but it just meant more public dissection. I felt like a frog in a high school biology lab. I was cut right down the middle with little needles stuck in me.

"Skye!" my father called out to me from behind the bar in our basement. I walked over to him.

"Hmm?"

"Lefty left a message on my cell. His wife won't let him go to the Bowl, and so he's staying home, the pussy. So how about you, me, Jimmy and your friend T.D. go?"

"I don't know, Dad."

"Remember, Skye, it's not about what's happening when the world is watching. It's about what happens when the two of you are alone."

"I'll think about it."

"Don't think. Thinking gets people in trouble. Just go for it, Skye."

TWENTY-SEVEN

"The Super Bowl, huh?" T.D.'s voice intoned over the telephone at eleven o'clock that night.

"Skybox in which to watch your favorite sport. Limo to the stadium. Suites in the Four Seasons down on South Beach. Women in thongs. Women in thongs in-line skating on the sidewalks."

"Skye..."

"You think I'm kidding? I have one word for you: *supermodels,* T.D. *Supermodels.*"

"I'll think about it. When you coming home?"

"Tomorrow. I have to find a baseball hat and dark glasses to travel."

"Heard from Mark?"

"No."

"You upset?"

"Yes."

Exasperated, I hung up the phone, plunged under the covers in my bed and fell asleep.

★ ★ ★

At twelve-thirty in the morning, my cell phone rang, the melodic tones of "Für Elise" by Beethoven ringing out from my jeans where I had crumpled them in a heap on the floor. I never could figure out how to change the bell tones.

Feeling around on the floor with my hand, I found my jeans and the pocket in them, and answered in a middle-of-the-night rasp. "Hello?"

"Skye?"

"Mark…" I felt a release of all the tension in my body in one breath.

"God, it's good to hear your voice. Where are you?"

"My father's house. Where are you?"

"In a hotel near the stadium. Listen, are you all right?"

"I'd be a whole lot better if the networks weren't broadcasting my mug shot every half hour."

"Why didn't you tell me, Skye?'

"Tell you what?"

"That you had a record."

"It slipped my mind."

"Come on, slipped your mind?"

"It did. Mark, it happened a long time ago. My father has a record, too. So does Jimmy. At the time I met you, it wasn't like I was thinking I had better fess up to everything I've ever done wrong in my life so that there would be nothing left for the tabloids to find."

He was silent.

"No, wait…you know, once when I was in ninth grade, I cheated on a chemistry test. And then there was the time when I was sixteen when the cops brought me home in a cruiser for underage drinking. Come off it, Mark, when the lawyers were through, it was a misdemeanor."

"But you were running your father's business."

"Yes, I was. All I can say is that was then and this is now. I don't gamble anymore."

"For what, two weeks now?"

"Forget it, Mark. I didn't ask for all this. *You* were the one who disappeared. I realize you had good reason to, but you're carrying around a mighty big secret, too. I'm not going to vilify my father. I've done that for long enough."

"What do you mean?"

"I've spent a lifetime blaming him for my addiction, Mark. My disease. I'm a compulsive gambler. And yes, he's a bookie, but God…there's another whole side of this I'm only beginning to see. He's a guy who was raised a certain way, in the world of tough guys and ex-cons. He's from the streets, Mark. And when my mother died, he didn't know the first thing about raising a daughter alone. He didn't hire a nanny or a housekeeper. He did it all himself, trying to make sure I felt secure. So yeah, he screwed up some. Most little girls don't spend their time playing Texas Hold 'em with two ex-cons and an enforcer. But they treated me like a princess in the best way they knew how."

"But that's a crazy life, Skye."

"True, but it's taken me twenty years to realize it's *my* life. I can't fault him for doing his best. He loved me, Mark. Thankfully, I didn't end up like my friend Annie. She turned tricks because her old man used to abuse her, Mark. She didn't know what love was. Our Higher Power…we just have to trust Him. Jesus Christ, I'm getting religion."

He laughed on the other end.

"Don't you trust me, Mark?"

"I do. This has just been grueling. Especially when I'm in the locker room with the doc. I want to kill him with my bare hands. I won't drink from any cup that's been touched by anyone else. All of a sudden the team's looking at me like I've got obsessive-compulsive disorder. Hey, can I meet you somewhere?"

"Why?"

"Please, Skye."

We agreed to meet at an exit on the Palisades Parkway. I left my father a note on the kitchen table and borrowed his Cadillac. Outside our house, the frenzy had died down. I drove onto the dark, empty streets of our town and headed through New York and across the George Washington Bridge to the Palisades expressway, which snakes its way through northern New Jersey and then New York and all the way up to West Point and Bear Mountain.

I pulled into the overlook point we chose and turned off my headlights. Fifteen minutes later, Mark pulled in. He was driving a Porsche. I unlocked my door, and he climbed out of his car and into mine.

There, in the front seat, he kissed me furiously, holding my face in both his hands. Then he moved his hands down to my breasts, then enveloped me in a passionate hug.

I shuddered.

"Hey," he whispered. "We're okay. I wanted to make sure you were real. You are a sight for sore eyes." Looking at him up close, I could see he was pale and had dark circles underneath his eyes.

"How did things get so out of control?" I whispered.

"It's all bullshit. I told my coach I wouldn't see you until after the Super Bowl…. It's not fair to the team to put them all through this, but I can't wait until then, Skye. I can't."

"Neither can I." I kissed him, and then leaned back against my car door and let him rest his head against my breasts. I wanted to make love with him. I thought back to high school, to all my years of gambling. I would feel sick if I didn't gamble, sick needing the rush of winning—needing something to feel my heart pounding as whatever team I bet on covered their spread. But I had never felt this kind of connection with someone. Not like this.

"I'm so sorry. I'm an addict, Mark. I've been betting for as long as I can remember, and only meeting you has opened me up to the idea that maybe I can live without gambling. But if I had known someone I cared about would get hurt, that my world would be so destructive to anyone besides me, I wouldn't have…"

He leaned up close to my ear, his breath hot on my neck, giving me goose bumps. "Let's go back to the desert. Let's just get away from here."

"I wish we could."

"In the desert that night, feeling the wind from the convertible rush around us, laughing, playing stupid Twenty Questions…everything else went away."

"And now I feel like everything is pressing in on us."

"Baby, Rialto thinks Hammond may be in bed with Big Easy, too. He and the evil doctor are very tight with each other. He followed the doctor to a lunch meeting the two of them had—but what was unusual was that Hammond drove himself."

"So?"

"You met the fat bastard. He never does anything himself. In my bones, I feel this thing is bigger than just the doctor. And meanwhile, I just want to tell the truth. Rialto is going to make contact with the FBI—he's a former agent, retired now. He'll make sure the Super Bowl is played, then they can raid the doc, Hammond, whoever. I've waited to play the Super Bowl my whole damn life, since I was old enough to dream of a world beyond the smog of my hometown. And I'm not going to play in a tainted Bowl game. I want to play for real. When I hold that trophy, I'll have won it fair and square."

He slid his hand up my shirt, caressing one of my breasts. "I want to put my head here and just get lost in you."

He unbuttoned my shirt and kissed his way down my belly. And then, out of nowhere, it seemed, someone rapped loudly on the driver's-side window, scaring the hell out of me. I screamed, and Mark shot upright in the seat.

"What the fuck!" Mark snapped. "Christ…it's Leon."

I rolled down the window, which was rather steamed up.

"What the hell do you want, Leon?" I asked.

"I was assigned to make sure he doesn't go AWOL again. You've had your little reunion, Shannon. Back to the hotel."

"Fuck, Leon, that's bullshit. I don't need a baby-sitter."

"I beg to differ, since you're here with Public Enemy Number One. Let's go." Leon wore an orange terry-cloth tracksuit that made him look like a short, furry tangerine, and he was stomping his feet to keep warm. His cigar was clenched between his teeth.

"Give me a minute, Leon," Mark said.

"Fine. You've got five."

I rolled up the window again.

"Mark?"

"Yeah, Skye?" He had slid his right hand in the waistband of my jeans.

"When we're alone, like this…does it work for you?"

He took his hand from my waistband, grabbed my hand and moved it to the zipper of his pants, where he was rock hard. "Does it feel like it works to you?"

"Men! I don't mean that! I mean away from all the Super Bowl hype, all of the craziness, away from the media storm, does this—me and you—work?"

"Skye, the last two weeks have been the most difficult of my life, but the one thing I know is that this works."

He leaned up to kiss me, not hungrily this time, but softly. Sweetly. Then he sat up, smiled and slid out of the car. He climbed into his Porsche and drove away with a wave, taking a piece of me with him. I felt like crying, but the fuzzy tangerine apparently wanted to talk to me. Leon had crystallized where Mark had sat seconds before.

"You love him?" Leon asked.

"I think so. But I have to tell you, Leon, I know next to nothing about love."

"If you even think you love him, you won't see him again."

"Leon, that's crazy. This isn't Romeo and Juliet. We're just two ordinary people."

"There's nothing ordinary about either of you. Did you see how he played today?"

"Leon, the media's hounding him. How could he concentrate?"

"Look, toots, you know what you are? You're poison to that kid."

"He's not a kid."

"Yeah, he is. First off, he's a couple of years younger than you. I pulled up your police record. I also noted you don't have a driver's license, and yet you are behind the wheel of this car. You're a real rule-buster. And you are poison, because he thinks you two could work."

"We can."

"I hear you had a meeting with Walt Squared."

"It went well."

"In your opinion."

"Yes." I was thinking of the contract I had—the secret one—allowing T.D. to be nominated into the Hall of Fame.

"You're not a naive girl. You know the score. Let me ask you again. Do you honestly think the NFL—his coach, the Mustangs' owners, Walt Squared—would allow him to get serious with a woman whose father is one of the biggest bookies in New York? Who has ties to organized crime? The NFL is an industry. It's an institution. There are millions and millions of people who live their lives around TV sets each Sunday. Who buy shirts with their favorite players' numbers on them. Who spend a lot of *money*. Skye, they can't let you two go on. Why pretend? It'll only torture him."

"They allow players who have beaten their wives, players who are drug addicts. They get them all the help they need. Christ, Dave Henderson has been to rehab five times. He's crashed his vehicles too many times to count, and he has three DUIs."

"But this is gambling. It's the ultimate sin to the NFL."

"I know. Have a gang bang and that's okay. Fuck the baby-sitter, and that's okay. This is hypocritical bullshit. Do you know how much *legitimate* sports book is taken on the Super Bowl in Vegas?"

Leon shrugged. "I suppose, as a resident bookmaking expert, you're going to tell me."

"Seventy million dollars. On one game. One day. Super Bowl Sunday. Worshipping at the altar of the end zone.

And that's legit book. Seventy million. So if you're going to spin some fairy tale that the NFL is beyond influence—even by legitimate sports book—you can go peddle that bullshit to someone else, Leon. 'Cause I ain't buying. My father may be a rich bookie, but he is not the biggest by a long shot. So-called legitimate book has it over him by hundreds of millions of dollars."

Leon wrinkled his face up.

"What?" I snapped.

"Look, kiddo, *maybe*—I only toss out a very small *maybe* here—you have something. But even so…the name of the game is image, not truth. You know that. You live in fucking Vegas, for God's sake. That city is built on image and neon. And silicone implants. It's not real."

"So?"

"So look at the Dallas Cowboys. They billed them as America's team and got pretty girls in tight red-white-and-blue outfits to rah-rah for the boys. Even you and I know that the Cowboys aren't all-American. Open the locker room door and you got bad boys same as every other team."

"And your point, Leon?"

"My point is that boy you love wants to play football. It's the only game he's ever loved, and that love predates you by a good twenty years or more. And if you insist on going forward with this relationship, you will ruin him."

"I won't."

"Sweetie pie, look, I got nothing against you, but you see your friend George Russell?"

"What about him?"

"You think it bothers him he can't be in the Hall of Fame?"

I blinked slowly.

"Come on, honey, just answer the question."

I sighed. "Yeah, it bothers him."

"You been around the track a time or two. Your dad's done time. Your mother died in a plane crash. You've been to the school of hard knocks. Your friggin' bookie's name is Heavy Harry."

"And, Leon? This lecture's getting long-winded."

"So come on, sister. You know that, yeah, you two may have something here, but you also know he'd get over it if you two didn't stay together. It's early in the relation-ship. Come on, you just met, for Christ's sake. Mark would get over it, and so would you. There's no such thing as a soul mate. Sure, maybe you fall in love, but there isn't any *one* love."

"My father's one love was my mother."

"And look how that turned out."

"Fuck you, Leon. That's cold."

"All I'm saying is that, if you really love this guy, you just back off. For him."

"Leon, get out of my car."

He held up his hands. "I'll leave, but you know I'm right."

Leon opened the car door, and the dome light went on. He turned around to face me once more before climbing out. "For the record, kid, I was rooting for you. But I've looked at this from every angle, and there ain't no way the NFL will leave you in peace. You mark my words, if you don't leave peacefully, do you know what Walt Squared will do?"

I thought of my agreement. "What?"

"He will crush your father like a bug under his shoe. That ex-husband of yours...he'll do time. Walt Squared will have assets seized. He will make sure your life is a living hell. You'll wish you'd never met Mark Shannon. Hammond—aka the Big Ham—will destroy you."

"Is that a warning, Leon?"

"Nope," he said as he stood. "Like I said, I was rooting for you two crazy kids. But I like you enough to tell you that, Skye, there's no way to survive this."

Leon shut my car door and walked away and toward a Town Car parked a few spots down. Mark and I hadn't seen him pull in. He drove away. And I was left, utterly alone, to look out on the frigid black waters of the Hudson.

CHAPTER
TWENTY-EIGHT

I was relieved to land back in Las Vegas. After the nightmare of the last week in New York, Vegas made sense, even as I drove down the Strip and surveyed the pleasure palaces and casinos. In Vegas, a giant Sphinx made sense, as did roller coasters indoors, a fake Venetian canal system, a replica of the New York skyline and a mock Eiffel Tower. This was my home.

After Leon's talk, I had become increasingly paranoid. In New York, until I left, every time the phone rang at my father's or there was a knock on the door, I thought it was the FBI. I remembered telling Jimmy that all I wanted was to not look in panic at the rearview mirror every time a cop pulled behind me. But now, that's all I did.

After he picked me up at the airport, T.D. and I discussed Leon's warning at the Big Buffet House of Hunan, which was off the beaten track enough that I didn't worry the *Enquirer* was hiding a photographer in the bushes outside. The Big Buffet pool was back down to zero after Huang's win, and so our arrival was heralded like the Second Coming.

T.D. had gone through three plates of egg rolls, shrimp toast and moo goo gai pan, in that order. Before that he'd had fried rice, shrimp and snow peas… Oh, I'd lost track.

"Mr. Touchdown, more water?" The busboy looked hopeful.

"Nah," T.D. smiled. "But I'll take another mai tai."

The busboy walked away and gave a thumbs-up to the bartender. They still bought into the notion that liquids seriously affected the outcome of T.D.'s trips to the table, but in T.D.'s case, I never saw a correlation.

Looking across the table, I asked him, "You were in the NFL. Is what Leon said true?"

He stared at me solemnly as he gnawed at barbecued spareribs—the food item from trip number four to the buffet. "Little Girl, I don't have to inform you that Leon's telling you the righteous truth. You know. Deep down. Walter Hammond II may have some people fooled with that Texas-drawl gentility thing, but inside he's a sociopath."

"Isn't that a bit extreme?"

T.D. shook his head.

"I tried to tell myself Leon was wrong."

"Skye, you and I weren't friends when I went through my unfortunate interaction with Walt Squared over my own predilection for gambling. I can tell you that never have I met a more rabid man. Like he'd been bitten by wild raccoons. Bitten by the dog in *Cujo*."

"When I met him, he wasn't rolling out the red carpet for me, but he didn't seem *that* bad."

"Little Girl, he is ruthless. When my team and I played against the Raiders, I used to stare down Tony 'the Cannibal' Vincetti—all three-hundred and twenty pounds of him, dripping blood out of his mouth because he used to chew *raw* beef before he came on the field to fucking *freak me out*. Well, Walter Hammond II was scarier."

"You're making me feel so much better."

He shrugged. "It's just the truth."

"But that's so unfair...I just want them to leave Mark and me alone."

"Now, didn't your daddy ever tell you life isn't fair?"

"No. His precise words were 'Life isn't fair, so make sure you check the odds before you make a decision.'"

"Unique way of lookin' at it."

"Exactly. And what about when Mark comes forward with the gambling thing—the doctor, the digitalis?"

"It will be a scandal the likes of which the NFL has *never* seen. There will be books about it. A movie about it. I guarantee you. But in the end, Little Girl, you'll be mixed up in it all. They'll paint the story with a wide brush."

"What do you mean?"

"As they vilify gambling and gamblers, and talk about cleaning up the NFL and all sorts of precautions and so on, you'll be seen as part of it."

"But I had nothing to do with Mark's problem."

"Of course you didn't. But since when has the public been very intelligent about figuring things like that out? The media spoon-feeds them the most juicy tidbits they can."

"So what do I do?"

"I don't know. If I always knew, I probably wouldn't have two ex-wives and be banned for life from the NFL."

"Come on—help me," I urged. "Since you stopped gambling, you...I don't know—it just seems like you have all the answers."

"If I had all the answers, I'd..." He looked down. "I wouldn't be hiding."

"Hiding? What the hell are you talking about?"

T.D. put down his sparerib. Our waitress brought over a mai tai, and he downed it like a shot. His hands were shaking. He signaled for another one.

"T.D....what's going on? What's the matter?" I felt my world spinning, and the palms of my hands grew icy.

"Little Girl," he whispered. "I don't have all the answers." He was hyperventilating, and one hand clutched his chest.

"Oh, my God, are you having a heart attack?"

He shook his head no.

"Are you gambling again?"

"No."

"What then, just tell me." I fought to keep the panic out of my voice.

"Little Girl...I got to tell you...I'm gay."

TWENTY-NINE

I leaned back in my chair. I would have laughed. Not a normal laugh, but a hyena-like nervous laugh just to hide my utter shock.

"*Gay?* How can—I mean…are you *sure?*"

"Sure as I'm sure of the color of my skin, sure as I'm sure I can't ever gamble again, sure as I'm sure that my Little Girl has fallen hard for Mark Shannon."

"That's just not possible," I whispered, leaning across the table. "I mean, T.D., you've been married—twice."

"I know that."

"And more than that…T.D., you just have no gay vibe."

"No gay vibe."

"Yeah. There isn't a gay thing about you."

He leaned his elbows on the table and started counting off on his fingers. "One, I have two Persian cats that I comb to perfection every day. Two, their names are Fred and Ginger. Three, I use Shiseido skin-care products. Four, my fondness for silk kimonos. Five, what is my favorite movie?"

"You like *South Park.*"

"I'm not talking cartoons, which I do happen to love. What is my favorite *movie?*"

"Singing in the Rain."

"Need I say more?"

I shook my head and stared at him. It was like finding out that Santa Claus was really an alcoholic who needed the money and dressed in a red suit at the mall for cold, hard cash.

"And, Little Girl?"

"Hmm?"

"When I see a movie with Richard Gere, I get all hot and bothered."

"Richard Gere? Now *that* disappoints me. I would have thought perhaps someone a little more exotic. Maybe an Andy Garcia."

T.D. shook his head. "I should have known it would be less than sixty seconds before you were mouthing off to me. But seriously, does this change anything between us?" he asked. "'Cause I feel a lot better for telling you, but if I lose you as my friend, I'll feel a whole lot worse."

"Is that what you're worried about?"

He nodded.

"T.D., nothing you say or do could change our friendship. This just means when I'm old and alone, I can't count on marrying you and having hot sex in my dotage."

He broke out in his trademark big grin and laughed that baritone laugh of his.

"T.D., how come you never told me before?"

"You're the first person I've ever told. I only started telling it to myself after my last wife left me. But once I started saying it to myself, a lot of things made sense."

"You didn't *know?* I mean, what about when you were in the locker room?"

He shrugged. "I was so closeted. I mean, I think if someone from the NFL came out, he'd be killed."

"Killed? By who?"

"Walt Squared. The team. I don't know. There was this guy—Chuck Streeter, the nose guard."

"Sure, I remember him. He retired three or four years ago."

"One time, me and Chuck, we went out for dinner. This was when we played together. And he told me. Flat-out told me he was gay. He guessed about me."

"How come he guessed, and I'm your best friend and had no idea?"

"I don't know. Maybe he got 'the vibe.'"

"Well, what happened?"

"I was having marital troubles. My wife said I was 'emotionally unavailable.' Anyway, I sympathized with him, but I told him he better get out of the NFL before someone snapped his neck on a play. I believed he was risking his life."

"He never came out, though. I don't remember reading anything about it."

"Nope. He quietly retired to the Florida Keys. My guess is he still keeps it quiet."

"So, did that make you wonder?"

"I don't know. Let me go get another plate of food."

He stood, walked to the buffet and heaped a plate full of sushi. It was piled high. Part of the house pool rules at Big Buffet is that T.D. is not allowed to know what anyone has bet—not even his favorite hostess. Not even the owner. That way, T.D. can't influence the outcome by taking smaller plates of food, or piling extra on a few plates in order to come in low. A restaurant with its own house rules on betting. Only in Vegas.

He sat back down.

"So…did Chuck talking to you make you wonder?"

He nodded. "A lot of things made me wonder. I guess deep down I already knew, but I kept along with this, 'if you walk like a duck and act like a duck, you'll be a duck' mentality. If I tried to get married, be with women, buy into the life, eventually what I felt would go away."

"Is that why you gambled?"

"Sure. That was part of it."

"So how come I've never met any of your, you know, dates?"

"'Cause I've never had one."

"What?"

"I'm a virgin, in that way."

"I don't know what's more shocking, the fact that my best friend has now told me he is gay, or that he's never made it with a man."

"I just need to keep it quiet until I figure it all out, you know. And being well known is not an advantage here."

As if to emphasize that point, two college-age guys, clearly tourists who had somehow stumbled on Big Buffet, came over to the table and asked T.D. for his autograph. He obliged; always a sweetheart to his fans. One of the guys, in a University of Wisconsin sweatshirt, looked at me.

"Are you someone famous?"

I shook my head.

"I know I know you. You're an actress, right?"

"No."

"Hmm." They both walked away, each stealing backward glances at me.

When they were out of earshot, I sat there staring at T.D., who was almost done with his sushi. Suddenly, I had a brilliant idea.

"I've got it!"

"I don't like when you have that look, Little Girl."

"My father invited us both to the Super Bowl, right?"

"Uh-huh."

"Where is the Super Bowl being held?"

"Miami."

"Precisely. You see where I'm going with this, don't you?"

"No, but that's okay, because it frightens me when I can follow your train of thought."

"Miami. Sexy Miami. Next to South Beach, which is like the gay capital of the East Coast. If we're going to find you a man, that's the city to do it in. We're going!"

"But—"

"Not a word, T.D. I know what I'm doing."

"And that, Skye, is what I'm afraid of."

"You need to have a fling of your own. You need to *celebrate* your gayness."

"I just want to keep this whole thing quiet. I'm still getting used to the idea. I don't want my sexuality being in the headlines. You've done enough headline-grabbing for the both of us."

"But, T.D., don't you deserve love? Don't we both?"

He looked at me across the table. "Yes, we do. But I'm turning this all over to my Higher Power."

"Higher Power, Schmigher Power. You leave it all to me."

"You're killing my appetite, Little Girl. Killing it."

"Just leave everything to me."

"God, I hate it when you say that."

THIRTY

That night, at T.D.'s house, I couldn't sleep. I went over my friendship with him round and round in my mind, looking for clues that he was gay, and finding very few. I suppose I was a little hurt that he'd kept this big secret from me. On the other hand, I was used to people who had secrets.

I had secrets.

Mark had secrets.

T.D. had secrets.

And my father had secrets.

"Honey?" My father's voice was feverish.

I was ten or eleven. Old enough that I had stopped dreaming of my mother every night, but young enough that I still believed in angels.

"Hmm?" I was sleepy, and rolled over, squinting as the light from the hallway hit my eyes.

Outside, I could hear a commotion, loud voices. And the pale red of reflected police cruiser lights pulsed on my bedroom wall.

"Put this in your secret hiding spot, baby."

My father shoved a huge wad of paper and cash, wrapped round with twenty or so rubber bands, at me.

Tired and frightened, I grabbed my old baby doll from the rocker by my bed, ripped off her head and stuffed the papers and cash down into the cavern of her body. What didn't fit there, I shoved up into her skull where her brains would be if she were a person and not a doll. Then I screwed her head back on and clutched her to my chest. We had rehearsed this.

The officers were downstairs, and I rolled over and pretended to be asleep, my doll clutched to my chest. At one point, a police officer shined a flashlight into my room. Pretending he had just awoken me, I turned over and said, "What's happening?"

The cop, a young guy in his twenties, came over to my bedside, shushing me. "It's okay, honey. We're just looking around. Your daddy said it was okay. You go on back to sleep now, all right?"

"Okay," I said in a voice as sweet as I could possibly muster. I curled up, innocent-faced, around my doll, who hid a good twenty thousand in her round plastic belly.

My father wasn't arrested. In fact, just before the police arrived with a search warrant, he'd been tipped off by a sergeant who was into my father for thirty thousand dollars—more than the sergeant made in a year. My father forgave him the debt.

The next day was Monday. My teacher asked me what I did over the weekend.

"I played cops and robbers," I said, smiling sweetly.

All my life, I'd been surrounded by secrets.

The next morning, my cell phone rang. I anxiously grabbed it, hoping it was Mark, but the caller ID read "James Sullivan."

"Hello?"

"Hey, baby, are you okay?"

"A little battered by the last week or so, but surviving. You know me. I've been through worse."

"Have you watched the news yet today?"

I felt nauseous. "No. Why?"

"Skye, if you want your father and me to kill this asshole, we will. No questions asked."

I grabbed the remote and turned on the television.

A TV reporter intoned into the camera, "If you're just tuning in, let's bring you up to date. Today, in a New York hotel, surrounded by attorneys, thirty-two-year-old financial advisor Bobby Corelli called a press conference to say that Mark Shannon's girlfriend, whose relationship with the quarterback superstar has caused one of the biggest sports scandals in history due to her ties to organized crime and gambling, used to work as a prostitute."

I stared in shock at the television, then fought the urge to jump out the window.

"Skye? Are you there?"

"Yeah, Jimmy."

"Your father says he's a two-bit nothing. Works for Big Teddy DeRosa's operation—financial advisor, my ass. You don't have to tell me if it's the truth. I don't care. Him calling this press conference is just dirty pool."

"It's a lie, Jimmy."

"Thank God. Your father's here. You wanna talk to him?"

"Not really. Look, this reeks of a setup to me. Walter Hammond II dug this slug up from under a rock."

"You know this guy?" Jimmy asked me.

"Yeah. Back in college. He went by the nickname

Bobby Buns. All the girls loved him. He and I were friends. He took book. I mean, strictly college stuff. He was a nobody then. We used to drink together. He liked me a lot because I was from the life he wanted. Easy money. Sports book. He was a hustler."

"So why's he sayin' this shit?"

"Like I said, it reeks. Like a cesspool. And I'm tired of swimming in it. Way back, Bobby and I decided to bet on the outcome of a St. John's basketball game. Just a straight bet. I bet they won, he bet they lost. We were drunk and stupid. We bet each other fifty thousand that neither of us had. I lost. We laughed. There'd be no way for me to pay it. One thing led to another, he smiles and says, 'Okay, McNally, I'll take it out in trade.' We sleep together…we kind of date for a few weeks. Now he's apparently saying I prostituted myself to pay off a gambling debt."

"I'll fuckin' break his neck and make it look like an accident."

"It's no use, Jimmy. This is bigger than me, you, Dad or Mark Shannon. I have to stop seeing him, or it will only get worse. Dad can't afford Walter Hammond's private eyes to start digging up dirt on him. Because I bet you that's how they found Bobby."

"So let 'em dig, the pricks."

"Jimmy, Dad can't do time. When he was fifty or forty, that's a different story. He'd probably still hold his own, but really, does he need to do time? Does he need to lose everything he has because of me?"

"Don't you think that's for him to decide?"

"Yeah, but I'm going to make it easy and decide for him. Let me go—I don't want to talk anymore."

I pressed the button to disconnect the cell phone. Now the news was onto something else. But in a half hour, *Headline News* would again air a snippet of the press conference—for anyone in America who missed it.

The phone rang again, and this time caller ID told me it was Mark. Whereas ten minutes before, my heart had pounded with excitement that it might be him on the line, now I knew I would never speak to him again. I couldn't. I ignored the ringing and let my voice mail pick up.

T.D. knocked on the door. "Can I come in?"

"Sure," I said without enthusiasm.

He entered, bearing two bourbons on the rocks.

"A little early for that, don't you think?" I asked, taking the offered drink.

"It's happy hour somewhere in the world."

"You saw the news, didn't you?"

He nodded.

"It's not true, you know."

"Wouldn't matter to me if it was."

"It's over, T.D. Me and Mark."

He nodded. He didn't even try to talk me out of it. I thought I had pulled one over on Walt Squared, but it looked like I was the one who'd been played.

I handed T.D. my cell phone.

"What's this for?"

"Throw it out for me? I don't even want to be tempted to listen to Mark's message. Just throw it out. I'll get a new one, a new number."

It started ringing again.

"It's him, isn't it?"

T.D. nodded. "I'm sorry, Little Girl." He turned the cell phone off.

"You want to know the most ironic thing?"

"Hmm?"

"For three years, I've been in Gamblers Anonymous, trying to cure myself of the itch to gamble. I go and I drink their lousy fucking coffee and I try for that stupid brass coin. I go because…I don't know what else to do instead of gamble. And everybody in that room talks about a Higher Power, and I couldn't even get past Step One. God must have a pretty strange sense of humor. Because not only is my life unmanageable now, but I have no desire to gamble. And it took all this shit to bring me to that conclusion. I finally get it, T.D."

"That's good."

"No, that's bad. Because now the man I am crazy about thinks I'm a paid whore. And I can't even talk to him because I'll cave. I'll tell him I love him. I'll drag me and you and my father and even poor Jimmy through a mess of epic proportions. And ordinarily, at least I could go sit in on a table. Find a game of poker. Bet the fights. And I don't want to. Now I have nothing but myself and all these feelings, and I don't know what to do with them."

"You just got to feel them."

"Like that's so easy."

"You think it was easy to tell you about me?"

I softened. "Here I am going on and on about me, but you're going through a world of shit, too."

"Yep. Just the two of us in a shit storm."

"Which leaves us only one choice," I said.

"What's that?"

"I told you. Road trip. We're going to sunny Miami."

"Isn't that kind of crazy? Going to watch Mark play in the Bowl?"

"The Super Bowl is a huge event, we can get lost in the crowd. I want to be out of Vegas. And I want to be with my family—you and Dad, and even Jimmy."

"You're not going to sleep with him again, are you?"

"No, but I do plan on getting good and drunk."

THIRTY-❤ONE

"Will you look at this suite?" I said.

T.D. and I were sharing one suite, and my father and Jimmy were sharing another.

T.D. smiled. "I'm scheduling a massage. And will you look at that view?"

In front of us, the azure blue waters of Miami Beach stretched all the way to the horizon. It was Friday of Super Bowl weekend. The city of Miami was insane. My father had a limousine waiting for us at the airport, but we rode in stop-and-go traffic all the way to South Beach, where the streets were lined with football revelers—Miami salsa-style. Women in thongs and little sunflower decals pasted over their nipples slipped in between people, riding on in-line skates. Buffed, tanned guys, their chests waxed to hairless perfection, strutted in jogging shorts that left little to the imagination. I elbowed T.D. a few times, though I had sworn to him I would not let my father and Jimmy know we were there to find him a boyfriend. Our mission—at least as defined by me: find a man for T.D. by Super Bowl Sunday.

I took my brass coin out of my pocket and put it on my dresser. I stared at it there. I had earned it. I had earned it the hard way. Thirty days and still counting.

Cowboy Hal had stood at the front of the room. "And will all those with thirty days come up here to collect their coin, please?"

I had stood—the only thirty-dayer. I walked, with my head held high, to the front of the room amid thunderous applause. T.D. and Fish-eye had even given me a standing ovation.

"Skye, would you like to say a few words to your home group?"

"When Cowboy Hal talked the other week about high bottoms and low bottoms, he was talking about me," I began. "Apparently, I didn't think getting arrested was enough of a clue that gambling was trouble."

The room laughed.

"And now my life is more unmanageable than ever, but something my sponsor said finally makes sense." I looked over at T.D. "Yes, I do actually listen to you. Sometimes. If you say it often enough."

More scattered laughter.

"He told me, 'Skye, all you have to do is not gamble.' And that sounds like kind of useless advice. Particularly to a gambler. But I get it now. If you don't gamble, if you just take care of that one thing, your Higher Power will take care of the rest. Lately, my heart's taken a beating, but gambling—I can promise you—wouldn't make it any better. It would just make it worse. So all I have to worry about right now is not gambling. Today. One day at a time. And yeah, Jesus, I never thought you'd hear me use one of those slogans…."

That brass coin now went with me everywhere. Since the fabricated story broke about my so-called days as a prostitute, I had cut my hair shoulder-length and dyed it platinum from its usual dark brown in an effort to totally change my appearance. Though the platinum was head-turning in a Marilyn Monroe way, no one guessed at my identity when I donned dark sunglasses with my new hair. T.D. had thrown out my cell phone, but if I thought it would be that easy to be rid of Mark Shannon, I had been mistaken.

After the story aired, a florist delivered ten dozen red roses, each bearing a card with the words "Call me." I had the florist take the flowers to the hospital with instructions to give them to people without visitors—and I tipped the deliveryman fifty bucks to make sure he did as I asked.

Next, a telegram came. I didn't even know telegrams existed anymore. When it arrived, I had visions of an old 1940s movie. My answering machine in my apartment blinked. I had so many messages that the tape was full, but I didn't play them. I didn't want to hear his voice.

And yet at the same time I was hiding from Mark, I had driven out to the desert, and even eaten at the diner where I met him. I was making myself insane with thoughts of him, and trying to do the right thing for once in my life. So, even though I told T.D. the road trip was to find him true love, or at least a fling, it was also because I couldn't bear Mark being at the Super Bowl without my being there to at least cheer him on in my heart. I decided I was a masochist where my heart was concerned.

I packed my suitcase, and T.D. and I flew to Miami to meet Jimmy and my dad. The entire time I kept fingering the brass coin in my pocket and tried to convince myself over and over again that giving up Mark was the only choice I had.

Now, in our suite, I talked T.D. into going with me to a bar on South Beach. I wanted to sit at a table outside and let the cool January breeze kiss my face while we searched out a suitable man for my fearless sponsor. My father and Jimmy had decided to take a limo to go bet on jai a'lai.

At six o'clock, T.D. and I were ensconced at a table sipping mai tais in honor of Big Buffet House of Hunan.

"How about him?" I gestured with my head toward a handsome Nordic-looking fellow with a tan, about six feet tall. He looked like a model.

"Not my type."

"What is your type?" I asked. "For the last three years I've set you up with women who were either the exact opposite of your ex-wife, or who resemble the hostess at Big Buffet that you always flirt with."

"I don't flirt with her."

"You do," I argued. "Are you sure you're not bi?"

"Positive."

"You haven't answered my question. What is your type?"

"I don't know."

"Come on, you must have a thought about it."

"Actually, I guess it would be someone like you, only a guy."

"What is that supposed to mean?"

"I'm not sure."

"This is not going to be easy."

"Tell me about it," he agreed.

While we sat there, me, in huge dark glasses, doing my best Jackie O. impersonation, a small-built man with a slightly graying brown beard, wavy hair and horn-rimmed glasses approached our table.

"George Russell?"

T.D. and I were so paparazzi-scarred, we each probably looked like the proverbial deer in a headlight.

"Ye-es," T.D. said slowly.

"I'm Max Robinson, from the *St. Louis Times-Dispatch*."

I threw up my hands. "Jesus, will you guys give us a fucking break?"

The reporter, dressed in crisp khakis and a pressed white oxford shirt, looked at me as if I was a woman out on a day pass from a mental institution for the criminally insane.

"I'm sorry," he said softly. "I didn't mean to intrude on a romantic evening for you two. I'm a sportswriter, and I'm a *huge* fan—I've followed George Russell since he was a college ballplayer. I know every stat, every Pro Bowl performance. Anyway, just wanted to tell you that you're one of the greats and you deserve to be in the Hall of Fame. I apologize for bothering you, really."

He hadn't recognized me. Gotta love the platinum hair.

"I'm sorry," I smiled. "I didn't mean to bark at you."

"Yeah." T.D. reached up a hand. "Sorry. We've had a long week."

Recognition crept into the reporter's eyes. But rather than looking as if he had found the scoop of the century by spotting me, his eyes were rather sympathetic and he dropped his voice to a whisper. "I bet it has been the week from hell. Listen, I won't tell anyone you guys are here for the Bowl. That Hammond is a bit like a pit bull."

"No, the pit bull is that Leon Krakowski, the fixer they sent to us," I said. "Hammond's more like Satan."

"Ah, Leon." Max smiled. "Does he still smoke those very fat Cuban cigars?"

"Chomps on them more than smokes them," I said. "Sputters cigar juice." I shuddered at the memory.

"Leon engineered the cover-up of Cory Dilliard's girl-friend-beating incident," Max said. "And he also was be-hind the scenes in that Roy Mallone vehicular man-slaughter case."

"So why aren't you going to trumpet the fact that you found us?" I asked.

Max shrugged. "To be honest? I'm not actually a sports-writer for the *Dispatch*—anymore. I used to be, but I was fired. I've been writing freelance articles while I figure out what to do with the rest of my life. I'm covering this for a magazine."

"We could be your biggest story," I said, eyeing him suspiciously.

He shook his head. "I love sports. That's why I'm here for the Super Bowl. But I'm a little burned out on scan-dal—it's a long story."

"Want to sit down with us?" T.D. asked. "All off the record, of course."

"Thanks." Max signaled a waiter, who brought over a third chair for our table and took his drink order. "I'll have what they're having."

I laughed.

"What?" Max asked.

"We're drinking mai tais. It's an inside joke. Trust me, you probably won't like them. We promise to switch to bourbon next round."

Max shrugged. "I'm actually not a bourbon man. I like froufrou drinks."

"The *St. Louis Post-Dispatch*… That paper's got a great sports desk," T.D. said. "I used to read it when we played there. I think we might have met."

"Good memory. Or lucky guess. We did, once. After the Pro Bowl. You gave me a pretty extensive interview."

"Sorry to hear you lost your job, man."

"Why were you fired?" I asked.

"Don't mind her, she's a bit pushy," T.D. said. He gave me a warning look.

Max turned a shade of fuchsia that matched the hibiscus tree growing in a huge urn by the hostess stand.

"Like I said, ignore her. She's nosy." T.D. gave me one of those *you're headed for a one-way bus ticket to a dry county where they won't sell you bourbon* looks.

"Well…" Max fingered his napkin. "Let's just say my editor and I didn't see eye-to-eye on a few things. Including whether the earth would spin backward on its axis and the anti-Christ would take up residence in St. Louis if it came out that a sports columnist was gay."

"Did you say *gay?*" My mouth dropped open.

He nodded. He glanced over at T.D. "I know—it really freaks out sports people. Anyway, thanks for the drink."

"Ooh, Max, don't rush off." I stared at T.D. with laser eyes. "We don't feel that way, *do we,* T.D.?"

"Not at all." T.D. was actually beaming. I recognized that look. It was the same look he had when he found a cashmere scarf at Nordstrom at fifty percent off. How could I not have known the man was gay?

"It was hard," Max said. "I'd kept it a secret for so long because of my profession. I mean, yes, I'm sure there are gay sportswriters out there somewhere, but it's not out in the open, especially not at the upper echelons of journalism."

I nodded understandingly. Sitting down at our table, I now noticed that Max had hazel eyes with longish lashes, and he was probably around forty years old. He had a great smile. A bookish look—but sexy, in a nebbish kind of way.

"Anyway, I wasn't happy about being in the closet. And then I wrote a column criticizing Rory Cullen—"

"The coach who supposedly hired hookers for his university team and then covered up a gang rape?" I asked. "What a creep!"

"I thought so. I just hated his insinuation that the woman deserved what happened to her because she got drunk with the team at a party. The guys were drunk, too. So if they beat up one of the younger guys on the team or sodomized him, would he have deserved it? Cullen's a bully."

T.D. shook his head disgustedly. I had never known him not to be anything but the most gallant gentleman. At his restaurant, if a woman was falling down drunk, he made sure she called a friend to pick her up, rather than leave with some guy she'd just met if the guy seemed suspect. He had a standing policy of calling cabs for people who'd had too much to drink—and paying for it out of his own pocket. And I'd seen him take more than one boorish man out of his restaurant by the collar of his shirt.

"So what happened when the column ran?" I asked.

"Cullen ended up getting fed the information that I was gay from some nutty fan who spotted me going into a gay bar two towns over. And Cullen not only had team members leaving me foul expletives on my answering machine, he called my editor and told him he didn't want me in the locker room. You'd have thought it was the 1950s, but that was only a couple of months ago."

"So where were your editor's balls?" I demanded, feeling my heart pound in fury. Around us was the chaos and carnival atmosphere of Miami, but for the moment, everything had receded except the three of us at the table, in our own intense world.

"This is weird telling total strangers this whole thing. I guess I had to get it off my chest."

"There's a lot of that going around," T.D. said dryly.

"Anyway…my editor acted supportive, but then he started picking on my stories. Fact checking them like mad. Found two people to say I made up quotes, which I had not. I had my notes, but it was like this chronic bullshit. Then he wanted me to work half my hours in the lifestyle section—to hard news or sports reporters, that's like sending us out to pasture. We ended up in a huge fight. I wound up being fired for insubordination."

"Couldn't you sue?" I asked.

He shook his head. "I mean, I guess I could, but it wouldn't be an easy fight, and I'd lose all my privacy."

"Which is why you won't write that you stumbled on the story of the year—with a new platinum hairdo," T.D. said.

Max nodded.

"You're all right in my book." T.D. looked at Max admiringly.

"Have dinner with us!" I blurted out.

"No, I couldn't." He smiled sheepishly. "I've pretty much monopolized your time here."

"Please stay." T.D. looked imploringly at him.

We ended up spending the entire night, under a full moon, along the romantic sands of Miami with a man I considered perfect for T.D. Worthy of him. The conversation flowed as easily as the champagne we ordered. Max was well-read, cultured, funny—and loved sports. Hell, I would have loved to date him. But at 3:00 a.m., I finally told them I had to go back to my hotel room or I would keel over. I fell asleep in the big king-size bed in the suite, lonelier than ever, without T.D. there to tell my own troubles to, which left me alone to dream about Mark.

THIRTY-TWO♥

The three mai tais and three bourbons I'd had caused my head to pound the next morning, and I had forgotten to pull the curtains, so sunlight streamed in, making my hangover worse. I looked over at T.D.'s bed. Empty. The clock read seven-thirty in the morning.

I was happy for him. But sad for me. Nursing my own broken heart caused me to picture T.D. and Max running off to Canada or Vermont, or someplace where they could get married, and then settling down somewhere and forgetting all about me. I pictured a picket fence, Fred and Ginger curled up and purring on a couch in a cozy living room. T.D. and Max would get a dog, maybe, and I would have to buy them a housewarming gift—perhaps a toaster oven. I rolled over and groaned. I was losing my best friend! Who else did I have? My bookie?

I had a new cell phone, having given T.D. my old one to dispose of when I feared even hearing Mark's voice would send me back to him. I hadn't plugged Heavy's phone number into it (though I *had* paid off my last debt to him). I knew his number by heart. I could call and bet on the Super Bowl. The Mustangs were no longer the favorites. The Vegas oddsmen now favored Green Bay based on Mark's dismal performance in his last game, his perceived instability, the lack of a deep bench—meaning if he got hurt, they had no real choice for backup—and the effect of all the bad publicity on the team's morale. Even *I* wasn't sure I'd bet on Mark Shannon.

Heavy's number was there in my head. I rolled over and gave out a small yell. *No. You've come this far.* So I started singing the words to "Sit Down You're Rocking the Boat" at the top of my lungs. And at that moment, I heard T.D. fumbling with the doorknob, and seconds later he came in.

"I could hear you all the way out in the hall, you know."

"Come here!" I shot up and scooted over, patting the bed. "Come tell me everything!"

He laughed and said, "I'm wiped. I think I'll just crash."

"Not a chance. I'll sing in your ear while you're trying to sleep."

"You do know you're tone deaf, don't you?"

He stood and started unbuttoning his shirt from the previous night. He walked over to the dresser and took out his wallet and put it there, and then took out a pair of soft, silk PJ bottoms from his drawer and stripped down and put them on. He did this all painstakingly slowly to drive me insane. If he turned his head to the side at all, I could see him smiling to himself at how he was killing me here.

I watched how neatly he folded his pants from the night before. We had traveled together before—the last time to Lake Tahoe. We were a study in opposites. I lived out of my suitcase, spilling clothes onto the floor and making a heap of dirty clothes, which I then shoved into the suitcase when it was time to fly home. He put all his things away in drawers. He even folded his dirty clothes.

Finally, T.D. must have decided he'd tortured me enough. He pulled the curtains and came over to the bed and climbed in, lying on his back, and I snuggled into his shoulder and started to cry—I wasn't even sure where the tears came from, they appeared so suddenly.

"Why are you crying, Little Girl?"

"Honestly? Because this is how we've always been. Me snuggled up right here. And I still fit here. I guess I worried, you know, that we wouldn't have this anymore—whatever this is."

"You don't think I worried about that? Little Girl, you disappeared into a desert, came back with a quarterback, and a few days later there were *helicopters* hovering over my house. Talk about wondering if things could remain the same between us." He pulled me tighter to him. "I got your back. You got mine."

I wiped my eyes and scrunched up to kiss his cheek. "Well? What happened?"

"You know I'm not a gory-details kind of person. Never have been. Even in the locker room, you had guys talking about having three girls in one day—hell, at one time. That was never me."

"Yes, but now we know there were obvious underlying reasons for that," I quipped.

"Nah. It's just me."

"You have to tell me *something.*"

"It was…perfect."

"I'm happy for you, T.D., I really am."

"What did you think of him?"

"I loved him. He seems like a smart, nice guy. He's cute. He's a catch, as they say."

T.D. sighed. A *happy, I'm-infatuated* sort of sigh. "I think so, too."

"And does he seem as...crazy about you?"

"Yeah, Little Girl. But what's not to love in a guy like me?"

I rolled my eyes. "There is your type-A personality, and your borderline obsessive-compulsive disorder with little shampoos."

"Point taken."

Though T.D. had more money than, well, anyone I knew except the Wentworths—and I didn't really know them, only collected money from my trust each month— he loved little hotel shampoo bottles. He'd apparently started collecting them when he played with the NFL, and so in each of his four bathrooms, he had baskets of them, arranged with fancy soaps, for when guests stayed. That way they could choose what shampoo they wanted and feel like they, too, were staying at hotels like the Four Seasons. The only problem with that scenario was I was his only guest, and though I have thick black hair, I could shampoo until I was *bald* and not make a dent in his collection. So the spillover from the baskets then went into a linen closet, where, I guessed, he had around eight hundred little bottles neatly lined up like an army.

"And there *is* the way you won't let me eat in bed."

"No, that's a positive. You can't count that in the negative column."

"I can. Besides, I'd bet now you'd let *Max* eat in bed."

"No. I wouldn't. Well, not crackers. He could eat something without crumbs."

"So what happens next with you and Max? Anything?"

"We're spending the day with you, once we all get some sleep. Then I figured you'd want to eat with your dad and

Jimmy—or you can come with Max and me to some sushi place a couple of blocks over."

"I don't want to be a third wheel."

"Look, Little Girl, no matter who I happen to be with, he would have to understand you are part of the package. Just like Mark Shannon seemed to get over the fact that the first time I met him, I gave him a shiner and tackled him into a plaster wall."

At the mention of Mark, I felt a pang. I tried to pretend it was hunger.

"I'll tell you what. I'll let you two have dinner, and I'll tag along with Dad and Jimmy and try not to get arrested or spotted. Frankly, with my platinum hair, I'm a lot less noticeable with my father and Jimmy than with T.D. Russell."

"Let's get some shut-eye."

"Will Max move to Vegas with us?"

"Man, you move fast. Come on. Let's get some sleep."

He yawned, and I put my head on his biceps the way I always did and waited until he started breathing heavily. I smiled. T.D. had found someone. And now I envisioned Max and me and T.D. living in that house with the picket fence. Definitely we'd get a dog—yet another childhood experience I'd missed. My father said they were too much trouble, and we—meaning him—kept hours that were too irregular for a dog.

I remember pleading for a golden retriever. I even had a name all picked out—Blackjack. Now that I had a thirty-day coin, I guess that was out. Jimmy had Gunther. I loved him for the brief time I'd had him. When I moved to Vegas, I could have gotten a dog, but a dog meant responsibility. It meant I couldn't go on a gambling bender and not come home. I saw now how much gambling impacted my life in a thousand decisions and a thousand little ways.

I climbed out of bed and went to get my brass coin. I tried to have faith that all I had to do was not gamble and the rest would fall into place. All I knew was that any hopes for a picket fence of my own had been blown to smithereens. On the other hand, I wasn't exactly a picket-fence kind of gal.

CHAPTER
THIRTY-THREE

T.D. woke up first and ordered us an enormous room-service breakfast. Elaborating on that, an "enormous" room-service breakfast for T.D. requires two trolleys for delivery. I woke up when I smelled coffee.

"Want some eggs?"

"Just coffee."

"Sausage? Pancakes? Muffins from the muffin basket? A little croissant?"

"Just coffee."

"Come on, we have a big day ahead of us."

"What big day? Tomorrow's the Super Bowl. Today I figured we'd hit the pool. Walk on the beach. Ogle men. The two of us can ogle men now!"

"Eat something," he ordered sternly.

"Yes, sir! I'll take bacon and a little scrambled eggs."

I watched as he filled a plate.

"T.D., I don't want two dozen eggs, just what amounts to a single scrambled egg. And two slices of bacon will do."

He put back about ten slices of bacon, but he left the

eggs. I climbed out of bed, pulled on a hotel robe, and sat down opposite him at the table. He had opened the balcony sliding doors. It was chilly. The pool was probably out.

"So, Little Girl, Max and I want to drive around, do a little sightseeing. Head over to the stadium, go for a drink—"

"Back up. What did you say?"

"Drive around. Sightsee. Go for a drink."

"No. There was something in the middle there."

"You have egg on your chin."

"T.D.! Stop changing the subject."

"Go to the stadium. I said go to the stadium."

"That's what I thought you said. You take too many hits as a football player? Your brains hit the side of your skull a few too many times?"

"Harsh."

"I am not going to the stadium. *We* are not going to the stadium. What are you thinking?"

He stopped buttering a croissant and looked at me. "You're the one not thinking if you let this thing with Mark end. I've thought about it, and you can't just give up. I never gave up. Not when my team was down twenty-one to seven with four minutes to go in the fourth quarter. So no, I am not insane. Max and I have a plan."

"A plan."

"Yes."

"Are you going to tell me what it is?"

"Not yet."

I shook my head and started eating my eggs, which were perfectly fluffy. The phone rang, and T.D. practically knocked over a trolley of food to answer it.

"Hello?"

I heard only his half of the conversation. It was obviously Max.

"Yeah…me, too. I know…yeah. Uh-huh… Yeah, she's on board with the plan….No, not yet. Trust me, with Skye, it's better to do it this way." He looked over at me and smiled. I felt ready to strangle him. "Okay. Yeah, me, too."

He hung up the phone, then barked at me. "Go get ready. Take a shower…and wear that black minidress with the pretty cashmere cardigan. Demure. Nice."

I stood up and rolled my eyes. "Suddenly he's gay, and now I'm getting unsolicited fashion advice."

"And make sure you curl your eyelashes. It makes your eyes pop."

"Pop?"

"Yeah."

"I think I liked it better when you were in the closet," I said, and marched into the bathroom.

Max had rented a two-door compact car. This was obviously before his new lover turned out to be a man who weighed a good 280 pounds and practically had to do a yoga contortion to fit in the front seat.

"Sorry, T.D., I didn't know we'd be driving around together when I rented this."

"No problem," T.D. smiled.

"No problem?" I piped up from the back seat. "Easy for you to say. You have friggin' shotgun. I'm back here, and I'm getting claustrophobia. Can you open a window?"

"No," T.D. said when Max moved to press the electric window button. "Use the air. When her hair is exposed to humidity, it starts looking like a fright wig."

"Gee, thanks. Why don't you tell him how bloated I get during my time of the month."

"She does," T.D. said.

"I give up!" I half shrieked. "Look, I am crammed in the back of this tin can, so would either of you care to enlighten me on the 'plan'? You make it sound like the invasion of Normandy."

"Here." Max passed back a press pass as we drove toward the stadium, driving over a causeway with water so clear and beautiful, it almost made me want to give up living in a desert.

"What's this?"

"You're my photographer."

"Your what?"

"See…in truth I'm writing about the Super Bowl for *Real Sports* magazine and their online division. They've assigned a photographer to this story. He's an alcoholic and is nursing the mother of all hangovers right now, so I took his press pass, screwed around with it on the computer he brought with him, along with a scanner and stuff to play with his digital pictures… Voilà, now you have a press pass."

"What about T.D.?"

"He'll wait in the car. If he's seen with you, even with that platinum hair, someone else may put two and two together."

"And your idea, gentlemen, is what? I take pictures of Mark and he'll suddenly 'get over' all he's seen about me on the news? Hello? Earth to Planet Stupid, they brought out some jerk to say I was a prostitute—which is not true, by the way, Max—"

"I never thought it was."

"What?"

He looked at me in the rearview mirror, his green eyes masked by sunglasses now, but still his face was warm and friendly. "You been around sports as long as I have, you see the games. I mean the games played by the front office. I guessed they were just trying to scare you off. Bury this thing before the Super Bowl."

"Well, thanks for the vote of confidence, but that doesn't mean Mark knows that."

"He sent you roses," T.D. said. "He's not buying it. Besides, he's got a bigger problem than media coverage of your past peccadilloes. His own situation. He sees through Hammond's games."

"Fine. Even if he does, by some miracle of epic proportions, still have faith in me, the impossibilities are endless. My father and his record. Heck, my record. The fact that I gambled on sports from the time I was eight until…well, it hasn't been that long."

"You're forgetting something," Max said.

"What?"

"The Cinderella story."

"As in you want me to wear a glass slipper?"

"No." He laughed as he drove along the Florida highway. "Look, sportswriters, and sports fans, love the Cinderella story. The boxer who isn't supposed to stand a chance against the champ scores a punch that knocks the champ flat. The team that doesn't have a prayer of making it into the World Series and then, lo and behold, they're all the way in game seven, two outs, bottom of the ninth, bases loaded, and the guy at bat hits a home run. And this team, the Mustangs, which didn't have a prayer, is now the Cinderella story of the year."

"The world according to T.D.…." I said dryly.

"All I'm saying is you can't count out the impossible. The Hail Mary pass."

I looked out the window. "I don't know. I can't hope for the impossible."

"Why not?"

I shrugged, which neither of them could see. "I don't know. Because I hope for teams to win, to cover their spread. I hope for things that are based on superstition. Like my father's friend Lefty, who got his name because he never touches any of his chips at the poker table with his right hand. You hope for things that have to do with luck, like your horse coming in, but you don't place your hope in people. At least I don't."

I thought back to wanting, for a while, to live in a world without flash paper and money hidden in my dolls' heads. It never came true. I hoped for my mother to come back. That didn't, either. I'd even hoped for a short time, that the Wentworths might want me—but they hadn't. Not really. So I had stopped hoping in people and instead hoped for teams. But I'd never pinned my hope on love before.

T.D. and Max exchanged glances. I know they thought their harebrained scheme would work, their big "plan," but ever since Mark Shannon got back to his team, nothing had gone according to plan. And I was the girl at the blackjack table who didn't know when to fold.

CHAPTER
THIRTY-F♥UR

"How do you work this thing?"

Max was giving me a ten-minute lesson on how to look as if knew what I was doing with a camera.

"You press this halfway down, then you wait, focus and shoot. You'll want to get some pictures this way. You may want to step back, half kneel, whatever. Watch the other photographers and just follow their lead. But snap a lot of pictures. We can't go straight over to Mark—too suspicious."

"And he'll be mobbed," T.D. said.

"Which could be good," Max added. "We considered that. You'll just be one of the crowd."

"And what if I'm recognized?"

"Context," T.D. said, and Max nodded.

"Could one of the two of you speak English?"

"The way we figure it, Little Girl, no one's expecting you to show up *as* one of the media. The media is the enemy. With the hair, the sunglasses, press pass. We got it all planned."

"Glad you two are so confident," I snapped.

"Good luck," T.D. intoned, giving me a thumbs-up.

Max and I turned and made the long trek from our parking spot to the stadium.

As I walked, I tried to figure out why I was going along with Max and T.D.'s plan. Everything in my life—my whole life—was a gambling analogy, and this was no different. I was taking all my chips and betting on black. Or red. Or the number seven. Any way I looked at the analogy, it was about coming to the table with everything on the line, like withdrawing your life savings and somehow finding the courage—or blind faith—to risk it all.

All my life, I knew the odds were with the house. The odds were still with the house. Walt Squared could crush me. The feds could crush my father. The conspiracy surrounding Mark and the digitalis could crush him. There were "forces"—things we couldn't necessarily even see, but we sure could sense—driving us apart. But every gambler—even a recovering one—has inside himself a spark. Maybe, I could at last see something *good* about my compulsion to gamble. Inside me beat a heart that wildly, against all odds, against the house, believed it could win.

The media had access to the teams before they practiced. As we walked, men—mostly men—with large cameras dangling from their necks, or teams of camera crews made their way into the stadium. We had to pass through a metal detector and checkpoints. My press pass was accepted, and Max and I were in.

"I feel like I'm going to throw up."

He patted my back. "Come on, it's a good plan."

"How did T.D. rope you into this?"

"It was actually a spontaneous thing—we both got the

idea sort of at the same time when we were in my room and saw my press pass on the nightstand."

"So he told you the whole story, huh?"

"Right down to the helicopters and having to re-sod his lawn again."

"I'm glad T.D. met you, just so you know."

"A few weeks ago, I thought my life was over...now I think it's just beginning. Now it's your turn. Come on." He grabbed my hand. His hand was warm and firm, comforting. I realized yet again I wasn't losing my best friend but gaining someone new to care about.

We walked with the crowds of reporters into the stadium. From the ground, the turf, looking up, the place felt huge. I couldn't imagine being Mark tomorrow, walking in with it filled to capacity and knowing the big game was on the line. You'd have to have nerves of steel. And right now, I was sure hoping he did. We made our way down a line of players, all offering sound bites.

Finally, we were part of a large group hovering around Mark. He stood, looking tired, but smiling, offering tidbits and quotes that would no doubt be used on the news that night. Reporters shouted questions out at him. I held up the camera to my face and looked at him through the lens. I felt dizzy. I wanted to rush at him and throw my arms around his neck so badly.

"Have you heard from Skye McNally since the prostitution story broke?"

"No comment."

"Do you feel ready to lead your team tomorrow after the turmoil of the last month?"

"Absolutely. We're ready. We're focused."

"How about you—is your mind totally on the game now?"

"I've been playin' ball since peewee leagues, fellas. I'm ready. This is the one I've been gunning for my whole life. I'm ready."

The camera I was using was huge. It totally hid my face.

"Has your team forgiven you for going AWOL?"

"Yes. I'm lucky they have. We've talked. There was some tension at first, but we're the same Mustangs we've always been. Maybe better for all we've been through."

Max shouted a question, "Mark, are *you* the same guy you've always been?"

Mark looked in our direction. I lowered the camera ever so slightly, feeling frozen, chilly. I pushed my sunglasses down the bridge of my nose so he could see my eyes for a minute. He blinked, hard, twice. Cameras flashed. Then he looked right at me and Max as he answered. "You know…I'm not. I think I'm a better man now, honestly. I think I know a lot more about myself. I know what I want." At the word *want* he looked at me.

"And what do you want?" Another reporter fired a question.

"To win, of course."

"What about your performance in the play-off game?"

"I'll admit I was just trying to deal with all you fellas." He flashed that toothpaste-commercial smile of his, and the press pool all laughed. "But I'm fine. I'm ready."

Even as he answered questions, his eyes kept coming back to rest on me, and Max, who now asked another question. "Do you think what happened to Skye McNally was fair? I mean, you're a football player, not a political candidate. Seems they really dug up a lot of dirt on her, regardless of what happened to the relationship."

"No. It wasn't fair at all. I think there were a lot of untruths, a lot of exaggerations. When it all comes down to it, the whole thing was my fault. If I wasn't AWOL, if we'd been having a quiet relationship instead of in the midst of my disappearance, then none of it would have come out— or mattered. And some day, soon, after the Super Bowl, I think the truth, the whole truth, will come out."

I put the camera up to my face so he couldn't see my eyes tearing, and I backed away from the crowd, pretending to take random shots of the empty stadium. Fifteen minutes later, Max was by my side.

"You ready to go?"

I nodded, not trusting my voice yet.

"What? Didn't you hear him? There's hope for you two. He didn't believe all the garbage put out about you."

I shrugged.

"Have you been crying?" Max got up close to my face. "You have, poor baby." He hugged me, the camera pressing against me and hurting me. "Come on. Nothing like a bourbon to mend a broken heart."

He held my hand as we walked out of the stadium. I whispered, "This was so nice of you and T.D., but it's a big so-what. The other part of this is that the world of gambling and the world of football have to pretend the other doesn't exist. Because of who my father is, if I went back to Mark, the dirt wouldn't stop. I can't do that to my father, or to Jimmy."

"You just leave that to me."

"Max, I'm beginning to think there's a lot more to you than meets the eye. What are you, CIA or something?"

"Now, I can't reveal all my secrets." He gave my hand a squeeze.

We exited the stadium and walked all the way down one of the long parking aisles to the rental car. T.D. was standing outside stretching his legs. And next to him was an

older man, cigar in mouth, wearing a Hawaiian shirt. Leon
Krakowski.

"Hello, Leon," I said unenthusiastically.

"I like the Marilyn Monroe look. Spotted it when you
got off the plane with your dear old dad and ex-husband. Sexy."

"Well, I *don't like* the Hawaiian shirt look. It looks like
somebody vomited on a Tilt-A-Whirl."

"I have to fit in down here in Miami."

"Leon, I bet you never fit in anywhere your whole life."

"You got me there, toots. Now, get in the car with your
new friend here and go bye-bye."

"How'd you find us?"

"Global positioning device."

"What?"

"Just kiddin'. Look, kid, I got eyes and ears everywhere.
I'll admit, coming here with a fake press pass? You get an
A for creativity. But Walt Squared is getting tired of this
whole thing. It was a *fling.* That's all it was. So do us all a
favor—most especially your dear old man and that ex-husband of yours—and go back home. Go back to your ex.
That's the kind of guy for you."

T.D., leaning back against the car with a cool expression on his face, suddenly turned around and lifted up
Leon by his pants.

"Christ! Put me down, you big schmuck. You're giving
me a fucking wedgie!" Leon kicked his legs back and
forth.

T.D. lifted him still higher. "I think, in grade school, they
call this an atomic wedgie. Now, listen here, Leon, we'll
go. But back off."

"I know your secret there, big boy."

"And I don't care. This is my Little Girl we're talking

about. Next time, I'll have that cigar so far down your throat, a proctologist will have to go find it."

T.D. dropped Leon, who crumpled to the pavement. Then T.D., Max and I climbed into the car and drove away.

"Well?" T.D. asked.

"He still loves her," Max said.

"He didn't say that exactly," I said.

"Close enough." Max took out a pocket tape recorder and rewound and pressed Play. Mark's voice filled our car.

"Sounds like he still loves her to me," T.D. said.

"But it doesn't matter, guys. This was a cute plan, but I personally don't envision spending the rest of my life with Leon Krakowski up my ass like a hemorrhoid."

"Well, that's a disgusting visual," T.D. said.

"I was just going with your proctologist image."

We drove back to the Four Seasons, and I told T.D. and Max to spend some time alone. "I'll find my dad and Jimmy."

"Don't get into trouble," T.D. said.

"Me, trouble?"

"As I recall, that's your middle name."

They drove off, and I rode in the elevator to the third floor. Seeing Mark left me depressed. He seemed to be dealing with the latest media punch, but I was back to imagining getting a golden retriever and growing old with T.D. and Max. Them together, and me, alone.

I knocked on my father and Jimmy's suite, and Jimmy came to the door in a pair of plaid boxers.

"Hey, wife, what's happening?"

"Nothing. I just was wondering what you two were up to today. Thought maybe I'd tag along."

"Your dad and I met a few guys from New York, and

they've got a high-stakes poker game going on in the penthouse."

"Surprise, surprise. And what about you?"

"I don't know. I haven't figured it out yet. Come on in."

I followed him into the suite. It was almost identical to T.D.'s and mine, though with my father and Jimmy sharing a room, the minibar had been raided, as evidenced by little bottles stacked on a desk, and towels and clothes were strewn on all the furniture.

"You know, Skye—" Jimmy turned around to face me "—we could always spend all afternoon in bed."

"No, we can't."

"Why?"

"Because, Jimmy, I'm in love with someone else."

He moved to me and started kissing my neck. "But we understand each other. We understand our world. No one's going to sit in judgment of us."

"I know, Jimmy, but even if I never see him again, I'm not ready to see someone else, either. And I'm not going back to gambling."

"I know. You showed me that coin. Tomorrow is the Super Bowl. You're going to tell me that coin is worth more than betting on the game?"

"Yeah," I whispered.

"You could go in on this one pool I got. You win, and it's a quick twenty-five Gs."

"Jimmy, like I said. I'll always love you. You were there for me when my father went to prison. You were the one who sat in those Dunkin' Donut shops, making me laugh, waiting for the cousins to come. But I'm not going backward, Jimmy."

He kissed me on the mouth, and I kissed him back. He was so familiar, Jimmy was. His kisses could make me sail through time to the night I lost my virginity. To nights when I needed someone to bail me out of a card game gone ugly. To tender nights when he'd made love to me all night long.

I pulled away. "Jimmy, you're always going to be a bookie. And that's who you are, and I don't judge you. But I can't do that life anymore."

"Fine," he snapped. "Then let's go drinking, 'cause I have a hangover and I could use the hair of the dog." He pulled on his jeans and a black T-shirt and ran his hands through his hair. "But I'm telling you, this guy hurts you any more than he has already done and I'll kill him. With my bare hands."

"Come on, tough guy." I smiled, and we went downstairs and out to walk South Beach in search of a place to drink and look at the waves. We didn't have to walk far before we settled into a place and ordered two Jacks and Coke.

"So what's next, Skye? You live in Vegas. You don't gamble. The man you supposedly love is off-limits. What's next? What do you do for an encore?" Bitterness had crept into his voice.

"I'm not sure. I had never pictured my life being about anything but the over-under and seeing what team covered the spread each Sunday."

"And that's another thing."

"Hmm?"

"Mark Shannon is now bad for business. No one's betting on the Mustangs to win, since he's been off his game. Do you realize most of New York is demoralized? They're talking about trading him."

I shrugged. "Trust me, next year, when this is all a faded memory, he'll be back better than ever."

"And you'll be a footnote."

"A what?"

"A footnote. You'll be like a Trivial Pursuit question. What was the name of the woman who almost single-handedly destroyed the Super Bowl between the Mustangs and the—"

"It was not single-handed. I had help."

"Still a Trivial Pursuit question."

"And what about you?"

"What about me?"

"You end up like my father? Sixty years old and still hustling? Find your own protégé? When you end up dead, they stick dice, a deck of cards and a racing form in your coffin?"

Jimmy stared across the table at me. He looked as if I'd hurt him, but then he grinned a little sadly. "And don't forget they'll throw me the biggest damn party as a send-off."

I looked away at the water, the revelers on the teeming sidewalks. That was how we'd say goodbye to my father. And that was how I'd say goodbye to Jimmy, my first love. But people rarely, if ever, change.

"To the point spread," I whispered, lifting my glass. "Good luck, Jimmy."

"To a lost weekend three years ago. I still don't regret."

"To Vegas."

We sat and drank the afternoon away. I felt melancholy. Tomorrow was the Super Bowl. The big one.

THIRTY-FIVE

Without revealing that T.D. was gay, we brought Max along in our limo the next day. My father was not, I would say, the most liberal man in the world. So we told him, simply, that Max was a friend we met along the way. Jimmy was immediately suspicious that Max was interested in me, but when he perceived there was nothing going on between us, we settled in for the ride to the stadium.

My father was on a gambler's high. Look at a cocaine addict during a rush and they're not a whole lot different. My father was talking fast, showing off, drinking and acting euphoric because he won $36,000 the previous night in poker.

When I was a little girl, I loved my father's highs. They meant ditching school to drive to Philadelphia for lunch because my father wanted me to have a "real" Philly cheese steak from the best spot in town, or ditching school to drive to Maine for lobster. Basically, I was happy because the highs meant ditching school, period. But now I was tired of the highs. I was ready for a life that was lived in the middle somewhere.

It was hours to kickoff. We snaked our way into the stadium parking lot, which was packed with tailgaters. People were grilling and drinking and waving banners proclaiming their team. There were ten different kinds of name-brand bottles of booze in our limo, and my father had the Four Seasons box us up some lunches.

I had a knot in my stomach and couldn't eat the five-layer club sandwich in the box on my lap. Right now, somewhere in that stadium, Mark was getting taped up and donning shoulder pads, and he was about to play, as my father said, "for all the marbles."

T.D. patted my knee. "I remember getting ready for my first Super Bowl. I threw up."

"Pussy," Jimmy said, joking.

"Yeah, well, think about the enormity of it. I was just *freaked* out. And then you go out there, and the adrenaline rush is overwhelming. That's part of what the coach has to do. He has to keep a lid on the team's adrenaline so nobody peaks too early."

"How'd you feel when you won?" Max asked.

"I didn't sleep for two days. I was on top of the world. No matter what happened the rest of my life, no one could take that from me. I played in the Super Bowl. And I won."

"Twice," said Max, proudly.

"And you made *me* a lot of money!" my father shouted. "Both times you were in the Bowl, I made a killing. Skye, I think that deck we have out back was paid for by this guy here. That and the Mustang I bought you. Whatever happened to that car?"

"I hocked it to pay my bookie four years ago," I said dryly.

"Shame. That was a nice car. Red, right?"

"Right."

The limo finally pulled up stadium-side, and we got out. With over thirty grand to burn, my father would pull out all the stops in our skybox—champagne, top-notch food and big tips for everyone, including our limo driver.

I walked up the line for Security. Nowadays they take no chances. I passed through a metal detector and waited for my father and everyone else. My father came through first and grabbed my hand.

"You're the best daughter in the world, and don't you forget it. I can tell you're still upset over this whole thing."

"I'll be fine, Dad."

"When this is over, I'm out of the business. That way you can honestly say you're the daughter of a retired gentleman, not a bookie. I want you to be proud of me."

I looked up at his face. "Daddy, I'm not ashamed of you. I'm angry at the people who've ripped us apart like a pack of wild hyenas on a dead animal."

"Well, I'm not dead yet—" my father winked at me "—and I've always got an ace in the hole."

T.D., Max and Jimmy joined us and we made our way up to our skybox, which came with our own waitress, who told us her name was Cammie. There was nothing to do but watch the pageantry and the excitement—and drink Jack and Cokes—until the teams took the field.

The woman who sang the national anthem was a pop star, and I was reminded why all pop records are nothing but studio mixes nowadays. She barely hit the "land of the free" notes, and I inwardly cringed. Not to mention she decided to wear a miniskirt so high she had to be lifted onto the little stage by two men so that she didn't flash the entire stadium.

The teams had been introduced, and the players high-fived one another as each one's name was read aloud by the announcer and they emerged from the locker room. Mark's face was blown up on the skycam when it was his turn.

"He's not that good-looking," Jimmy said. "I don't see what all the fuss is about."

"Oh, yeah, he's really ugly," Max quipped.

The coin was tossed. It came up heads. In Vegas, you can bet on the coin toss. You can bet on the over-under—betting on the total score of both teams being over or under a certain number—on which team will score first, on any one of a number of things. My father didn't sit down. He stood to watch. He had a lot of money riding on the game. Most of his clients were betting that Green Bay would win. They were favored by eleven points. That meant if they won by more than eleven, those that bet for the spread won. If Green Bay won—but by less than eleven, you could bet on Green Bay and still lose, which is why once the "spread" is covered in a game, you'll usually see a euphoria spread throughout the stands from the bettors rejoicing their potential winnings. Of course, they have to hold on to whatever that lead is, and as they say, "It ain't over until the fat lady sings"—or at least until that last pass. If, by some miracle, the Mustangs pulled out a win, or lost by less than eleven points, my father would be on a high that would likely last a month or so—at least until baseball season started—or until the Stanley Cup series in hockey. He had season tickets for the Rangers for hockey. And the Yankees for baseball. And the Knicks for basketball. But nothing, *nothing* compared to football season.

In the opening kickoff, the football was sent spiraling

through the sky toward a Mustang receiver, who promptly fumbled. The ball rolled, end over end, and players scrambled.

"Nerves," T.D. said. "A lot of mistakes happen in the first few minutes."

A big pileup of players was on the field, and one by one, they were pulled off by referees who announced that the Mustangs had already lost the ball.

"They'll settle down," Max said. "Don't worry."

But the Mustangs never settled down, and by the end of the first quarter, they were losing by ten points. As in ten to nothing. Not one point.

"I think I'm going to be sick," I said. Mark looked so sloppy out there. He was unfocused. I could see it. Rather than stepping back and looking for an opening, he rushed his passes. He kept getting sacked—tackled by the defense. And each time they threw him to the ground, he got up slower and slower. Each hit was like getting trampled by stampeding bulls.

Max slipped out to the rest room muttering, "How do I write about this one? Crap!"

The second quarter began, and Green Bay immediately scored another touchdown. They made the extra point. It was seventeen to nothing—more than Green Bay's allotted eleven points.

"A fucking blowout!" my father screamed. "Christ! What's wrong with him? Where's his head at?"

Everyone in the skybox turned to look at me.

If Mustang fans in the stadium knew I was there, I was certain I would be burned in effigy from the goalposts. Either that or they would hurl me onto the field and let the opposing players tackle me for fun.

I didn't hold out much hope that Mark was suddenly

going to pull himself together. This was shaping up to be even uglier than I had thought. I felt anger rising up inside me. If Walt and Leon and the media had left us alone, Mark would be playing better—not worse. I wondered how much lower the Mustang's fortunes could sink.

THIRTY-SIX

By the middle of the second quarter, people had started to boo the Mustangs. *Boo them*. Mark had been intercepted four times. I felt terrible for him. And guilty. Maybe Max and T.D.'s big scheme had been the worst possible idea. Seeing me hadn't helped matters, it had made them far, far worse. Mark was a basket case out there. And even when they showed him on the JumboTron, he looked defeated, as if the other team had already won.

The door to our skybox opened and a voice said, "Miss me?"

I turned around to see Leon Krakowski, in a tailored gray three-piece suit, grinning and chomping on a fatter cigar than usual.

"You have a lot of nerve coming here," T.D. said, rising from his chair and facing off against Leon, who looked like he barely came to T.D.'s thigh.

"Easy, big boy." Leon held up his arms. "I'm barely over the atomic wedgie you gave me, and I'm not looking for another one."

"Then what do you want now, Leon?" I asked, my voice utterly weary.

"What do I want? *What do I want?* Can't a man come and pay a visit to an old pal?"

He strode over to me, and in a quiet voice said, "Can I talk to you alone?"

"No," I said, and crossed my arms. "Whatever you have to say, you can say in front of my family—and friends." I looked over at my dad, whose stance said that if Leon fucked with me, he would be victim of more than an atomic wedgie.

"Well, it seems that Walter Hammond has some freaked-out owners on his hands. Ever hear of the Carter brothers?"

"Too bad."

The Carter brothers owned the Mustangs, and they were arguably the most boisterous owners in the league. They wore loud shirts and plaid pants, and they arrived in limos painted the team's colors of orange and white.

"Anyway—" Leon ignored my comment "—Walt Squared was wondering if perhaps you might pop into the coach's booth and talk to Mark. You know, with a head-phone. Seems Hammond is willing to invoke, and he said to tell you this specifically, 'All letters of the agreement,' and he's perhaps willing to admit the whole press confer-ence recently was a bit of, how shall we say, a misstep on the part of Hammond's office. An unfortunate misunder-standing. Bottom line—he wants a competition, not con-troversy. He wants Mark in his true playing form."

"Tell him to go fuck himself." I shook my head. "You guys are a real piece of work. A real goddamn piece of work. Crawl back under the rock you came from, Leon." T.D. came over to my side.

"Look, Skye…" It was the first time Leon had called me by my name, not Toots or some nickname. "If it matters to you, I didn't agree with Hammond on what he did. I argued against it. That's not how to fix things. I was rooting for you and Shannon. I told you that. But I did warn you. I did do that—friend to friend. Remember?"

"Leon, you're a fixer. You're not my friend."

"And what about T.D. here?"

"What about me?"

Leon stared at me. "You didn't tell him about the clause?"

"What clause?" T.D. asked, brows knit together.

"Nothing, T.D. Nothing. Forget the clause, Leon. Just forget it. It's not worth the piece of paper it's printed on. Look…Hammond can't be trusted. You know it, I know it. So let's just assume I did talk to Mark. And let's just assume he started playing better. Just for argument's sake. Once the game is over and people have had their entertainment—and I don't mean a nipple-baring halftime show or trotting out Aerosmith—Hammond will double-cross me again. He will use me for what he needs and then discard me like a piece of trash. What will he dig up next? An illegitimate love child? An affair with someone else to make Mark believe I've betrayed him?"

"No. This time, if Hammond pulls any crap, I'll call a press conference."

"I don't believe you, Leon."

"You think Hammond is who I work for? I work for the teams, the owners. I have no problem hanging Hammond out to dry. He's an ass. He mishandled this from start to finish. *I'm* the guy to trust. Come on." He looked at T.D. "Tell her, T.D. I sat across from you at your kitchen table and tried to fix things. I tried to help them."

"What clause?" T.D. asked again.

"Nothing, T.D. Will you leave this to me?" I snapped. "I can handle this."

Now my father came to stand shoulder to shoulder with me. Then Jimmy and Max stood next to him. A little solidarity to challenge short little Leon Krakowski. We were our own defensive line.

"You'd let your boyfriend blow the Super Bowl? You'd do that to him? You won't even talk to him?"

"I'm not even sure it would help. He saw me yesterday. He knows I'm here. And he's playing the worst he's ever played in his life. Just leave it alone, Leon. I trust none of you, and I won't put my family—" I grabbed my father and T.D.'s hands "—through this anymore. I'm done. Tell the Carter brothers—better luck next year."

"But, toots—"

"I think," said Jimmy, moving over to Leon and grabbing him by the throat, "that it's time for you, my weasel friend, to leave. The lady considers the conversation *over.*"

"You just want your wife back," Leon said hoarsely. "That's why you're tossing me out."

Jimmy looked over his shoulder at me, then back at Leon. "You know, she's not a gambler anymore. And I, my friend, am a bookie. So, no. We're through. She just ain't going to play your games."

"Lemme go. I'll leave."

"Fine. 'Cause we can do this the polite way, or we can do it the bookie way. And you won't like that way." Jimmy released his grip on Leon's throat. Leon's face, beet-red a moment before, started returning to its natural color.

Leon gave me one last long look, and then he left, saying, "I'll let Hammond know, no deal."

"No deal is right!" I called after him. Then I walked over and shut the door behind him.

I turned around to look at the scoreboard. While our little drama was going on, the Mustangs had managed to score a measly three points on a field goal—and Green Bay had scored another touchdown. I looked over at T.D. and Max. "He's playing so badly. I sure hope I'm doing the right thing."

"What clause?" T.D. demanded again.

"Drop it."

I turned to face the stadium. Mark's face was blown up on the JumboTron. He had taken off his helmet and was casting his eyes skyward, his lips moving, saying an internal prayer, I assumed.

And in my heart, I said one, too.

Lord, Higher Power, help him. Give him guidance. I'm holding up my end of the bargain. I didn't gamble today. The biggest game, the biggest day, of the year for us gamblers. And I don't have so much as a dollar riding on it. Please help him.

Then I prayed to my mother to be his guardian angel. He needed all the help he could get.

THIRTY-SEVEN

The halftime show was not an MTV slut extravaganza, but a pop singer-filled, balloon-releasing piece of fluff. They got Gloria Estefan to sing—she being the resident patron saint of Miami—as well as a number of Latin-influenced singers to shake their bon-bons. I watched it dejectedly. Swirling schoolchildren waved flags in formation to form the red, white and blue of the American flag.

Suddenly, T.D.'s pocket started ringing.

"Your mother's calling you?" I asked questioningly, knowing she and I were about the only ones who had his cell phone number—and I assumed soon Max would have it, if he didn't already.

"No…" He looked at caller ID. "It's for you." He held out my old cell phone to me.

I stared at it. It kept ringing its "Für Elise" tones.

"If you don't answer it, Skye, he's going to get your voice mail."

My eyes teared up. I took the phone in my hand, shaking and pressed Talk.

"Hello?" I said, swallowing hard, not trusting my voice.

"Skye? Baby? Is that you?"

"Yeah," I sniffled.

"Did anyone ever tell you that you look sexy as hell as a platinum blonde?"

"I think Leon might have said something sort of along those lines."

"Baby, I never believed anything they said about you. And more than that, I don't care. Not for one second. I ache for you. I…can't do this without you. I know you're up there in a skybox."

"How do you know?"

"Your friend Max has a press pass. He got a note to me. Said to call the cell phone at halftime." I looked over at Max and T.D., who were beaming.

"Please tell me you love me, Skye."

I was tired of being frightened of what the media and the NFL would do to me. "I love you," I whispered, turning my back on my father and everyone so I could have some semblance of privacy.

"Say it again."

"I love you," I said louder, flushing a little.

"Marry me."

"What? You can't ask me that. Not in the middle of the Super Bowl."

"Marry me. I can't function without you. I need you, Skye. I think I've needed you from the moment I saw you sitting at that counter in Joe's diner."

I thought back to my last quickie marriage. But this was different. I wasn't sure how, but Mark and I knew each other in a short span of time the way lovers hope to know each other after ten years.

"Yes," I said.

He yelled, *"Amen, baby!"* At the top of his lungs. I laughed.

Then he said, "Halftime's about over…when this game is done, I'm through with the game. Me and you, we're gonna go buy that old diner in the desert and sling hash and grow old together."

"You're crazy, you know."

"I know. Look, I've got a meeting with the FBI tomorrow. I have to go, Skye."

"Wait! One more thing."

"What's that? My coach is motioning for me. I have to go, Skye."

"Do something for me?"

"Anything."

"Win."

THIRTY-EIGHT

"Folks...I don't know what Coach McBride said in the locker room, but the Mustangs are on fire. Mark Shannon is a different man—*a different man!*" the NFL announcers said into the TV. We had a set on in the skybox.

"This is a nailbiter. I have rarely seen such an exciting Super Bowl. Or at least the second half of one. The first half and the second half, to be honest, Dan, feel like two entirely different games, wouldn't you say?"

None of us—Max, T.D., Jimmy, my father or I—was sitting down now. Not that many of the people in the stadium were, either. It was the fourth quarter with minutes to go, and the Mustangs had staged the comeback of the decade.

"Sweet Jesus, let them win," my father muttered.

"What clause?" T.D. demanded again.

"I can't talk now," I said, slapping him hard in the arm. "And Max?"

"Yeah."

"Thanks."

"Anything for love," he said, grinning over at T.D.

"T.D.?"

"Yeah, Little Girl?"

"How come you didn't throw out my cell phone?"

"Let's just say when the worst gambler in our home group—the Little Girl who couldn't earn a thirty-day coin in three years—stops thinking about gambling, stops caring about placing a bet each day…it's love. And I wasn't about to let you let that go. Your sponsor always knows what's best for you."

"Thanks." I rubbed his arm where I'd slapped him a minute before.

Our backs were to the door. We heard it open, and Leon walked in again.

"Jesus, you're like shit on a shoe," I said.

"I know you talked to him."

"How do you know everything? You can't be every-where. What is the skybox—bugged?"

"I can't give away all my secrets, now, can I?" He winked at me. "So we gonna watch the end of this game together?"

"Come on in and grab a bourbon," I said, rolling my eyes.

Two minutes to go, and the Mustangs were down by seven points. One touchdown away from tying the game and forcing it into overtime. Mark had the ball.

"Now I really am going to puke," I said. "I can't watch."

"You have to," Jimmy said. "That's your guy down there." I looked over at him. His eyes were lonely look-ing, but he was smiling at me. My sweet Jimmy, the boy I'd always loved. I mouthed a silent "thank you" to him and turned my eyes to the field.

Mark found his receiver. The kicker made the extra point, and it was a tie game. Our skybox erupted. We started hugging one another. I think I was crying. I even hugged Leon.

Now the Mustangs only had to hold on. Force it into overtime. They kicked downfield to Green Bay. Despite the Mustangs' comeback, it didn't look good for them. Green Bay would try to run the clock down by taking up as much of the two minutes as possible getting the ball up the field. If they could, they'd leave no time on the clock.

I was hyperventilating. I started pacing, not looking at the field.

"Come on, kid," my father said. "You've watched this far. You have to see how it ends. My God…New York Super Bowl champs. Can you imagine what that will do for business?"

"I thought you were retiring," I said wryly.

"Now, Skye, honey, you can't expect me to retire with sitting New York champs, can you? If they win, I can't retire."

I looked at him and smiled. "Mommy loved you as a bookie, and I do, too. No, I don't suppose you can retire."

"And you're my daughter, so look at the field, for God's sake. I raised you to have guts, kid."

I stared down at the field. Green Bay had driven the ball to the thirty-six-yard line. Close enough for a field goal if their kicker didn't blow it. That would be it, basically. I felt deflated. My father, of course, would be richer than ever, but Mark would have lost.

The kicker made the three-point field goal, and the Mustangs immediately called a time-out.

There were twenty-one seconds on the clock.

I stopped breathing.

"Christ!" Leon shouted. "I can't take it. I can't fucking take it! I'll need a friggin' pacemaker after this game at this rate. Come on, kiddo. Come on, boy."

"*You* can't take it? Think how I feel!"

"What clause?" T.D. said again.

"Shut up!" I screamed.

The ball was in play.

Twenty seconds. The ball was in the air.

Again, Mark found his receiver. The stadium roared. I screamed. They called their last time-out.

Jimmy got down on his knees and made the sign of the cross three times. Once an Irish-Catholic, always an Irish-Catholic. He was muttering the Hail Mary. I wondered what he would say in confessional. "Bless me, Father, for I have sinned. I invoked the Blessed Virgin to help a team win a football game."

The ball went into play again.

Eighteen.

Seventeen.

The Mustangs huddled. They moved into position fast at the fifty-yard line. Their only hope…their only prayer… was a Hail Mary pass….

Sixteen.

The crowd started chanting the countdown with the clock. The numbers were huge and digital on the scoreboard. The announcers counted down. An entire stadium, Green Bay fans and New York fans, and people along for the ride, chanted the numbers. I gripped my father's hand. Max grabbed T.D.'s hand. Leon hugged T.D.'s arm.

Fifteen.

Fourteen.

Thirteen.

Twelve.

Eleven.

The center snapped the ball.

Ten.

Nine.

Mark caught the snap. He took one…two…three steps backward.

Eight.

Seven.

His running back moved downfield, chased by two defensive players.

Six.

"Take your time," I whispered.

I held my breath.

Hail Mary.

Five.

Full of grace. The Lord is with thee.

Four.

He threw the ball.

Blessed art thou among women.

It went spiraling in a perfect arc across the field.

Three.

And blessed is the fruit of thy womb, Jesus.

His receiver was in the end zone.

Holy Mary, mother of God.

Two.

Hail Mary. Dear God, let him make it. I promise I will never gamble again.

One.

The receiver caught it. No flags were thrown on the play. The referees lifted both arms up.

"Ladies and gentlemen…" the announcers screamed into their microphones.

Touchdown!

THIRTY-NINE

"Oh, my God!"

I kissed Jimmy on the mouth. I kissed T.D. on the mouth.

I kissed Max on the mouth. Hell…I kissed Leon on the mouth.

T.D. and Max kissed each other on the mouth—but I don't think anyone noticed, we were all so busy shrieking and shouting. Jimmy crossed himself three times—something he used to do for good luck.

"Hail Mary, I love you!" Jimmy shouted at the ceiling.

I ran screaming all over the skybox. I literally ran around in circles.

"Oh, my God! Oh, my God! Tell me that just happened."

My father came over to me and hugged me, knocking the breath out of me and lifting me up off the ground. Tears rolled down both our faces.

"They did it!" my father shouted.

"*He* did it!"

"I can't wait to meet that boy!"

My heart was beating a mile a minute.

I ran over to the window of the skybox and looked down on the field. The sidelines were full of players hugging one another.

Players were making their way off the field in a hurry, with microphones being shoved in their faces and cameras on them. Some jumped up and down and were bounding out. The Mustangs' coach was on his players' shoulders and someone had dumped a gallon of Gatorade on his head, turning his white shirt an orangey color.

Green Bay's players and coaches walked dejectedly off the field toward their locker room, quickly, trying not to chat with the media. My cell phone rang again.

"Hello?"

"I did it, Skye. I did it for you."

I scanned the field trying to find Mark in all the confusion. I spotted him, and he was looking at all the skyboxes, not that he could make me out.

"I'm in the skybox to the left of the commentator's booth—four down."

He turned his head to the left. "I can see your hair."

Media swarmed him, and the next second, I couldn't see him. He was lost in the middle of a sea of cameras and lights.

I looked up at the TV and could see his face on camera. "I see you on television."

"I love you!" He had to shout it over the mass hysteria. "I won it for you!"

"You won it for you, Mark. And the Mustangs. I'm so happy for you."

"I can barely hear you. Come to the locker room."

"I don't think so. Too much commotion."

"How about I come to the Four Seasons, then? Tonight."

"How'd you know I was there?"

"Leon told me."

"Leon?"

"Yeah. He said if I blew the game, at least I'd get the girl."

I squealed aloud. "Oh, my God, Mark, I'll see you later!"

I hung up the phone. One of the on-camera commentators had him on TV now, and I turned up the volume.

"How do you feel, Mark? Do you feel vindicated in any way? Your critics have been pretty harsh in recent weeks."

"Yeah, I do feel vindicated. I'm proud of the way our guys came back today. I'm proud of the whole team. Our coaches. The fans for not giving up on us."

"You've just been named Most Valuable Player. How do you feel about that? What a performance!"

"Man…it's icing on the cake. But it was a team effort. That award belongs to the whole team. To my offensive line. To the defense, who really held Green Bay off in the second half."

"Two weeks ago, they were talking of trading you. It was all over the news in New York. You've had a crazy month—one of the strangest in the annals of football. Now you've won the Super Bowl, what's next?

"What's next? I'm getting married!"

"To Skye McNally?"

"You bet."

"Well, folks, you heard it here first. In yet another strange turn of events, Mark Shannon is going to ride off into the sunset with the woman who almost derailed his career permanently. Truth can be stranger than fiction. But I guess all the controversy will be forgotten now that you've won the trophy, Mark. Good luck!"

Mark shook his hand and moved off the field.

Riding off into the sunset.

From what I remembered, a desert sunset—a desert night—was how it all started.

CHAPTER

F♥RTY

On the way back to the hotel, we were all drunk. Me more so with the thrill of the game than drinking. I think the adrenaline rush pushed all the alcohol out of my system.

When we got to the Four Seasons, my father and Jimmy decided to take the limo on to South Beach. The city would be partying all night long, and neither of them was one to miss a party.

"Behave yourselves," I said, thinking of the thirty grand or so still burning a hole in my father's pocket. I imagined that some strippers that night were going to be very, very happy young ladies.

"Behave ourselves?" Jimmy grinned as he stuck his head out the car window. "Not on your life!"

Max, T.D. and I stood on the sidewalk with Leon and waved goodbye to them. My father was standing up with his head and shoulders out the sky roof.

"Well, Leon, no more fixing until next season, I guess," I said. I reached out my hand to shake his.

"No handshake," he said, and came over to me and

hugged me. His face landed right in my breasts he was so short. "Good luck, toots."

"Guess you won't have much to do now that it's all over."

"What, are you kidding?" he asked, stepping back. "You think those knucklehead football players don't get into trouble in the off-season? Trust me, baby-sitting the NFL is what I call, in my business, job security."

He turned to T.D. "Big man," he said, and stuck out his hand. "Your secret's safe with me."

T.D. looked over at Max and then down at Leon. "Eventually, I guess it won't be a secret."

"Well, until then, it's safe with me. And if you need help 'fixing' your media image when it comes out, you just give me a call. It's a freebie. For old times' sake."

"Thanks. And sorry for the atomic wedgie."

"All part of the job sometimes. All part of the job. Well, kids, it's been real." Leon turned and walked away.

"Where you going, Leon, anyway?"

"Me? I got a six-foot-tall supermodel waiting for me in my hotel room."

I shook my head. "Have fun."

"I intend to." He headed down the sidewalk, weaving between the partying citizens of South Beach.

I tapped T.D. on the shoulder. "T.D.? Can I ask a favor?"

"Sure, Little Girl."

"Can you and Max…um…stay somewhere else tonight? His room, maybe?"

He broke out in a broad grin. "Well, Little Girl, I think that can be arranged."

I hugged him, and then hugged Max. "Have fun tonight."

"Sure thing," T.D. said as he hugged me. "Don't do anything I wouldn't do."

I looked up at him and winked. "I love you."

"You know I love you, too."

The two of them walked in the opposite direction of Leon, their arms touching as they made their way through the crowd. I watched them until they disappeared in the mass of people. Horns beeped. People were screaming. I heard Spanish and English and French being spoken rapidly. Police strolled, trying to keep the traffic flowing and the crowds from congregating too heavily and spilling onto the road.

I walked into the Four Seasons. The doorman was grinning. "Great game." I spied a small television set over at his podium.

"Sure was," I said. I took the elevator up to my suite. My body was numb from the excitement, and I took a deep breath. I went into the bathroom and played with my hair and touched up my makeup. I changed into a cocoa-colored silk nightgown and turned on some soft music to unwind a little bit. I opened the sliding glass doors just a little to let the ocean breeze drift in, and I could hear a reggae band playing outside somewhere. I walked back to the couch in the sitting area. And then I waited.

Around twelve-thirty, there was a soft knock on the door. I threw it open. There he stood, my quarterback, freshly showered, hair wet and smelling of shampoo. I threw my arms around his neck and hugged him to me, feeling his heart beating hard against his chest.

"God, that feels good," Mark whispered. His voice was husky.

"Come on in." I let him go, and he followed me into the suite.

Inside, I had just one lamp on, a small one that softly lit the room. I turned it out and allowed the moonlight to illuminate us through the open curtains. The streets had quieted slightly, and we could hear the waves crashing to shore. I faced Mark.

"I didn't know for sure if you were going to do it. To pull it off."

"When I heard your voice, I knew it."

"I'm so proud of you, so happy for you." I bit my lip. "Mark, I'm sorry about everything. It's been a real mess. Everything."

"Oh, baby. No, I'm so sorry about Hammond. The hypocrisy. The bullshit. But you don't have to say you're sorry to me. Not me, Skye. You and me—when it's just us—it all works. We're the perfect team. Don't ever forget that."

He leaned in and kissed me. Maybe, for a brief moment, or maybe during our whole ordeal, I wondered if what we had was just fleeting. I wondered if it had all been the desert air, the sky, the stars, the wind in our hair. If it had been a mirage, like the shimmering heat off the road in the desert playing tricks on me.

But it wasn't. He loosened my nightgown from my shoulders, and it fell to the floor.

"You are so beautiful," he whispered.

I unbuttoned his shirt, kissing his neck. He moaned softly. He took off his shirt and unbuttoned his jeans, letting them fall to the ground, and slipped out of his shoes and his pants. I felt his stomach, his six-pack abs. Then I put my hand to his heart. It was beating so strongly.

I walked over to the bed in the moonlight, and he came and lay down next to me, his perfect quarterback body rock solid and strong. We faced each other and just stroked each other with featherlight touches, letting the stress of the week fall away. My breathing was shallow. I wanted him.

And then he rolled over to lie, gently, on top of me, maneuvering me beneath him. "Hey, are you going to keep that platinum hair?"

"I don't know. I've kind of gotten used to it." I grinned.

"I like it." He twirled a curl around his index finger. He kissed my forehead.

"Promise me something?"

"What?"

"You won't ever let anything tear us apart again. Because if there's one thing I've learned from all this, it's that if you don't have the people you love, you don't have anything at all. And all the trophies in the world won't help fill the empty spot."

"I promise," I whispered. "Nothing will ever break us apart again."

And then he kissed me hungrily, more intensely, searchingly. I wanted him inside me as I've never wanted anything so badly in all my life. Not even a pair of aces or a trifecta. And then Mark Shannon made love to me, all night long.

And that's what I call…

A perfect touchdown.

EPIL♥GUE

"Tonight," Cowboy Hal said, "we've got a special anniversary. I myself thought this group would never see the day, but we've got the one-year anniversary of Skye. Come on up here and get your coin, young lady."

T.D. squeezed my hand and I made my way across the metal chairs and gamblers to the front of the room, where Hal sat with a gavel. He stood and gave me a squeeze and handed me my brass coin. Everyone applauded and stamped their feet in the old church basement.

I took the one-year anniversary coin. I earned it. The hard way. By loving and losing and then finding love again. By figuring out what it all meant. I liked the way the coin felt it my hand. It had weight. It weighed as much as all I had gone through, all I had let go of.

Since that amazing Super Bowl eleven months or so ago, a lot has happened.

Mark met with the FBI. His hired P.I., Rialto, had been thorough. A former fed, he'd left no stone unturned. The doc, it turned out, was in even deeper. Besides Big Easy, he had gotten a line of credit from *another* bookie on the strength of his plan to make Mark Shannon too ill to play well. He had doctored Mark's sports drinks with just enough digitalis to make him think he was going crazy, that he was under a lot of stress, but not enough to take him out of the game. The doc counted on his playing—but poorly.

The scandal that broke brought gambling to the front pages. But Mark had his win—without the taint of the gambling scandal and the doctor marring it.

My father decided to retire after all, and he passed the reins to Jimmy. Dad moved out to Vegas to be near me. I couldn't believe he sold our old house. It had always been like a shrine, first to my mother, his beloved Christina, and then to me, to the old days when I lived with him. He packed up our house. Every bit of it. He took her pictures, and he took the furniture. He took the little ceramic turtle I made—and yelled at the movers to make sure the boxes marked Fragile arrived safely. He even took the door frame that had all the years and how I'd grown written in pen on it. He replaced the frame with a crisp white one. The people who bought our house were a young couple with two kids, and my father showed them the door and where he'd measured and said he'd be taking it with him.

"I'll replace it, and you can make your own memories in this old house of ours. We were happy here."

I'm not sure what the new owners thought of the twenty-some-odd phone lines in the basement and the built-in beer keg, but they were touched and let Dad mark off their kids' first heights and dates on the door frame for good luck.

My father bought a replica of our old house. Well, actually, he had one built, as it's not really a very "Vegas" house. It still looks like it should be sitting on a lawn in Long Island somewhere, with snow and a plastic Santa on the lawn. He wanted an upstairs and a downstairs, and a slightly smaller house. But he wanted a Dutch colonial with a long hallway for the family pictures. He putters around in his yard trying to figure out how to grow cactus.

He actually started dating, too. A widow named Peggy. Not too serious, but now that he's left the Shrine, he even lets Peggy come over and cook him dinner. She's a very nice woman, a brunette with a soft smile. She doesn't gamble, though she'll go to the track with him. She makes an amazing pot roast. And I think, after all this time, my mother would definitely approve. I do. I like her a lot.

Dad plays in a standing Wednesday night poker game with some high rollers. I'm pretty sure under the floorboards and stuck inside dolls' heads there is a lot of cash in that house. But it's good to see that he doesn't collect book anymore. I no longer have to reconcile the man who isn't afraid to use a crowbar with the man who raised me as best he could after Mom died. He's living a quieter life now, and it's good for both of us.

Jimmy? Well, he ran the business through the start of a second successful Mustang season. Then he decided to come to Vegas, too. He had parlayed all his winning seasons into quite a bankroll and opened a pizza parlor that takes book on the side. He does very well for himself. On both counts. People like good New York pizza in Vegas. And they like to gamble. What can I say? He combines the best of both worlds.

Jimmy started dating, too. CoCo is a showgirl with a French accent. She's very tall. Taller than Jimmy, even. She likes to play cards, and they seem happy together. He's sworn off marriage, but he says she's good company. She's very sweet—and if you have a thing for fake breasts, she's got a very lovely pair. She doesn't mind that he wants to have dinner every Sunday with me and my dad; half the time she comes along. And don't get the idea that CoCo isn't bright just because she wears plumage and shows her breasts in a show. She's smart enough to keep Jimmy on his toes.

Gunther, Jimmy's old dog, passed away. I talked him into getting a golden retriever. He named him Gunther II.

T.D. was named to the Hall of Fame. Ol' Walt Squared actually kept his end of the bargain. He lifted the lifetime ban, and T.D. made it by a commanding vote. I was there for the ceremony.

Max left St. Louis and moved to Vegas. He and T.D. live together. They're very, very happy. They even got a dog. I tried to talk them into a golden retriever named Blackjack, but they didn't go for it. Instead, they got a little dust mop of a dog. A maltese they named Monroe, after Marilyn Monroe, a salute to my—and the dog's—platinum hair. Monroe gets along with Fred and Ginger, and he is the most spoiled dog in the world.

Max decided to get out of the newspaper business. Turns out that he worked as a bartender to put himself through college. So now he tends bar at the steakhouse. He's a very good listener. Excellent, in fact, and he's brought even more regulars into the place. T.D. is richer than ever. I suspect he's even richer than he was when he was in the NFL.

T.D. and Max haven't come "out" yet. There are rumors, of course. Every once in a while, there's a little furor in one paper or the other. Someone hints or prints a blind item. But they're left alone, and they're happy.

The Big Buffet House of Hunan is still there. Now we take Max, and he's learned that this is serious business. The last time we were there, the pool was up to eighteen hundred dollars and no one won.

Leon? We hear from him every time he has to come to Vegas to "fix" a mess. Not surprisingly, since Vegas is a big playground, that's fairly often. NFL players who end up with showgirls who then have babies—that sort of thing. He always comes to the steakhouse, and we all have dinner together and laugh about the "old times"—that crazy month a year ago when it seemed as if the entire world had fallen apart for Mark and me. He makes sure that what happens in Vegas, stays in Vegas.

The Carter brothers were very happy with the Mustangs. In fact, Mark got a big bonus. He didn't retire after all...but he commutes to New York from Vegas, and the Carter brothers and I have actually become friends. After all, when Mark is happy, the team plays well. In fact, I share the skybox with the Carters. I said they were flamboyant, and indeed they are. Usually at least one of them is dating a stripper. They wear their shirts backward for good luck, and they're very superstitious. One of them wears bunny ears—something about losing a bet to his brother. It makes the games even more interesting is all I can say.

Walt Squared? Max apparently had some inside dirt on him, courtesy of a confidential tip from a Deep Throat informant, who sounded an awful lot like Leon Krakowski. Turns out Walt Squared was once caught in a dress. A pink sequined dress. So that, and my secret clause, were what prompted Walt to back down. Sadly, the big old guy had a heart attack. He survived it, but retired. He lives in Palm Springs now with his new wife, a former *Playboy* bunny named Destiny—at least that's what he calls her.

So who did they name as new commissioner? A nice guy named Charlie Abrams who is one of Leon's best friends. They play poker together every other Wednesday. Charlie met me and my father and agreed with Leon that there was no reason to make a big deal about the whole issue of the McNally family anymore—especially in light of my father's retirement. So we've been left alone, and we like it that way. Besides, the team doctor scandal—he accepted a plea and was sent to prison for ten years—was enough for the NFL. The next season, it was all a memory, and everyone was ready to move on, to the next scandal, the next trial, the next case. That's America…we never tire of our stories.

As for Mark and me, we wanted to go to the Little Wedding Chapel here in Las Vegas, but my father wouldn't hear of it. "The pictures!" he said. "Think of the pictures!" We were going to walk down a real aisle in a real church and do it properly. Mark's parents came out to Vegas. Lovely people. Mark's father is a great guy. He and my father and Max and Jimmy and T.D., they all played poker for the bachelor party—with Mark, of course. T.D. bet with fake money to avoid feeling like he was cheating on his gambling thing. At the end of the night, Mr. Shannon had won a tidy sum. He and his wife come out to Vegas often now, and he and my father play golf.

After the wedding we had a reception at the steakhouse. We invited Cowboy Hal and the entire home group, Mai and Huang and the gang from Big Buffet, Leon and all the Mustangs. Following the reception, there was apparently an incident involving three hookers and four players, but Leon fixed it. Job security, like he says.

Mark and I moved out of my condo and into a real house about a half mile from T.D. and Max's place. It's a mansion, which I have to say takes a little getting used to. We bought it from a wacky casino owner, and the pool is shaped like a pair of dice. It also has plenty of bedrooms for babies....

The first one is on the way.

And of course my father can't wait. Because at the end of the hall, next to his and my mother's wedding day picture, and next to my and Mark's wedding picture, will be a spot for a picture frame to hold a photo of the baby.

And finally, important, I don't gamble anymore. That was what I had to learn all along. If I just don't gamble, everything else will fall into place. I talk to my Higher Power a lot. This Higher Power filled up the empty place. I figured out, finally, that was what my addiction was all about. I was like my baby doll. The hollow one. Inside me was a big hole that I filled with gambling. It was the hole of a motherless girl, the hole of a girl raised in a dark world. That world had bright spots. There was laughter and love, and a father with a ceramic turtle. But it was also a world of crowbars, broken fingers and even whispers of murder. Prison. That hole is filled with other things now. Love. Serenity. God. Now I don't gamble. Ever. I don't even miss it. Well...that's not true. Not quite.

I do have one bet right now. We started a baby pool. We all put in ten bucks and whoever guesses the actual delivery date wins.

Leon's hoping to induce labor by feeding me chili peppers when it comes close to my due date. Max and T.D. hope to stick me in bed with my legs crossed so they win. Only in Vegas.

Oh, and one more thing. I almost called the Wentworths to tell them they could keep their damn trust fund money. But then I changed my mind. So Mark and I took that monthly money, plus a million dollars that Mark put in, and we founded a charity that helps kids with cancer. I think my mom would be happy with the good work that they do. It's called the Christina McNally Memorial Charity.

And once a month, on the anniversary of the day we met, my quarterback and I drive to Joe's diner. No, we didn't buy it—at least not yet. And afterward, we take a drive in the desert.

Las Vegas. An oasis of neon.

And, for some, the city of dreams.